RUNNING
with
SCISSORS

L.A. WITT

Copyright Information

This is a work of fiction. Names, characters, places, and incidents are either the product of the author's imagination or are used fictitiously. Any resemblance to actual persons living or dead, business establishments, events, or locales is entirely coincidental.

RUNNING
with
SCISSORS

L.A. WITT

L.A. WITT

CHAPTER 1

"Hey, Jude?"

Jude looked up from a stack of invoices and turned to Steve, his cubicle mate. "Hmm?"

"You're doing it again."

Jude's foot stopped moving, and he realized he'd been tapping it against the leg of his desk. Again. Tucking his feet beneath his chair, he muttered, "Sorry."

No reply. At least Steve was more or less polite about it. Their other cubicle mate, Grant, was constantly on Jude's case, and never even tried to hide his irritation.

Jude knew it annoyed them, and he tried his best not to do it, but telling a drummer not to tap his foot was like telling an eye not to see.

You're not a drummer anymore.

He gritted his teeth. He'd always be a drummer. Always. Just because he wasn't in a band at the moment didn't mean—

Whatever helps you sleep at night, dude.

Cursing under his breath, he scrubbed a hand over his face. His leg itched with the need to mark time to the rhythm he had stuck in his head.

He couldn't listen to the radio.

Couldn't wear headphones.

Couldn't tap his foot.

Couldn't fucking concentrate.

"Jude?" Steve sounded concerned this time. "You okay?"

Grant muttered something. Jude didn't catch it, but he recognized the tone and glanced at his own fingers.

Which were tapping beside his keyboard.

Fuck.

"I'll be right back." He snatched his phone off the desk and left. Head down, heart thumping, he hurried through the maze of cubicles. His cigarettes and lighter were already in his hand. He didn't even remember pulling them out of his pocket, but whatever.

As the door to the communal patio came into view, he put a cigarette between his lips. He sensed one of the receptionists glaring at him—*it's not even* lit, *for God's sake*—but kept his gaze fixed on the door in front of him.

And finally, he was there.

He pushed it open with his hip, and before he'd even stepped all the way out into the SoCal heat, he'd cupped a hand around the end of his cigarette and flicked the lighter.

One drag brought his pulse back down. The second stilled his hands. Sort of. His fingers might as well have had a mind of their own, and were tapping out the bass line of a song he'd heard this morning on the radio. That tapping, much like the nicotine easing its way into his system, settled him. Centered him.

And naturally, drove his coworkers *insane*.

Holding his cigarette between two fingers, he rubbed his forehead with the heel of his hand. He'd long ago given up telling himself he was just having a bad day. If that were the case, he wouldn't be out here every fucking afternoon, smoking two or three cigarettes in a row just to keep himself sane until five o'clock. And there wouldn't be two more in the car. Three if traffic was exceptionally bad, even by Los Angeles standards.

At least in the car, he'd have music. The radio worked, and he had his iPod as backup. He'd be able to get the beat out of his system on the steering wheel because there'd be no one around to get on his case about it.

He lowered his hand and glared at the cigarette. His mom kept telling him these things would kill him sooner or later. After a year and a half behind a desk in a cramped cubicle, he was pretty sure the job would do him in well before the smokes did.

It's your own fault you're here.

Jude swore under his breath. Then he took another long drag and held it for a moment as he gazed out at the hazy LA skyline.

Every day, it was the same shit. He worked until he couldn't anymore. Then he made his escape to this patio. And smoked. And kicked himself for being here in the first place.

This job was hell. The monotony and the buzz of fluorescent lights seemed to numb everyone else into some weird state where casual Friday and birthday potlucks were things to legitimately look forward to, but he had never adjusted. Day by day, he grew surer that he never would.

I could be on the road with them right now.

The thought didn't even make him flinch anymore. Well, not much. Okay, not as bad as it had when he'd first found out the band was going on tour.

Six months. If he could've just hung on for six more goddamned months, he'd have been there when the record company offered them a deal. He'd have signed. He'd have been on tour *right now*. He'd have been onstage under the hot lights instead of dying inside under fluorescents while he crunched numbers he didn't care about to make people he didn't know rich. If he were onstage, he'd be whoring out albums to make record company execs rich, but at least he'd enjoy the work.

Well, he couldn't go back and change the past, but he definitely needed to change his future. Maybe he'd give the job websites another look tonight. And of course, five minutes into that, he'd be all over Craigslist and any other place where someone might post that they were in search of a drummer. Even if it was just a part-time gig where they played twice a month in shithole bars for less than gas money, and he had to come into the office every morning with his ears ringing and his shoulders aching, that would be better than what he was doing now.

But nobody was looking for a drummer these days. Not many were looking for twitchy idiots to work in accounts receivable, either, but that was worth a look too unless he wanted to spend a decade or two trying not to disturb Steve and Grant.

All because he'd quit the band like a fucking idiot. Not that he'd had much choice by that point, especially since the circumstances that had driven him out of Running with Scissors were, at least in part, his own fucking fault.

Well, you made your bed. Now go back in there and lie in it.

He crushed his cigarette beneath his heel, tossed the butt into the ash can, and went back inside.

Two hours and too many cigarettes after five, Jude keyed himself into his second floor apartment. The place was quiet, thank God. None of his roommates were due home anytime soon.

He tossed his keys on the counter and shot the sink a glare—it was Tim's turn to wash dishes, and there were still plates and cups in there from Gordy's turn two nights ago. Jude rolled his eyes. Something told him if it didn't get done tonight, he'd be washing it all tomorrow when it was his turn. Tim would be too tired or too stoned later, and he'd forget like he always did.

Jude looked under the sink for detergent and a serviceable sponge. He'd need to make a run to the grocery store before too long, but he could get the job done for now.

He went to work on the dishes and promised himself an evening of binge-watching *Game of Thrones* on his laptop. He needed the relaxation and the distraction. From his job. From the band out there on tour without him. From the roommates who couldn't seem to remember when it was their turn to do chores. At least they managed to pay their portions of the rent on time. Usually.

Mostly he needed a distraction from the miserable, stagnant state he'd been in since he'd left the band. After he relaxed a bit, then he'd start looking at new jobs. And then, of course, he'd depress himself with how few options he had, and he'd be back in the tire-spinning cycle of needing to change something and having no idea where to start.

He'd figure it out. Eventually. All he knew right now was there were only so many times a man could pretend his roommates hadn't once again dumped a sink full of moldy dishes in his lap after he'd spent a day walking on eggshells for some jackass in a cubicle before *something* had to give.

Sighing, he put a plate into the drying rack. There were also only so many times he could tell himself he needed to change things before he had to actually, like, *change* something.

Once he'd finished with the dishes, he smoked another cigarette on the balcony and then went into his bedroom. With his laptop on his knee, he lounged on the bed and pulled up *Game of Thrones*. He'd fallen almost a season behind, so he clicked on the first unwatched episode and—

His cell phone startled the shit out of him. Especially since it was his generic ringtone, the one that only went off when it was someone who wasn't in his contact list.

He picked it up and eyed the screen. Though there was no name, something about the sequence of numbers seemed familiar. If memory served, that was—

No, it couldn't be. Could it?

He accepted the call. "Hello?"

"Jude, thank God. It's Kristy."

"Hey. Uh." He hadn't heard the band manager's voice since the day she'd tried to stop him from quitting, and the last thing she'd said to him had involved the words "fucking" and "idiot." He cleared his throat. "Long time no talk."

"Too long, honey." She paused. "Listen, I'm gonna keep this short. The band needs you."

A cough of laughter burst out of him. "What?"

"We're . . ." She sighed. "Wyatt quit tonight. Just walked out."

Jude's lips parted. "What? What happened?"

"Let's just say you and he apparently have the same taste in men," she growled.

"Jesus." He rubbed his eyes. Hadn't Wyatt learned anything from him and Connor? They'd fought more often than not, and spent most of their stupidly volatile relationship on the brink of a catastrophic breakup. As friends, they'd been fine. As boyfriends? An utter disaster. And Wyatt had watched the whole thing.

Jude exhaled and shrugged for no one's benefit but his own. "Okay, so? Why are you calling me? I don't know any bass players anymore."

"You *are* a bass player."

"I . . ." He blinked. "I'm a drummer, remember?"

"But you play bass. I've heard you, sweetheart."

He glanced skyward and bit back a groan. "Okay, fine, but I haven't picked up a bass in forever."

"You haven't played the drums in forever either, but I'm pretty sure you could fill in there if we needed you to."

Touché.

He swallowed. "*Do* you need me to fill in on the drums?"

"No. The guy who took your place is—" She hesitated. "What we need is a bass player."

"Why me?"

"Because the band's got a lot of back-to-back shows coming up." The desperation in her voice was suddenly palpable, thrumming down the line and into his ear like an off-key chord. "We don't have time to audition anyone, and even if we did, there's no way they could learn the music that fast. You know it. You might be rusty, but you *know* the music."

"I don't know any of the new stuff."

"The band can play all old school for a few sets if they have to. But we *need* a bassist, or the band is fucked."

Jude gnawed his lip. The band's music leaned hard on the rhythm section. The bass line wasn't as in-your-face as the guitar or the vocalists, but if it was absent? The whole thing fell apart just as it would without the drums.

He swallowed. "I have a job now, Kris. It's not like I can just drop everything and go on tour."

"Yeah? How's that job working out for you?"

He flinched, and before he even realized it, he'd picked up his cigarettes off the nightstand. "It's—"

"That's what I thought. Honey, I know you. And I never believed for a second you'd be happy doing the nine-to-five thing."

Jude gnawed his lip. She was right, wasn't she? And how many months had he spent agonizing over how to un-fuck his life?

He was out of vacation days, but he could always take a leave of absence. Or, hell, quit. His job was miserable anyway, and it didn't pay enough to keep him afloat for much longer. It'd be just his luck that his landlord would raise his rent again and he'd have to move back in with his folks or something. Awesome.

He looked around his shithole bedroom. A mattress on the floor. Secondhand IKEA furniture on its last legs. Bare walls with water stains to match the ones on the ceiling.

"So," she prodded. "Are you in?"

Well. Are you?

What did he have to lose?

Well, for starters . . .

Jude swept his tongue across his dry lips. "What about Connor?" Just saying his ex's name filled his mouth with a bitter taste and his stomach with guilt.

"He knows how desperate we are. If you can be civil, so can he."

I'll believe that when I see it.

"Look." Kristy's voice sharpened. "I'm gonna tell you the same thing I've been telling him: get along with each other, keep your dicks out of the other band members, and we won't have drama. It's that simple."

The second part of that *was* simple. The first part? Not so much.

But would restraining himself from choking his ex be worse than dealing with the shithole apartment and miserable job? Hadn't he been telling himself for months he'd rather put up with Connor's crap and his own conscience than work another day at that desk-in-a-box?

This was the opportunity he *needed*. He'd been an idiot to walk away from the band. How big an idiot would he have to be to pass up this chance?

"There's one problem, though. I can't just take that much time off from work." He swallowed. "If I'm going to do this, it can't be halfway. Either I'm in or I'm not."

"So, what? You want to rejoin the band permanently?"

"Or at least longer term than a few shows. I can't afford to lose my job for that."

Kristy didn't speak for a moment. "And if I can bring you on board for, say, the rest of this tour, the next album, and the headlining tour?"

Well, that would give him a good year, year and a half before he'd have to start polishing up his résumé again. "Do you think the band would go for that?"

"They're in a panic like you wouldn't believe over losing Wyatt. I'm pretty sure they'll go for having a semipermanent bassist."

"In theory. But after the way things ended with—"

"Nobody has the luxury of being picky right now. They've got a lot riding on this, so if there's a solution— especially one that could be more than a Band-Aid solution—they'll roll with it if they know what's good for them."

"True." He knew damn well he should sleep on it, think about it, really grill himself over it, but what was the point? He'd been hoping for something like this for too long to think twice. He closed his eyes and blew out a breath. "Okay. If they'll agree to keep me on through the next tour, I'm in."

"Oh my God." Kristy released a long breath. "Thank you so much. You have no idea how much you're saving our asses."

"Don't mention it."

"There is one other thing, though."

Of course there was. "Yeah?"

"We need you back, but . . ." She fell silent for several seconds. "Keeping you on for the next tour and everything? I'm sure I don't have to spell out for you that part of the arrangement is contingent on everyone behaving."

He glared up at the ceiling. "I assume 'everyone' means me in this context?"

"Yes. Don't get me wrong, sweetheart. I'm grateful and the band will be too. But after last time . . ."

He cringed, guilt pressing down on his shoulders. "Yeah, I follow. I'll stay out of Connor's way if he'll—"

"Perfect. I'll make sure he toes the line too."

Good luck with that.

"Where are you guys now?"

"Some godforsaken town in the Bumfuck Egypt Midwest." She paused. "I'll text you with our stops. They're not performing again until we get to Des Moines, and that's on Wednesday."

Jude coughed. "You're aware that today is Monday, right?"

"Uh-huh."

"And . . . are you expecting me to be onstage in Des Moines on Wednesday?"

"Um . . ."

"Kristy, I—"

"They're the opening act, so they can afford to bail on one show. *Maybe* the one in Omaha the next night. But more than two in a row, and we're fucked. The headliner's manager doesn't have a lot of patience, so I guarantee he'll be bringing in another opener if we bail more than twice."

He swallowed. "Where are you after Omaha?"

"Denver. On Saturday."

"Okay." His heart sped up, and the cigarette pack crinkled between his twitchy fingers. "I'll meet you guys in Omaha. That should give us some time to rehearse a bit." A tiny bit. Not nearly enough. Jesus, what was he doing?

"You're a lifesaver, sweetie. I'll see what the band says, and assuming everything's a go, I'll book you a ticket and we'll see you in Nebraska."

"Yeah. See you in Nebraska."

After they hung up, Jude collapsed back on his mattress.

Panic and excitement mingled behind his ribs. Everything about this seemed reckless and stupid and . . . right.

Like it was the first time he'd made the right decision since before he'd quit. After that, he'd had about a week of feeling like he'd done the right thing, before spending the next eighteen months wallowing in regret.

Maybe this would blow up in his face. Maybe it wouldn't. But it was a change. At this point, he'd take any opportunity to get out of this bullshit rut he'd gotten himself into.

Even if it meant being in close confines with the ex-boyfriend and band he'd screwed over.

L.A. WITT

CHAPTER 2

A.J. fidgeted in a chair beside the rickety table in the band's motel room, tapping out a nervous rhythm on the armrest. Everyone was wound up, waiting for Kristy to come back in. Nobody in the group was thrilled about their manager's long shot of an idea, but without any better ideas, they all waited impatiently for the verdict.

When the door opened, every member of Running with Scissors sat bolt upright.

Kristy stepped in from the motel's breezeway, cell phone in hand, and shut the door behind her. The band members exchanged glances. A.J.'s heart pounded—he was pretty sure he didn't hear anyone breathing, and he was holding his breath too.

"Well?" Richie fidgeted against the headboard of one of the beds. "What'd he say?"

She exhaled hard. "He's not in a good spot to drop everything and leave for a handful of shows."

That prompted a few frustrated sighs and some whispered swearing. Someone thumped a fist on something.

"*But.*" Kristy held up a hand. "And you all need to hear me out on this one. He is willing to come back for a semipermanent position."

"Semipermanent?" Shiloh cocked her head. "Meaning?"

Kristy ticked the points off on her fingers. "The duration of this tour. The upcoming album. And the headlining tour. After that, we'll have to play it by ear."

Beside Richie, Connor muttered a few curses.

Shiloh shot him a glare and then turned to Kristy. "He'd really come back for that long?"

Kristy nodded. "It's the only way he can justify leaving his job on short notice. And quite frankly, I can't blame him."

"Then maybe he doesn't want the opportunity after all," Connor said through his teeth. "He did quit, remember?"

Kristy narrowed her eyes. "He did, and he also knows the music as well or better than anyone in this room."

A.J.'s chest tightened. Jude's command of music was legendary, but A.J. wasn't too sure he liked the idea of having him around, especially in the long term. It would be great for the band as a whole, of course. But not necessarily for him.

Not that he—or the band—had any choice.

"So." Kristy folded her arms loosely. "What'll it be? Do I book him a ticket? Or do we keep looking?"

"I say bring him back," Shiloh said. "I know things are tough between Jude and Connor, and yeah, it was a dick move on Jude's part to leave like that, but let's face it—we'd be stupid to let him go again."

"What she said," Vanessa chimed in. "Jude can eat shit and die for all I care, but we don't have a choice. We don't have to like it, and we don't have to like him, but we need the jerk."

The rest of the band gave nods and murmured affirmatives, aside from Connor. He definitely wasn't thrilled.

"I don't believe this," he grumbled. "He's the reason we almost didn't get signed!"

"But you *did* get signed," Kristy said in that tone that meant her patience was wearing thin. "And I assume you want to stay that way, so it's either bring in Jude, or pack your shit and go home while another opening act takes over, and kiss your headlining tour good-bye."

Every head turned toward Connor, the unspoken question thrumming in the air: *Is that what you want?*

His lips pulled tight as he glared up at Kristy. "There's no way Jude's going to be ready to go onstage in Denver. No fucking way."

"Well, maybe you should've thought of that before you and Wyatt—"

"I get it," Connor snapped.

"Somehow I don't think you do. Look, nothing can be done about Wyatt, and Jude is the only one who can get in here and save your collective asses. Connor, look at me." When he met her gaze, Kristy said, "Unless you want to go back to playing for double-digit crowds who just want to drink with a little background music, I would suggest you and Jude leave your bullshit in the past."

Connor scowled. "It *is* in the past. I'm over it."

A.J. and Richie exchanged incredulous looks. If Connor was over Jude, then that had happened in the past fifteen seconds or so. Hell, one of the first things A.J. had learned upon joining Running with Scissors was that if you wanted to fuck with Connor, all you had to do was mention Jude. And if you fucked with Connor, you'd be on your way out of Running with Scissors on a moment's notice. That had been a bone of contention that helped drive Wyatt away.

Over Jude? My ass.

Kristy didn't look convinced either. She folded her arms and arched a thin eyebrow.

Connor sighed, deflating a little. "I'm serious."

"So am I. Jude is bailing us out big time. We just need the two of you to get along, and everyone—*everyone*—to let the past go and be adults about this. All right?"

More nods. More murmurs.

Kristy lowered her arms and rolled the visible tension out of her shoulders. "Bottom line is our problem is solved, at least for the foreseeable future. I'll have Jude meet us in Omaha, and from there you guys are going to need to find any time and space you can, and rehearse, rehearse, rehearse. He knows the music, but he's going to be rusty, and none of you have played with him since he left. If anyone wants to hash out any bullshit, suck it up and wait until we aren't in hot water if someone walks out. Got it?"

Connor muttered something A.J. didn't understand, and no one asked him to repeat it.

"Everyone get some sleep." Kristy started for the door. "We're on the road bright and early tomorrow."

She left, and after the door had closed, Connor sagged back against the chair opposite A.J.'s. "This is bullshit."

"It's the only option we have," Richie said.

Connor rolled his eyes. "You don't think I could go on Craigslist right now and find a desperate bassist who—"

"Oh, save it." Vanessa shook her head. "Running with Scissors doesn't need a random desperate bassist. We need someone who knows our music and won't make us all sound bad. Like it or not, that's Jude."

"Connor, please." Shiloh touched his shoulder. "We all know this is going to be hard on you. None of us are thrilled about the idea either, but we don't have any other options. Can you guys just, you know, get along until—?"

"We'll be *fine*." Connor shrugged away from her and pushed himself to his feet. "I need some air." He stormed out of the room and slammed the door so hard it rattled the whole building.

In silence, everyone stared at the door as if Connor might suddenly come back in. Yeah, right. One of the *other* first things they'd all told A.J. was that when Connor said he needed some air, let him go. He'd be back—eventually—but for the love of God, do not go after him.

Shiloh turned away. Folding her arms, she leaned against the wall beside the brown burlap drapes. "Why am I suddenly hoping they'll get back together?"

Every head snapped toward her.

Richie's eyes got huge. "Please tell me you're joking."

Shiloh scowled. "Well, if they were fucking again, then they wouldn't be trying to kill each other."

A.J. sat up a little. "That might—"

"You're probably right." Vanessa pursed her lips. Then she sighed and shrugged. "Part of me wants to choke them if they even look at each other, but I can't really argue with you, to tell you the truth."

Richie grunted in agreement. A.J. couldn't argue either. Connor was easiest to deal with when he and his guy du jour were on speaking terms and sleeping together. But God help them all if there was even the slightest lover's quarrel. Bringing an ex—especially *that* ex—into the picture was going to make things interesting.

Vanessa cursed. "Well, Connor's going to be easy to live with for a while."

A.J. sat up a little. "Maybe we'd—"

"Can you blame him?" Shiloh asked. A.J. gritted his teeth. Why he tried to interject in these conversations, he didn't even know.

"Uh, yeah," Richie said. "Actually, I can blame him." He sat back against the headboard, lacing his hands behind his head. "He has nobody to blame but himself for this shit with Jude, and he fucking knows it."

"That wasn't entirely Connor's fault," Vanessa said. "Remember? Wyatt quit, and so did Jude."

Richie huffed. "Connor brought that on himself— and us—both times. If someone treated me the way he treated Jude, I'd cheat too."

"Wouldn't you just have broken up with Connor before things got so ugly?" Vanessa said. "I mean, why bother sticking around until it's that bad? They were both idiots for dragging it out, just like Wyatt was an idiot for thinking Connor was over Jude." Rolling her eyes, she added, "And Connor *is* an idiot for being hung up on that jackass."

Shiloh scowled. "Enough. Come on. Jude's not a bad guy, and neither is Connor. They just suck at relationships, and Connor's super protective of the band. Fact is, we wouldn't have gotten this far without either of them."

"Yeah, they got us really far," Vanessa said. "And that almost didn't matter since Jude decided to fuck *us* after he was done fucking Connor."

"Okay, yes." Shiloh shrugged. "And Wyatt quit, so— "

"So I'll smack him if I ever see him again," Vanessa said, "but I have to work with Connor, and now Jude too. I'm pissed at all of them, but those two are going to be here."

"True," Shiloh said. "But the fact is, Jude's just here temporarily. It was his choice to do what he did, and he knew what was at stake. If he and Connor don't get along this time, we all know who's getting the boot."

A murmur of reluctant agreement rippled through the group.

"Well." Vanessa stretched her arms as she stood. "Kristy's right. We're on the road early tomorrow. I'm going to call it a night."

Shiloh nodded. "Same here. Let's go."

The girls left. Connor hadn't returned yet, so the tension in the room had eased, at least for the moment. Richie went out for a smoke, leaving A.J. alone with his thoughts.

A.J. sat back and stared up at the ceiling. His fingers kept time with his heartbeat, tapping softly on his leg, and his other knee bounced as his heel tapped out the piece he'd been practicing earlier. Try as he might, he could not get comfortable. Even though the bassist crisis was averted, and things weren't as up in the air as they'd been since Wyatt's departure, A.J. didn't like this. He didn't like it at all.

He'd been at the recent meetings where they'd all panicked over what to do now that Wyatt was gone, but he was fairly sure there'd been conversations behind closed doors too. This group had been friends since they were kids, and Kristy had been their manager since the band's early days. A.J. had been part of the group for a year and a half, coming in on the heels of Jude's departure, but he still felt like an outsider.

What if the band settled their drama and decided to keep Jude after all? And what if they decided he was better behind the drums than he was on the bass, and decided to—

Easy, A.J.

He slowly released a breath. Jude was coming back temporarily. He wasn't going to replace A.J.

He screwed them over. They're not going to boot me out and keep him.

I hope.

Three days later, Running with Scissors arrived in Omaha. While Schadenfreude prepared to take the stage without their opening act, Running with Scissors settled into a shithole motel on the other side of town. Hopefully their crappy tour bus would be repaired soon—in addition to a volatile lead singer and a missing bassist, the band had been dealing with a bus with no running water for the last week and a half. Because they weren't at each other's throats enough already. And yes, they were lucky to even *have* a shower and a toilet on their bus, but God help them when those things quit working.

Kristy came into the guys' room, where everyone was hanging out, and jingled a set of keys. "I'm going to get Jude from the airport. Anyone coming with me?"

Connor smirked. "He can't get a cab?"

"He could, but since he's saving our asses, I thought picking him up myself was the least I could do."

Connor's lip curled, but he didn't argue.

A.J. shifted and then stood. "Do you mind if I come with you, Kristy? Since I've never met him?"

"Not at all." Kristy smiled. "Let's roll."

He thought he felt some invisible daggers coming his way, but didn't bother checking if Connor was glaring at him. Or if any of the other band members were. He just followed Kristy outside to the parking lot, and they climbed into a black Ford Explorer.

"His flight is on time," she said. "So we shouldn't have to wait long. I'm going to park, though, instead of waiting for him on the curb. In case he needs a hand with his stuff."

A.J. didn't protest. Neither of them said much while Kristy's phone directed them from the motel to the interstate. When the first sign for Eppley Airfield came into view, a nervous feeling twisted in A.J.'s stomach. This was it. He was going to meet the legendary Jude. And hopefully—*hopefully!*—he wouldn't get replaced by the guy.

He drummed his nails on the armrest. "So, you really think Jude's going to be able to perform?" His cheeks burned at the accidental double entendre. "I mean, he hasn't played in ages."

"If it were anyone else, I'd be concerned. I'm not sure I'd trust any other musician to get onstage after so little rehearsal time, but he's . . ." She was quiet for a moment, and A.J. marveled at how still her hands were on the wheel while she seemed so lost in thought. "Jude was born to be a musician. No two ways about it. He plays by ear, too. Once he hears a song, he only needs to run through it a couple of times before he nails it. He was one of those child prodigies, and if his parents'd had their way, he would've gone to Juilliard or something. And if I have *my* way, he'll be back in Running with Scissors *permanently.*"

A.J. gulped. "As . . . the bassist?"

"What else would—" She glanced at him. "Oh honey. I'm not looking to replace you."

"He's a drummer, though."

"Drumming is his passion, yes. But he's a *musician*. In every sense of the word. He could easily fill the shoes of any member of that band except vocals, and even then, he could pull it off in a pinch. The thing is, whether he's on the drums, the bass, the keyboard, or the damn cowbell, he's amazing. And personal drama aside, the band is better with him than without him." She sighed. "I just hope he'll stay with us this time."

A.J. pressed his lips together. If he'd been nervous about Jude before, he was a wreck now. He was good, and he knew he was good, but he wasn't child-prodigy good. It was just as well the band was still pissed at Jude. Apparently he'd walked out days before a major festival—one that had been teeming with people from record labels—and they'd had to bail on the performance. A.J. couldn't say he blamed them for the grudge.

Kristy reached across the console and patted his arm. "Listen, hon. You have nothing to worry about. I promise." She withdrew her hand and put it back on the wheel. "You're a rock-solid drummer, and quite honestly, you're one of the saner members of that band."

He laughed halfheartedly. "Really?"

"Oh yeah. And that sanity, it helps the morale for the whole band. Even Connor. Hell, especially Connor. When he gets pissed off, almost everyone involved in this group just pours gas on the fire, but you've got a calming effect on all of them." She glanced at him again. "I've seen you stop Shiloh and Vanessa from getting into catfights, and Richie's just mellower all around when you're there. Musicians are volatile creatures, honey. Anyone who can keep them from killing each other is worth his weight in gold."

"I do my best."

"In fact, with Jude in the band?" Kristy whistled. "That calming effect of yours is going to be even more crucial than ever. Trust me, A.J. You're not going *anywhere.*"

Great. His life's ambition—to be the second-best drummer in a band, but to be kept around because someone had to keep them all from killing each other.

But at least he wasn't getting kicked out of Running with Scissors anytime soon.

Inside the tiny airport, Kristy and A.J. loitered in baggage claim by the escalator. She alternately scrolled through emails on her phone and looked up at the escalator. A.J. did the same, though his nerves were holding his attention more than Facebook or Twitter. A few fans had tweeted at the band, and a handful had messaged him directly. He'd reply to those when his brain was functional. Hopefully they wouldn't mind the wait.

Beside him, Kristy straightened. "There he is."

A.J. turned around, and his heart went into double time. There was no mistaking who this man was, coming down the escalator with the guitar case on his back and the elaborate sleeve of ink covering his right arm, but he looked a hell of a lot different than he had in the photos and videos A.J. had seen. Either those images hadn't done Jude a bit of justice, or a year and a half had been enough for him to quantum leap from good-looking to *holy shit*.

As the escalator brought Jude closer, A.J. stared. Jude's nearly black hair was cut short now. Instead of hanging in sweaty strings over his face and falling over his shoulders, it was cropped like he'd walked into a barbershop with a copy of *GQ* and said, "*That's* what I want." A hint of five-o'clock shadow dusted his sharp jaw, and though they looked exhausted as all hell, those dark eyes were just spectacular.

Jude must've seen Kristy right then, because a tired smile spread across his lips. A moment later he stepped off the escalator, oblivious to the effect he was having on A.J.'s blood pressure, and embraced Kristy.

The manager hugged him tight. "It's good to see you, baby."

"You too."

As they separated, Kristy gestured at A.J. "Jude, this is A.J. Palmer. He's—"

"My replacement." Jude studied A.J. His comment hadn't been laced with any malice. Just an observation, it seemed. "Jude Colburn."

"I know." A.J. extended his hand. "Good to meet you."

"Likewise." Jude started to return the gesture, but hesitated. "I, uh . . ." He glanced down, and A.J. followed his gaze. At first, A.J.'s attention went to the elaborate tattoos going from beneath Jude's T-shirt sleeve to just below the heel of his hand, but then he realized what was making Jude hesitate—his fingers were wrapped in white tape. They'd even bled through in a few places.

"Oh. Shit." A.J. withdrew the offer. "Don't worry about it. I understand."

Jude smiled faintly. "Thanks. I've been, uh, practicing. So . . ."

"Good." Kristy's lips quirked. "Are you going to be healed enough to play?"

He shrugged. "I've played through worse."

"Just don't wear your fingers off, okay?"

"Promise."

Behind them, the baggage claim belt groaned to life.

"I'd better get my bag." Jude adjusted the bass on his shoulders.

"Okay. Why don't I go get the car?" Kristy gestured at the door. "I'll meet you two outside."

"Perfect."

She left, and suddenly A.J. was alone with the unexpectedly hot incarnation of Jude Colburn. All six foot something of him. He only had an inch or two on A.J., but it felt like much more. Even standing there, tired as fuck and waiting for his luggage to come down the belt, he had a larger-than-life presence about him.

Or maybe A.J. just hadn't been laid in way, *way* too long.

He cleared his throat and turned away before he made an ass of himself.

A moment later, Jude hauled a drab green duffel bag off the belt. "All right, that's everything."

"Just the one bag?"

"Well, and . . ." Jude tapped the bass still slung over his shoulder. "I travel light."

"So I see." A.J. gestured at the duffel bag. "You want me to carry that?"

"You don't mind?"

"Nah, it's fine."

"Cool." Jude handed it over. "Thanks."

"Don't mention it." A.J. returned the smile as he hoisted Jude's bag onto his shoulders.

Outside, as they waited on the curb, Jude turned to him, his expression blank. "So how's the tour been going?"

"It's been awesome. Beats the hell out of playing in clubs."

A barely perceptible wince flickered across Jude's face. "Glad to hear it."

"Thanks, by the way." A.J. shifted his weight. "For bailing us out."

Jude smiled. "Don't mention it. Honestly, I've been hoping something like this would come along."

"Oh yeah?"

"Yeah. The corporate world is just . . ." He grimaced and shook his head. "I was starting to wonder how much longer I could handle it before I went on a stapling rampage or threw a printer at one of the guys in my cubicle."

A.J. laughed. "That bad?"

"Worse." Jude sighed. "Okay, it's not *that* bad. But it's definitely not for me. This"—he adjusted the bass on his shoulder—"is what I was born to do."

"I know the feeling. I was doing retail before I joined the band."

Jude wrinkled his nose. "Sorry to hear it."

"Eh, it was a paycheck. A small one, but a paycheck."

"There is that. I'll be fucking thrilled if I don't have to go back to a day job, though."

"Yeah, same here." An uncomfortable knot grew beneath A.J.'s ribs. Jude had been itching for a change. Wanting to get back onstage. What if he liked being back in his old band and stayed indefinitely? Beyond the next album and tour? How long before he started eyeballing the drum set?

No. No. Not going to think about that. I'm part of this band. Jude is the bassist. The temporary *bassist.*

I'm not going anywhere.

Please, God . . .

Oblivious to A.J.'s worries, Jude reached into his pocket and pulled out a wrinkled pack of cigarettes. He slipped one between his lips, then patted the pockets of his jeans—front first, then back, then front again—and cursed around the cigarette. "You don't have a lighter, do you?"

A.J. shook his head. "Sorry."

"Damn it." Jude shoved the pack into his pocket but kept the single unlit cigarette in his mouth. "Fucking TSA took mine."

"Bastards."

"Right?"

A.J. wasn't a fan of smoking—it didn't bother him but didn't do anything for him either. Still, there was something weirdly hot about Jude with the cigarette. About this whole picture of Jude—clean-cut with some scruff and a hell of a lot of ink, standing beneath a No Smoking sign with a cigarette hanging from the corner of his mouth and an elbow on his bass—that did inexplicable things to A.J.'s pulse. It was a damn good thing Jude wasn't playing his bass just then, long fingers on the strings and narrow hips cocked just so . . .

A.J. shook himself and tried not to pass out from thinking about Jude with a bass across his lap.

Breathe, dude. Get a fucking grip.

A pair of headlights caught his eye, and he waved at the approaching Explorer. "There's Kristy."

"Perfect," Jude said around the cigarette. "Maybe she's got a lighter."

A.J. had never seen Kristy smoke, but she'd pulled stranger things from that giant handbag.

When their manager stepped out of the Explorer, though, she took one look at Jude and gave him that ball-withering scowl that kept most of the band in line. "Jude Colburn, when did you take up smoking again?"

Jude smiled sheepishly, his cheeks coloring. "Uh . . ."

She sighed loudly. "Idiot. Well, no smoking in the car. You'll have to wait until we get to the motel."

"Motel? They don't even have a bus?"

"They do, Princess." She opened the trunk. "But we're stuck in motels until it's fixed."

"Joy." Jude hoisted his bag and bass into the trunk.

"Hey, you've got nothing to complain about." She wagged a finger at him. "The mechanics are working on the bus as we speak, so *you* only have to spend *one* night in a shitty motel. We've been staying in them since Little Rock."

"Ouch."

"Yeah. Ouch. Okay, let's roll."

Everyone climbed into the Explorer. While Kristy shifted gears, A.J. settled into the backseat. As it happened, the seating arrangement gave him a perfect vantage point to surreptitiously check out Jude.

So, heart pounding and palms sweating, he fixed his gaze on the ridiculously hot bassist-slash-drummer.

And wondered just how screwed he was.

L.A. WITT

CHAPTER 3

Jude hadn't expected the new drummer to show up at the airport with Kristy. He hadn't expected anyone, really, but especially not the guy who'd taken his place.

Good thing he'd been on the escalator when he first saw A.J., or he'd have tripped over his own feet, because he sure as hell hadn't expected . . . that.

The kid definitely took the "I'm a fucking rock star" look seriously. His bleached blond spikes with "I don't give a fuck" dark roots were eye-catching, as were the eyebrow piercings and the nose ring. Jude was willing to bet money this kid never went onstage without eyeliner, and that thought . . .

Shiver.

The drummer behind him was the least of his concerns tonight, though. All the way here from California, his stomach had been in knots that those

35

twelve-dollar bottles of booze on the plane hadn't been able to touch. His bandmates had every reason to want nothing to do with him. Kristy had undoubtedly warned them against giving him shit since he was bailing them out. That didn't mean they'd be thrilled to see him.

Kristy pulled into a parking space outside one of those cheap motels where people either got knocked up or murdered.

He craned his neck, scrutinizing the decrepit clapboard shithole beneath a faded sign. "Record company's really making you guys travel in luxury, aren't they?"

Kristy sniffed. "Yeah. If Schadenfreude's bus had broken down, they'd be staying in the goddamned Four Seasons. But whatever. It's only until after this show."

He turned to her. "What's wrong with the bus?"

"Plumbing issues." She dropped her keys into that giant ever-present purse. "If the mechanics value their lives, we'll have it back by the time we hit the road tomorrow, and y'all will be sleeping in it in Denver."

"Great." He swallowed. "Do I need to sleep with one eye open?"

She laughed uncomfortably and patted his leg, something she only did when she was trying to sell somebody bullshit. "Oh come on, honey. It's all in the past."

"Yeah. Not-the-very-distant past."

She sighed. "You'll be fine."

"At least let me have a cigarette first." He paused. "You got a light?"

Kristy rolled her eyes and then dug through her purse. After a moment she found a cheap BIC lighter and handed it to him. "Do we need to have a talk about your smoking?"

"Not if you want me to get through this tour without turning into a nervous wreck."

She scowled but shrugged. "Okay. When the tour's over, we're—"

"Yeah, yeah."

"I mean it."

"I know you do."

They got out of the truck, and Jude lit up a cigarette before he helped A.J. unload what little luggage he'd brought along. He'd been itching for a smoke for hours, especially since the Denver airport, where he'd spent a way-too-fucking-long-layover, had cruelly eliminated its smoking lounges. Now he needed two or three in a row, not only to kill the craving but to settle his nerves. There was no telling how this was going to play out, but he wasn't all that optimistic.

He extinguished the cigarette beneath his heel. Kristy pushed herself off the truck, which she'd been leaning on, but A.J. didn't move. He stood beside her, and he studied Jude, holding his position as if he knew without a doubt that Jude wasn't stopping with a single cigarette.

Smart kid.

Jude pulled out a second smoke.

Kristy glared at him but didn't say anything. She probably wanted to get this over with as much as he did, but she was apparently willing to cut him some slack this one time.

Through the thin cloud of smoke, Jude surreptitiously watched A.J. The drummer was playing on his phone now, so those intense eyes were focused elsewhere, giving Jude a chance to stare for a minute. And checking A.J. out was easier than thinking about what awaited him behind one of those numbered doors, so he damn sure took the opportunity and stared.

Drummers always developed gorgeous muscles in their arms and shoulders, and A.J. was no exception. His biceps and shoulders stretched the limits of his tight T-shirt, and even the subtle motions of his fingers skimming across the phone sent subtle, mouthwatering ripples up his toned forearm.

I wonder if he takes his shirt off when he's performing.

Jude coughed and looked away, hoping A.J. hadn't noticed him choking on his own smoke. Or staring at A.J.'s arms.

It wasn't just that Jude couldn't help drooling over what drumming did to a man's physique. He also missed the effect it'd had on his own body before he'd stopped drumming. His tattoos masked some of the new softness, but it was still obvious to him. A constant reminder that he was trading a life of percussion for the slow onset of carpal tunnel.

The carpal tunnel was a moot point now, though. He had his wrist splints with him in case he needed them, but it wasn't like he was spending forty hours a week at a keyboard anymore. He might shred his fingers on the strings or strain his muscles and tendons a million different ways onstage, but the days of plunking data into spreadsheets and wearing the numbers off a ten-key were behind him.

Yep. It's behind me.

Whether I like it or not.

As he blew out some smoke, he fidgeted. His skin itched, as if reality were pushing itself in through his pores. There was no turning back, was there?

"We're sorry to see you go," his boss had said without an ounce of sincerity. *"Are you sure you can't give me a full two-week notice, though?"*

"I wish I could. This came up kind of . . . suddenly."

"I see." The look—piercing eyes over wire-rimmed glasses—had told him in no uncertain terms this resignation was a one-way ticket. *Don't even try to come crawling back in a few months when you're done playing wannabe rock star with people who wouldn't piss on you if you were on fire.*

"Jude?" Kristy's voice startled him. "The band's waiting, honey."

He swallowed. There was nearly three-quarters of an inch of ash on the end of his cigarette after he'd let it burn unnoticed for . . . however long he'd been lost in thought. "Right. Yeah." He tapped the ashes, took another drag, and then crushed this butt beside the first. Then he picked both up and, since there was no ashtray nearby, tossed them in the gravel where they wouldn't ignite anything. "Okay. Let's do this."

A.J. picked up Jude's duffel bag, and Jude took the bass, and they followed Kristy up to the second floor breezeway. At the door of room two twenty-one, she paused and turned to him. "You ready?"

"Not really."

A thin eyebrow rose. "Jude, are you—"

"I'm never going to be ready." He nodded toward the door. "Let's just . . . get this part over with." *Before I decide to stand out here and smoke every cigarette I have left.*

His skin prickled, and he glanced at A.J. Their eyes met briefly, but the drummer quickly lowered his gaze.

I hope you aren't this timid onstage, kid.

Kristy swiped her keycard, pushed open the door, and gestured for him to go inside.

He stepped in. And stopped. And swallowed.

Holy shit, was this weird.

Time ground to a halt, and no one in the room seemed to be moving or breathing. Everyone just stared at each other. He absently tapped the tips of his fingers against his thumb, tape clicking against tape and the dull impacts stinging his raw, bandaged skin. He couldn't stop, though. He needed some sort of release for all this nervous energy, and this was the subtlest thing he could manage.

Everyone had changed, and everyone was the same.

Shiloh's hair had been almost white when Jude left, hanging halfway down her tattooed back. Now it was black, cropped so short it barely reached the edge of her tightly clenched jaw. Was the third eyebrow ring new? He couldn't remember for sure.

Richie was a little heavier. Vanessa was a little thinner. Not surprising—Jude had heard that touring took its toll. Nobody made it from one end to the other without wearing the effects of sleep deprivation, eating like a coyote, and performing night after night. He wasn't looking forward to those effects himself, but he envied his bandmates—*former* bandmates—for those visible reminders of the past few weeks. He'd have preferred that form of self-destruction over chain-smoking his way through a miserable job beneath fluorescent lights.

As they stood in silence, it slowly sank in just how long it had been since they'd all been in the same room. The people looking back at him—they were strangers now despite almost twenty years of history.

Wyatt was conspicuous in his absence—Jude couldn't remember a time when the band was all together and Wyatt wasn't kicked back in a chair, his fingers moving constantly across his bass strings like a spider perfecting its web.

And farthest away from Jude, sitting up against a headboard with his legs crossed and his fingers working at a loose thread on his laced-up black boot, was Connor. His blond hair was pulled back, dark eyes fixed right on Jude, and no, a year and a half hadn't been enough time to let bygones be bygones. The time apparently hadn't done a thing to temper the anger that smoldered in his eyes just like the night Jude had come clean. God knew how much worse it had gotten when Connor found out that Jude had quit the band—like a coward, Jude had told Kristy and the others, but hadn't had the balls to face Connor again. The guilt had been too much then, and it was still too much now.

Jude tore his gaze away from his ex and shook himself. "Wow. It's, um, been a long time."

Connor glared at him, and though he didn't speak, the *Not nearly long enough* came across loud and clear.

Richie sat up, brushing a few black curls out of his face. "How you been, man?"

Jude rocked from his heels to the balls of his feet. "Good. Good." *I should've smoked three.* "How's the tour been going?"

"It's been great up until recently." Shiloh stood. She glanced at her bandmates, then the floor, and finally met Jude's gaze, a tentative smile forming on her lips. To his surprise, she stepped closer and hugged him. "It's good to see you again."

"You too." Jude swallowed, returning her embrace. She let him go, and no one else got up to offer so much as a handshake. "Well, um, I'm a bit late, but congrats. On the record deal."

"Thanks," each muttered, aside from Connor.

Jude tapped his fingers harder against his thumb, letting the sting and the percussion ground him. His gaze shifted from one bandmate to the other, and his stomach sank deeper. He'd grown up with them, and now they couldn't even make comfortable small talk. Fuck—this was going to be a long tour.

Kristy checked her watch. "It's getting to be about dinner-thirty, so why don't you all figure out something to eat." She cast a sweeping glance at the band members. Immediately, Richie, Shiloh, A.J., and Vanessa were on their feet and heading for the door.

Shiloh slung her purse over her shoulder. "I think I saw a Chinese place up the road."

"Chinese again?" Vanessa made a face. "Ugh. Can't we just get a damn pizza?"

"I think there's a Subway close by too." Richie held open the door. To Kristy he said, "We'll bring back whatever we find."

"Good. *Go.*" She shooed them out, and when the door closed, suddenly the room was almost empty. Voices and footsteps faded down the breezeway, leaving Jude and Kristy and—

Connor.

Jude gulped. *Fuck.*

He locked eyes with his ex, and the hatred written all over Connor's face faltered for a second, his features softening just long enough to twist the guilt a little harder in Jude's chest. Even as Connor's cold expression returned, Jude couldn't help—for a couple of seconds— seeing the man he'd been in love with at one time. Had it really been that long since he'd woken up looking into those eyes? He didn't miss the Connor who was sitting there glaring at him. Seeing the other side of him, though—that "how could you?" beneath the veil that had briefly lifted—hit him harder than he'd thought it would.

He swallowed, breaking eye contact. This was a mistake, wasn't it?

"So, what now?" Connor huffed sharply. "Do you want us to dance or something?"

"Enough." Kristy stood between them, arms folded, and gave them each a pointed look. "All right, you two. Here's the thing. I know you guys have all kinds of baggage and shit that neither of you has let go, and I don't need a couple of powder kegs on this tour."

Connor opened his mouth to speak, but a glare from their manager shut him up fast.

"Listen," she snapped. "I'm going to step outside, and you two have until the rest of the band gets back with dinner to settle this enough you can function as bandmates for the next few weeks, and work together on the next album. You don't have to like each other, but over my dead body are you going to make this tour miserable for the rest of the band. Talk. Get it out of your systems, and then I don't want to hear another word about it, or see so much as a dirty look while Jude is back in the band. Clear?"

Jude nodded. "Yeah."

"Whatever," Connor growled.

Kristy eyed them both.

Sometimes she struck Jude as a frazzled mom trying to keep a handle on a half dozen rowdy kids who refused to stay in line. That was probably how she felt too, especially since she was sometimes the only thing that kept Running with Scissors from imploding.

She adjusted her purse on her shoulder. "You've got about half an hour, depending on where they decide to go get food."

With that, she walked out, letting the door slam behind her.

For the first time in a year and a half, he was alone with Connor, and the air between them was as fraught as it had been the last time. Connor didn't get up. Jude stayed where he was, standing in the middle of the orange carpet like an idiot, wondering what the hell he was supposed to say. Finally he managed, "It's, um, been a while."

His ex's lips pulled tight. "That's what you wanted, isn't it?"

"Come on. Don't start. It's been long enough. We can—"

Connor snorted derisively as only he could. Then he got up from the bed and came around the foot. Face-to-face, he and Jude locked eyes again. "Long enough? Maybe for you."

Jude gritted his teeth. "Listen, everything that happened was in the past. Can we . . . I mean, we've got to work together. Is there any way we can put the past behind us?"

"The past *was* behind us," Connor snapped. "And now, here you are."

"Do you want me to leave?"

His lips twisted. "What I want and what the band needs aren't the same thing."

"Glad you finally understand that."

"Oh, fuck you." Connor's lips pulled back across his teeth. "You're the last man alive who can get on that high horse. After you—"

"What do you want me to say? Kristy called me. It wasn't the other way around. You guys need—"

"We need a fucking bassist who knows our music. Just because you're bailing us out doesn't mean you didn't fuck us over in the past."

Jude exhaled hard. "Okay, look. I messed up back then. I know I did. And I'm sorry."

"Yeah? For which part?" Connor narrowed his eyes. "The part where you screwed over the band? Or the part where you screwed *me* over?"

Jude winced. "All of it. I—"

"It really doesn't matter." He stepped closer, still looking Jude right in the eye. "Let's be clear about one thing. As far as I'm concerned, you're here to fill in until we find someone to sign on permanently. If that means through the next tour, fine. But don't think for a minute that you're a part of this band anymore."

"Connor, I—"

"There's nothing else to say." Connor set his jaw. "You had your shot. You're nothing but a touring bassist now, and the minute we find someone to—"

"I get it," Jude ground out. "But the fact is, we have to be onstage together."

"Yeah. We do." Connor raised his chin. "And the stage and rehearsals are the only places we need to cross paths."

"Is that right? Because I heard tour buses are pretty tight confines."

"They are."

Jude shifted uncomfortably, running his thumb back and forth along his fingers as if they were guitar strings. "I don't know what you want me to say. We're stuck together for a while."

"Yep." Connor shrugged. "And Kristy can try to make us kiss and make up all she wants, but this is the best you're getting from me. Personally, I think it's a hell of a lot better than you deserve." Another shrug. "Pity you can play the bass, isn't it?"

Jude rolled his eyes and exhaled. "Jesus, Connor. I fucked up back then, but don't you dare act like you didn't—"

"Like I didn't what?" Connor got right up in his face. "Like I didn't deserve for my best friend and boyfriend to go off and fuck someone else just for spite? Are you saying I did?"

Jude didn't back down. "No, you didn't. And I'm sorry. But don't act like you didn't walk all over me for a year leading up to that."

Connor blinked. Genuine hurt flickered across his face, cutting Jude right to the bone, but it was quickly replaced by fresh anger. "If you were that miserable, why didn't you just man up and break up instead of—"

"I tried. Several times."

Connor laughed humorlessly. "Well. Guess it worked the last time, didn't it?" He stormed past Jude, clipping his shoulder as he went by and muttering "motherfucker" under his breath. Before Jude could stop him, he snatched his wallet off the table, threw open the door, and stormed out.

The door banged shut. Jude's shoulders dropped.

Maybe he should've kept that cubicle job after all.

L.A. WITT

CHAPTER 4

To keep the peace, Jude roomed with Kristy that night while Connor stayed with Richie and A.J. For a while, Richie tried to talk Connor down, but eventually gave up and put on his headphones, leaving A.J. to listen to Connor ranting and sniping about Jude.

A.J. kept his mouth shut. There was no point in trying to reason with Connor if the subject was Jude. He couldn't blame the guy. From what everyone had said, Jude had left them all in one hell of a lurch back then, and he'd hurt Connor. Though the lead singer was a volatile son of a bitch, and maybe not the easiest person to live or work with, A.J. couldn't imagine he'd deserved to have his heart stomped on and his band left hanging in one night. A.J. didn't envy the situation he was in now.

But the show had to go on, and they'd be on the road at the crack of dawn, so despite Jude's presence next door, they settled in to grab some shut-eye.

Not surprisingly, it was one of the worst restless nights he'd had so far on this tour. It didn't help that Connor spent most of it tossing and turning. In the next bed, A.J. was wide-awake because even when Connor was still, his frustration was so palpable, it might as well have been feedback through an amp—constant, shrill, impossible to muffle or ignore. Great. The rest of this tour was going to be like living in his parents' house during the final weeks of their marriage.

He sighed into the taut silence. No wonder Shiloh had lost her shit the night she'd realized Connor and Wyatt were sleeping together. A.J. had thought she was overreacting—so what if two adults in the same band were dating? Who cared?—but she must've known what the aftermath would be. The inevitable breakup. The three excruciating weeks of Wyatt and Connor gnashing their teeth at each other. A screaming match that almost killed Connor's voice an hour before a show.

She'd probably seen all of that coming, but A.J. doubted even she had imagined that Wyatt would pack up and walk out. None of them had expected that. Not from the band member who'd been most vocal about his resentment toward Jude. And now, like an evil prophecy coming to fruition, Wyatt was gone, Jude was in his place, and Connor was losing his mind.

A.J. shifted beneath the covers, doing his level best not to wake Richie. He wasn't sure why he bothered. The guitarist could've slept onstage during a show. Lucky bastard.

A.J. swore into his pillow. Then he closed his eyes, took a deep breath, and tried like hell to go to sleep.

Kristy sent them all wake-up texts at six fifteen, including one to A.J. to remind him to wake Richie. At six forty-five, she was at their door, making sure everyone was out of bed.

"You guys can shower tonight if you have to, but we need to get on the road. Let's *go*."

Richie rubbed his eyes. "The bus is here already?"

"Yep." She gestured over her shoulder. "And it's leaving as soon as you all get your butts on it."

A.J. glanced past her, beyond the breezeway's railing. Below them the tour bus took up a sizeable chunk of the parking lot, its diesel engines idling while Vanessa and Shiloh shuffled toward it, dragging their suitcases behind them.

"Let's go," Kristy said again, and left the room.

A.J. bit back a string of curses. Connor didn't. Awesome. It was going to be one of those days when everyone within earshot would know exactly how displeased the lead singer was. That would make the bus ride through corn-covered plains just *fly* by.

Trying to stay out of everyone's way, A.J. dressed, gathered his things, and left the room. Brushing his teeth in the parking lot with an ice-cold bottle of water was a bit more "roughing it" than he liked, but it kept him from being underfoot.

He rinsed his mouth and toothbrush and then joined the others on the bus. Richie was sprawled across the sofa, seat-belted and snoring. Still no Connor, but he was always the straggler. This morning, he was probably in even less of a hurry than usual.

Outside, with his back to the bus, Jude rocked from the balls of his feet to his heels, a cigarette between his taped fingers. Through the tinted window, A.J. couldn't see much of Jude's face—even when he turned, his baseball cap and sunglasses kept his eyes in shadow.

A.J. couldn't help wondering how much of his smoking was due to nicotine addiction and how much of it was nerves. He'd heard Jude step out of the room next door, and in the stillness, he'd been able to make out the click of a lighter. At least once, Jude had either been playing with the lighter, or he'd smoked two cigarettes in rapid succession. Yet he didn't have the voice or cough of a chain-smoker. And when he'd smoked in the parking lot yesterday before meeting up with the band, his hands had gotten progressively shakier, where most people's would've steadied after getting their fix.

Jude turned, and his spine suddenly straightened. A.J. followed the trajectory of his gaze toward the motel and wasn't at all surprised to see Connor walking across the parking lot, a duffel on his shoulder and a coffee cup in his hand. Both guys wore dark sunglasses, but the lenses did nothing to temper the poisonous glares that passed between them.

Then they quickly broke eye contact. Connor sipped his coffee. Jude took a drag off his cigarette. Neither looked the other's way again.

Connor boarded the bus. He stashed his duffel and took a seat at the table. Shiloh was sitting opposite him, playing on her phone, but neither spoke. After he'd fastened his seat belt, Connor gazed out the window as he nursed his coffee.

A moment later, Jude boarded. Connor's gaze stayed fixed on something outside. For his part, Jude focused straight ahead as he continued into the back of the bus where the racks were. Something unzipped, and something else rustled, and then Jude returned, a pair of earbuds in his hand. He found a seat that put some distance between himself and Connor—a deliberate choice, no doubt—put in his earbuds, and pulled his cap over his eyes.

The engines groaned, and the bus eased into motion. As the bus rolled down the interstate, most of the band members dozed, and thanks to the motion and the steady hum of road noise, even A.J. drifted off.

The next thing he knew, the bus was decelerating and nosing down an off-ramp. His bandmates were stirring too. He sat up, yawning as he rubbed his stiff neck, and looked out the window. They were somewhere in the middle of nowhere, with nothing but a gas station and a junkyard to break up the monotony of cornfields.

"I'm going in for more coffee," Shiloh announced as the bus pulled into the gas station. "Anybody want anything?"

Everyone raised a hand. A.J.'s temples were already throbbing. Coffee? Yes, *please*.

"Of course," she grumbled, and as soon as the bus had come to a stop, she headed inside. One by one, the band followed. They browsed the racks for junk food, caffeine, and cigarettes before they paid and got back on board. Richie and Jude both smoked, then joined everyone.

Sitting at the table across from Connor, Shiloh cleared her throat. "So. I guess we should get rehearsing."

Vanessa groaned. "I haven't had nearly enough caffeine for that."

"You're not the one who needs to rehearse." Shiloh shot Jude a look. "How about you? Had enough coffee yet?"

"I'm good." Jude sat up. "My bass is in one of the compartments under the bus, though."

"Well." She nodded toward the door. "We aren't moving."

Jude chuckled. "All right, all right." He rose, throwing over his shoulder, "Back in a second."

Richie went with him, and the two returned with their instruments. This wasn't the best place for rehearsing, but their opportunities were going to be limited and they were short on time, so this would have to do.

Connor stayed in his seat, playing with the edge of his coffee cup, while the rest of the band gathered in the cramped living area, belting themselves in and making the most of what little space they had. Since A.J. wouldn't be much use during this rehearsal, he sat across from Connor and stayed out of the way.

He watched uneasily as Jude tuned his bass. Desperate or not, this was madness. They were performing tomorrow night. A little over twenty-four hours from now, they'd be taking the stage in Denver, playing for a crowd that was already impatient for Running with Scissors to get the fuck through their set so they could see Schadenfreude like they'd paid through the nose to do.

Jude rested his bass on his leg and positioned his hand on the neck. He absently warmed up, plucking his way through a few scales. The medical tape was gone now, revealing raw fingertips, but they didn't seem to hinder his ability to play.

Shiloh handed him a tattered page. "Here's the set list for tomorrow night. Where do you want to start?"

Jude's lips quirked as he scanned the list. "The bass line for 'I Never' was pretty complicated, wasn't it?"

"You tell me." Shiloh shrugged. "I'm just a lowly singer, remember?"

Jude laughed. "All right. Let's start with that one. Everything else is fairly simple, if memory serves." He handed the list back to her. "I don't suppose you've got recordings, do you?"

"I have them on my phone." She pulled her iPhone out of her pocket. "Everything we ever recorded."

"Good. Could you play 'I Never' for me?"

She cued up the song, turned the volume to max, and hit Play.

As the song started, no one spoke. Eyes closed, Jude bobbed his head and tapped his foot in time with the music. No, that wasn't right. His chin dipped and his fingers drummed in time with the bass line, but his foot tapped in time with the percussion.

When the track was almost over, Jude put his fingers on the strings. Without opening his eyes, he said, "Play it once more?"

Shiloh restarted the track.

This time, Jude played along. At first, his fingers skimmed over the strings but only grazed them, not drawing a sound from the bass beyond the faintest hiss of skin over steel.

Then he actually started playing, and almost immediately fell into perfect sync with the track. His tone, his tempo—it blended perfectly. Even when he screwed up a note once, it was subtle, and Jude recovered so quickly that A.J. wondered if he'd imagined the slip.

"Stop the track," Jude murmured.

Shiloh pressed Pause, and the music stopped.

Except it didn't. Jude kept playing, and it was as if everything on the MP3 had shut off but the bass line.

Then he too stopped. "Okay. I think I've got it."

"You think?" Shiloh laughed. "I don't know. You want to try it a few more times to make the rest of us feel better?"

Jude chuckled. "Let's see how the set goes, and we'll work on whichever ones need it."

Each piece was the same routine. Jude listened to the track. Then he played alongside it. Then he played alone. And every fucking time, he nailed it. A.J. had heard the stories of Jude as a musician, and seeing—and hearing—was definitely believing.

Once Jude had been through the entire set list, he went through it again. This time Richie joined in, and A.J. tapped out the percussion on the table. It wasn't perfect, but he was quickly becoming convinced that it would be enough for Jude to learn the piece and hold his own onstage. A few more hours of this—assuming Jude's hands could take it—and he'd be golden.

All the while, Connor watched silently from the sidelines. His expression was neutral, his gaze shifting from his coffee cup to his bandmates to something outside. He was difficult to read, but at least he didn't seem so hostile at the moment. People could say what they wanted about him—when it came down to it, he was a hard worker who put his career and his band ahead of most things. If A.J. had to guess, he'd have bet money that no matter how much Connor would've liked to choke Jude, he was grateful as hell for competent fingers on strings right then.

A.J. was grateful too. Whether anyone liked the solution or not, Running with Scissors had averted a crisis, and they had Jude to thank for it.

CHAPTER 5

The rolling rehearsal gave Jude some hope that things might level out with his bandmates, but that hope didn't last.

He hadn't even finished retaping his fingers before a heavy, conspicuous silence set in. As soon as the instruments were back in their cases, everyone had dispersed to their various seats, putting as much space between each other as their confines allowed. The "leave me the fuck alone" radiating from Connor was damn near visible to the naked eye, which was no surprise. And Jude supposed it wasn't much of a surprise, either, that Richie kept his headphones on most of the time, Vanessa wouldn't look at him, and even Shiloh kept her distance. A.J. buried his nose in a Kindle and didn't talk to anyone unless he had to.

As he surreptitiously watched his bandmates—his childhood best friends—from behind his sunglasses, his mind went back to their optimistic early days. Back when they'd all practiced until blisters turned to calluses, dreaming about an inevitable future with Running with Scissors in lights on the sides of stadiums. Shiloh coveted a shot at playing Madison Square Garden. Connor would've sold his soul for Wembley. Richie and Wyatt wanted to headline one of the big festivals like Coachella.

And time and again, they'd all fantasized about what it would be like to cruise around the country in a tour bus. They'd imagined themselves playing practical jokes on each other, stopping to take ridiculous photos in front of landmarks, and creating new music while the scenery rolled past. Icy, uncomfortable silence hadn't been part of the agenda.

Which meant that right now, damage control needed to be a little higher on Jude's agenda. He needed to figure out a way, little by little, to reconcile with everyone. There was no point in approaching Connor yet, but maybe he could nip some of this tension in the bud.

So, when the bus pulled into another rest stop and everyone wandered off, he stepped outside for a cigarette and waited for his opportunity.

Vanessa was the first to return. She glanced at him, then lowered her narrow-eyed gaze, stuffed her hands in her pockets, and hurried past him.

"Vanessa, wait." He dropped his cigarette on the pavement. "Can I talk to you?"

She turned around, glaring at him. "About what?"

"About—"

"Actually, I don't care." She put up a hand. "Whatever it is, I'm not fucking interested."

He sighed. "Vanessa, please. Can—"

"Don't even try to get put out with me." She stepped closer, lips pulled back across her clenched teeth. "Let me guess: you want to make things right and smooth everything over so we can all have peace and quiet. Am I close?"

He gulped. Then nodded.

"Yeah? Well, you can kiss my ass."

"Look, it—"

"Do you have *any* idea how much you fucked us back then? Any idea at all?" She threw up her hands. "StarFire Records was at that festival, Jude. StarFire. Records. And you know what? They were looking for us. So were Vista and B&I. They'd heard our demos, and when they found out we'd gotten one of the unsigned slots at RockClimb, they were going to be all over us."

His stomach clenched. "Yeah, I knew they were going to be there."

"Did you know we tried to contact them after the festival?"

He winced.

She folded her arms tightly across her chest. "They'd all signed other bands at RockClimb. The guy at StarFire even said if we'd been there—"

"I get it. I do. I really do. And if I could change—"

"You can't change it," she snarled. "That's the fucking point. You can't. The only reason we have a record deal now is that Shiloh and Kristy begged and pleaded with Hurricane Records to give us the fucking time of day." She shook her head, lips contorting with disgust as she held his gaze. "We could have been with StarFire, Jude. All you had to do was suck it up and deal with Connor for one more fucking week, and *we could have been with StarFire.*"

Before he could say anything else—and she probably would've cut him off anyway—Vanessa spun on her heel and stomped onto the bus.

His shoulders slumped. Okay, so maybe damage control was going to be harder than he thought. As the other band members came back, he couldn't even look them in the eyes.

I screwed you guys out of a StarFire deal. I'm sorry. I don't know what else to say.

Once they'd all come back, he joined them on the bus, put in his earbuds, and listened to anything that drowned out the lack of conversation.

When it came time to stop for lunch, they were well into Colorado and not too far from Denver. They were ahead of schedule, so there was no reason they couldn't stop, sit down, and have a relaxed meal, but the consensus was fast food. No one was objecting to anything that could be acquired, brought on the bus, and eaten with minimal interaction. After his spat with Vanessa, Jude had to admit he was grateful for that today.

As he picked at his cooling fries, silence echoing in his ears whenever his MP3 player changed tracks, he cast subtle glances at his bandmates. What he needed now was an ally. Maybe he couldn't bury the hatchet with the entire band at once, but one-on-one, it was possible.

Connor was obviously not an option. A.J. was a stranger. Vanessa was out of the question for the time being. Richie avoided conflict and confrontation at all costs.

Which left . . . Shiloh.

Her back was to him now, though, her own earbuds separating her from the tense silence, and there was no privacy on this bus. He'd have to wait. But if he had a shot at making peace with anyone, it was her.

He just had to find the opportunity and hope she was willing to hear him out.

Jude didn't find his opportunity until that afternoon.

Kristy, Connor, and Vanessa had gone off to deal with some issue or another with the venue, and Richie and A.J. were hanging out with Schadenfreude's roadies.

Shiloh was alone at the table on the bus, typing away on her phone beside a steaming mug of tea.

"Hey." He stopped beside the table. "Can I talk to you for a minute?"

Shiloh thumbed the handle on her cup, but nodded. She tapped her throat and shrugged apologetically.

"Yeah, I know. It's okay." To save their voices, she and Connor both stayed almost completely silent in the hours leading up to a show. Shiloh had nearly fucked up her voice beyond repair a few years ago, so she was extra careful now, and it wasn't unusual for her to go on vocal rest for a full twenty-four hours before performing.

He slid in across from her and folded his hands in his lap. "I think . . . I think I'm the one who needs to do the talking anyway. Just stop me if you want to."

Shiloh nodded again.

"So all this tension, it's . . ." He swallowed. "Connor's not the only one who isn't thrilled about me being here, is he?"

Shiloh bit her lip. Her eyebrows pulled together, and the way she held his gaze seemed to ask, *What do you want me to say?*

He rested his folded hands on the table. "I get it. I do. And there's no way I can change what happened. What I did. All I can say is that I'm sorry. There's . . . I can't say that enough."

She lowered her eyes, her expression offering nothing.

Not sure if he really needed to say more, or if he just needed to fill this uncomfortable silence, Jude went on. "I fucked up, and nobody knows that better than I do. I've been kicking myself ever since. Connor and I, we weren't happy, and I . . . I should have just called it quits with him instead of doing what I did. At least that would've done minimal damage to the band. And believe me, if I could go back and change it, I would. In a heartbeat."

Without meeting his eyes, she picked up her phone and started tapping on the screen. He gritted his teeth, thinking she was ignoring him and responding to a text.

Okay. Message received. Apparently you don't want to—

But then she turned her screen toward him, and on the notepad app, she'd typed out: *Why?*

He swallowed. "Which part?"

She typed again and held up the screen. *Why did you quit?*

Jude took a deep breath and pushed a hand through his hair. "Because I felt like an asshole. For cheating on Connor, and for letting my thing with him cause so much strife within the band. It was a stupid, shortsighted thing to do." He paused. "Leaving the band, and cheating on Connor in the first place."

Shiloh nodded, as if to say *Go on*, but he wasn't sure what there was to add. Any explanation he gave would just sound like he was trying to rationalize things that had been dick moves, plain and simple. There were only so many ways he could apologize, only so many ways he could express how much he knew he'd fucked up.

Finally, he decided on a different approach. "You want to know what I've been doing since I left?"

She cocked her head, but nodded again.

"Would you believe I've been pushing a desk?"

Shiloh's eyes widened. She pointed at him and mouthed *You?*

"Yeah. Me. And yes, it was miserable. Especially since I'd spend my breaks googling the band and seeing what you guys were up to."

Her chin dipped slightly, and she arched an eyebrow as if to say, *Really?*

He nodded. "Especially after I'd heard you guys had signed. I kept watching because I was curious how things were going, and because I was . . ." He cleared his throat. "Look, what I'm getting at is that I was doing it to beat myself up. And to remind myself that I'd pissed away the opportunity to be there with you guys. Not just signed and touring, but . . . playing music with my friends like I've been doing since middle school. I'm not kidding when I say I've regretted everything for the last year and a half. Not a single day has gone by that I haven't hated what my life has become, and hated myself for making it turn out that way. I missed my friends. I missed the music. I even missed Connor. And yeah, I envied your success, but mostly, I . . ."

He swallowed, forcing that fucking lump back. "The thing is, I'm hoping that by filling in for Wyatt now, I can make even some of that right. Because I miss being a musician. I miss playing music and just being with you guys. Yeah, I wanted all this." He gestured at their surroundings. "And it's nice to get a taste of it, even temporarily, but it's not the same because the band is barely speaking to me. I'm not saying I blame any of you. I just, you know, hope we can eventually find a way to bury the hatchet."

Shiloh didn't say, mouth, or type anything, and the silence made his skin crawl. The band had been through stupid immaturity-fueled fights when they were teenagers, and had come out stronger on the other side, but he didn't know how to fix it this time. He didn't know if it could be fixed.

"The thing is, we were all good friends once. You guys basically *are* my childhood. I don't expect everyone to forget what I did and let it go, especially not overnight, but what can I do to at least *try* to go back to—" His voice cracked, and he stopped, lowering his gaze. "I miss you guys."

After a moment, Shiloh reached across the table. He hadn't even realized he'd been drumming his wrapped fingers until her hand stilled his. His raw skin buzzed with the lingering vibration, throbbing beneath the tape. Under the table, he started tapping his heel, nerves increasing the tempo until his knee was shaking.

With her other hand, Shiloh typed out another message—a much longer one this time—before she turned the phone around and slid it toward him.

Everybody just needs time. It hurt when you left. But I think they want you back. & you know Connor. He doesn't let things go easily. Give him time. He'll be the last to come around, but he will.

That lump rose in Jude's throat again as he pushed the phone back. "You really think they do? Want me back, I mean?"

He didn't know what to make of her split-second hesitation, but when she smiled, it seemed genuine.

His heel kept tapping beneath the table. "I am so sorry, Shiloh. I hurt everybody, and there's all this tension because of . . ." He exhaled. "I am so sorry."

Squeezing his hand, Shiloh smiled. Then she got up and came around to his side of the table. To his surprise, she hugged him, and in his ear, she whispered, "I'm glad you're back."

Jude squeezed his eyes shut and hugged her tighter. "Me too."

Later that evening, most of the band had gone off to find food, but Jude had hung back. Eyes closed, he leaned against the bus and slowly blew out a lungful of smoke. This was his third cigarette in an hour, and he wondered more than once if he'd finish off the pack before the night was through. So much for music tempering the need for nicotine. Turned out that being in close proximity to people he'd screwed over didn't help with stress levels.

But at least he'd made some headway settling things with Shiloh. Now he had enough confidence to approach Richie, and when he had half a chance, he fully intended to do so. Vanessa would be a challenge—hopefully she just needed some time. If Jude was honest with himself, so did he.

And Connor, well . . . he'd cross that bridge if the band kept him long enough to get there.

Until then, he hoped his meager savings could handle two packs a day or more.

Beside him, the bus door opened, and he turned just as A.J. stepped out in a half-zipped hoodie.

"Oh. Hey." A.J. smiled shyly, closing the door behind him. "Didn't realize you were out here."

Jude gestured with his cigarette. "Outdoor habit."

"True." A.J. paused. "I'm, um . . ." He cleared his throat and gestured toward the other end of the parking lot. "I was going to get some food. Do you want me to bring anything back for you?" Another pause. "Or, you know, if you want to come with me . . ."

Jude mulled it over. Now that he thought about it, he was hungry. Quite hungry, actually. "You're sure you don't mind?"

"No. No, of course not. It'd be kind of nice to not eat alone."

Jude dropped his cigarette and crushed it under his heel. "Most people *want* to be alone after being in a sardine can with the rest of the group."

Chuckling, A.J. shrugged. "Sometimes, yeah." He didn't offer anything more, though, and Jude didn't push the issue.

Together, they started across the parking lot. In twenty-four hours, it would be wall-to-wall cars—Schadenfreude almost always sold out—but for now, it was deserted.

He shifted his attention to the soft-spoken drummer beside him. Tomorrow they'd be performing together for the first time, and he was still struggling to imagine A.J. onstage. The band's percussion lines were always hard and wild—not something to be played by the faint of heart. And A.J. just didn't seem . . . aggressive enough.

Shy drummers weren't that unusual, but every move A.J. made and every word he said bordered on apologetic. Still, if Running with Scissors had hired him on, then he could obviously hold his own behind a drum set. It was just difficult to picture, and now that Jude thought about it, that made A.J. intriguing in a way he couldn't quite put his finger on.

A.J. glanced at him, and Jude realized he'd been watching him out of the corner of his eye long enough to be conspicuous. He quickly focused ahead, though he didn't have a clue what to say to divert the awkwardness.

After a more few steps, A.J. asked, "So, you've never played a stadium before?"

"Nope." Jude laughed quietly. "To be honest, I have no idea what to expect."

"It's kind of overwhelming the first time." A.J. paused, his shoulders bunching a little as he slid his hands into his pockets. "At least Schadenfreude is good to work with. And they let us have a sound check. I mean it's short, but at least they're willing to *give* their opening act a sound check."

"That's a plus."

They continued from the parking lot to the sidewalk, then followed it toward some shops and restaurants. After a while, Jude asked, "So, how was the tour going before all the shit with Wyatt and Connor?"

"Good. It was going good." A.J. slid his hands deeper into his pockets and kept his gaze fixed on the pavement. "Chaotic, but I guess that's part of touring."

Jude laughed dryly. "Keeps it from getting boring, right?"

"Something like that." A.J. paused. "I can't believe this is your first tour."

"Believe it. Running with Scissors is the only band I've ever been in, and we just played locally."

A.J. was quiet for a moment. "Did you miss it?"

"Like you wouldn't believe. Even the really rough years when no one would give us the time of day."

"Yeah?"

Jude nodded. "We played in some of the shittiest clubs. Hell, we played for some school dances when we started." He sighed, looking out at the road but not really focusing on anything in the present. "Sometimes there were maybe a dozen people in the room. But goddamn, it was addictive."

Beside him, A.J. shivered. "Yeah. It really is, isn't it?" He turned. "So are you looking forward to it? The bigger venues?"

"Like you wouldn't believe."

A.J. grinned, and Jude's spine tingled even before the drummer quietly said, "Just wait until tomorrow."

Jude swept his tongue across his lips. "I'm looking forward to it."

A.J.'s grin broadened. The knowing look in his eyes did nothing to put that tingling to rest. Jesus.

Then he faced forward again and cleared his throat as he gestured at something up ahead. "This place looks decent. Want to try it?"

Jude shook himself, trying to get that grin and tomorrow's show out of his mind long enough to answer. The place A.J. had indicated was a burger joint. Not top of the line, probably the kind of shop that catered to people heading into or out of the stadium, but the smell of burgers on the grill made Jude's mouth water.

"Yeah. Sure. That'll work." He smiled. "After you."

CHAPTER 6

A.J. could've sworn his stomach had been growling earlier. That was the whole reason he'd ventured off the bus in the first place. And the food in here smelled absolutely amazing.

But standing here now, staring up at the electronic menus above the cashier's head, he went completely blank.

"A.J.?" Jude nudged him with his elbow. "You know what you want?"

Probably something I shouldn't have.

"Um . . ." A.J. quickly cleared his throat, heat rushing into his cheeks. "I'll just have a regular cheeseburger and fries."

The cashier shot him a puzzled look—*It took you that long to decide you wanted the basics?*—but she rang him up without a word. He paid her and took his cup over to the soda fountain to fill it while Jude placed his order.

A.J. snagged an empty booth near the back. Both hands around his cold cup of Coke, he watched Jude from the corner of his eye. Though he couldn't quite explain why, Jude fucked with his head just by being there. Yeah, he was a musical god. Yeah, he was hot. But A.J. had been around good-looking, talented musicians before. What the hell?

He took a deep swallow of Coke. He wasn't even sure what had possessed him to extend the invitation to Jude. Well, besides the fact that Jude had been standing there, and it had seemed like the polite thing to do, but he should've known it wouldn't bode well for his appetite. Or his nerves. Or his fucking brain.

Everything about Jude threw him. For God's sake, this afternoon he'd picked up a bass and played almost every one of the band's songs with all the ease of playing a scale. Even the songs Wyatt had struggled with, the ones he'd rehearsed until his fingers bled, were nothing for Jude. And allegedly, the bass wasn't even his strongest instrument. If he ever touched the drums . . .

No, A.J. wasn't intimidated in the slightest.

And he couldn't hate Jude for his musical prowess, but it didn't seem fair that the dude also had eyes that fucked with A.J.'s body temperature, tattoos that pulled A.J.'s focus right to his powerful muscles, or . . . anything, really. A.J. couldn't put his finger on anything he didn't like about Jude. Well, aside from the fact that he couldn't literally put his finger on any of it.

He shook himself and shifted his attention to his receipt, as if the printout of his order was somehow more interesting than the drummer-turned-bassist who screwed up his balance and jeopardized his position within the band.

He exhaled. That was why he'd invited Jude along, wasn't it? To make some kind of subtle preemptive peace offering. Gain an ally before Jude had a chance to turn into an enemy.

And maybe steal a few glances. Jude was intense. Something about him—something beyond musical talents and raw good looks—intrigued A.J. Maybe it was knowing that this was a guy who'd been with Connor for a good many years. After all, Connor was *not* for the faint of heart.

Oblivious to A.J.'s mind coming unraveled, Jude slid into the booth across from him.

"I hope this place is as good as it smells." Jude set his receipt down beside his drink. "Because I am fucking starving."

"You and me both." Well, that wasn't entirely true anymore, but A.J. didn't really want to explain why his appetite was MIA.

I'm insane, and paranoid, and seriously *fucking attracted to you. Wait, where are you going?*

He took a gulp of soda.

Jude drummed his fingers rapidly beside his own drink. "So, how'd you get started drumming?"

"School band." A.J. played with the edge of his cup's lid. "I started out as a brass player, believe it or not."

"Yeah? Trumpet?"

"Trombone."

"How'd you get from the trombone to the drums?"

A.J. tapped a nail on his front tooth. "Braces. First time I tried to play after they were put on, I turned the insides of my lips to hamburger."

Jude shuddered, sucking his lips into his mouth. "Ouch."

"Tell me about it. Didn't want to drop out of the band, though, so I asked the band director if I could switch to drums. And I was hooked."

Jude smiled. "Something about the drums, am I right?"

"So right." *Back off my drums, dude.*

Jude opened his mouth to speak, but the cashier called A.J.'s order number.

"Back in a second." He got up and went to the counter to get his food. While he was putting on condiments and mixing ketchup and mustard for his fries, Jude's number was called.

Moments later they both took their seats again, this time with food in hand. Though A.J.'s stomach was still fluttering from being alone with Jude like this, he did find enough of an appetite to take that first bite of his burger. That was all he needed—the food was delicious, and neither of them said much of anything until the burgers were gone and there was nothing left but two huge mountains of fries.

Jude drenched a fry in barbecue sauce and, after he'd washed it down with some soda, asked, "So, you been in any bands before this one?"

A.J. nodded. "Three. One kind of ran out of steam, the second had zero chemistry, and the third was a little . . . I don't know. Out there."

"How so?"

"It's hard to explain. Our lead vocalist had all these grand visions about changing the world with our music, and every time we played a small gig somewhere, or even when we were opening for a solid headliner, he'd get depressed and pissed off that we were wasting our time. He thought we were being unappreciated. Apparently the world was supposed to magically recognize his genius or something. I don't know." He rolled his eyes. "Didn't have the slightest idea about the concept of 'paying your dues.'"

"Yeah." Jude snorted. "That's a foreign concept to some people, I think."

A.J. chuckled. "So what about you? Any other bands?"

Jude shook his head, lowering his gaze. "No. Running with Scissors was the only band I was ever in."

"Oh. Right. You said that." A.J. hesitated, not sure how raw this nerve might be for him. "Even after you left, you never—"

"Nope. It wasn't for lack of trying, though." Jude sighed. He picked up a fry but then dropped it back on the pile. "I looked for bands who needed—" He met A.J.'s eyes. "Bands I could join. But . . ." He gnawed his lip, and then shook his head. "Anyway. I never did start playing again." A faint smile formed. "But I'm playing now, so I can't complain, right?"

"Wait, wait. Back up." A.J. studied him. "You haven't played at all since you left?"

"I couldn't, to be honest. I fucked around on a guitar once in a while, and my mom couldn't keep me away from her piano whenever I went home, but otherwise I didn't really have the opportunity. Roommates, paper-thin apartment walls . . ." Another shrug, this one tighter than before. "I wanted to play, but I couldn't."

"But I heard the way you played this afternoon. I . . . How, man? How do you do it?" He tried to be casual, dragging a fry through the ketchup-mustard mix and hoping he didn't sound too much like a squealing fanboy. "You listen to a song one time, and then . . . *How?*"

A hint of pink bloomed in Jude's cheeks. "To be fair, I've heard those songs a million times. I helped write some of them."

"Still."

Jude lowered his gaze, watching himself dip a couple of fries in barbecue sauce. "It's . . . hard to explain. Once I hear it, I know it. That's how music has always been for me." He munched on his fries and washed them down with a swig of soda. "It drove my instructors and band directors crazy. I never wanted to fuck around with scales or exercises or any of that shit, because I knew the fucking music, you know?"

"But they still made you do it?"

"Yeah, and to a point, they were right. I needed the practice and the exercises so I could develop the muscle memory, and working on my precision and all of that. Just because my brain knew the music didn't mean my hands did."

A.J. nodded. He understood the need to develop muscle memory, but it was weird to imagine a time when Jude had anything less than flawless technique. Of course that was ridiculous. All musicians, even the prodigies, had to start somewhere. But all A.J. had to go on with Jude was what he'd seen on the bus, and that hadn't been someone who'd ever struggled with the basics. The bass wasn't even his primary instrument; put him behind a drum, and he'd probably wipe the floor with A.J. and every drummer before him. Making him practice rudimental drumming or scales seemed like a colossal waste of his genius.

Easy, Palmer. You're going to start drooling.

He fidgeted, reaching for his drink. "Well, you've obviously got the muscle memory down." *Way to sound like a fucking tool.*

Jude chuckled and held up a taped hand. "Now if I can build a decent callus, I'll be good."

"I know the feeling." A.J. showed his own hands, which had long since callused where the drumsticks rubbed. "And shit, there's building up a callus, and there's building one up for a fucking tour." He whistled, lowering his hands. "Amazing what happens when you go from one or two gigs a week to performing every other night."

"I can imagine. Good thing I brought more of this tape. I have a feeling I'm gonna need it." Jude dragged another fry through the barbecue sauce. "I'm looking forward to hearing you play, by the way."

A.J. gulped. "You . . . really?"

"Well yeah." Jude's smile threw every one of A.J.'s vitals out of whack. "I know my bandmates—if they hired you on, then you're good."

A.J. swallowed. "So, no pressure, right?"

Jude laughed. "You've already impressed anyone whose opinion counts. I'm just a drummer who appreciates other drummers."

"And you're talking to a drummer who gets nervous as fuck around other drummers." *Especially when they're that good.*

Jude held his gaze for a moment, then shook his head. "There's nothing to be nervous about. Relax. You've already done your audition."

So have you . . .

A.J. nudged his half-empty basket of fries away. "Well, if I screw up the first time you hear me, just promise me you'll write it off as nerves."

"Sure." Jude half shrugged, adding a wink that didn't help A.J.'s nerves or any of the other systems that were going haywire. "It'll be all right. Besides, I'm the one who'll be getting up in front of a few thousand people, playing an instrument I've only picked up in the last week."

"Yeah, and I heard you play it today. Pretty sure you'll be fine."

"We'll see, won't we?"

They ate in silence for a few minutes. Or rather, Jude ate in silence while A.J. pondered whether he had any appetite left for the cooling fries he'd pushed away. He needed to eat today. Tomorrow, preshow nerves would keep him from holding anything down, so unless he wanted to pass out onstage . . .

He brought the basket back toward him and made himself eat a few more fries. Slowly, his stomach settled. Maybe he'd finish them after all.

"So." Jude drummed his fingers rapidly on the table. "As long as we're here and it's just the two of us, maybe we should, um . . ."

A.J.'s tongue stuck to the roof of his mouth. So much for finishing his meal.

Jude continued. "Look, I'm sure you know about all the shit that's happened between me and the band. And I'm not going to lie—I did what they say I did." He held A.J.'s gaze. "You weren't a part of it, and I don't want you getting caught in the middle."

A.J. cleared his throat. "I . . . don't really feel like I am. It's not really my business."

"No, but being part of the band, it's sort of inevitable to get pulled into everyone else's drama." Jude chewed his lip and played with the lid on his soda cup. "I mean, it's good to have a shot at getting to know you and being friends. At the same time, though, with all the other shit going on, I don't want to put you in a bad spot. I'm a temporary member. You might as well think of me like a touring bassist—I'm part of the group onstage, but after the show's over . . ." He shook his head.

A.J. shifted uncomfortably. "I don't really want to get involved in the drama. You seem like a pretty cool guy, so if I'm hanging out and talking with you, it's not really anyone else's business."

Jude lowered his gaze. "I'm sure you've been with this group long enough to know it's not that simple."

There was that. Everything about this band was starting to feel like the days leading up to his parents' divorce—just speaking to one side of the volatile pair had been an affront to the other side. Neutrality had been grounds for suspicion. A.J. rarely resented anything more than the implication that he was either with or against someone. He hated being forced—implicitly or explicitly—to either take sides or stay away completely.

He took a drink to wet his mouth. "Is this where I'm supposed to throw up my hands and scream, 'Can't we all just get along?'"

Jude laughed. "Yeah. Good luck with that." He winced. "Sorry. Sorry. I'm . . . I'm really not helping, am I? Here's the thing. I'm trying to mend fences with the band. They're my friends. Or at least they were, and I'm trying to get us back to there. It's a slow process, but . . ." He waved a hand. "Anyway. That'll happen in its own time, but I'd . . . I'd like to be friends with you."

A.J.'s insides flipped.

Jude stared at his food for a moment. "The thing is, I haven't been around musicians in a long time. And I miss it. I miss being friends with people who get it." His eyes flicked up to meet A.J.'s. "I guess I just want us to get off on the right foot."

"Oh." A.J. took another drink. "To be honest, I'm not all that close to everyone else anyhow. It would . . . I guess it would be kind of nice to have someone to bullshit with on this tour."

Jude smiled, but it quickly faded. "If it starts making things weird with everybody else, though, we can—"

"Don't worry about them." A.J. gestured dismissively. "You deal with your shit with them, and I'll deal with mine. I'd rather not let other people dictate who I'm friends with."

Jude studied him, and slowly, his smile came back to life. "Cool. But, um, if by some chance you get dragged into the middle of this bullshit, or you feel like you are, just say so, okay?"

A.J. nodded. "I will. Thanks." He knew himself well enough to know he'd never take Jude up on it. Push back? Say "enough"? Yeah, right. Not this guy.

But still, although there wasn't a snowball's chance in hell that he'd ever do anything with it, he was grateful that Jude had made the offer.

Late the next morning, everyone in the band was slowly rolling out of their racks and taking their turns in the bus's tiny shower, which was actually functioning for once. They'd start getting ready for the show in a few hours, after the roadies had set up the stage, but for now it was coffee, breakfast, and smoke 'em if you've got 'em. The usual routine, except for two *minor* problems.

One, having Jude and Connor on the same bus.

Two, the coffeepot picking that day to refuse to work.

"You've got to be fucking kidding me." Connor pushed out a breath and ran a hand through his wet hair. "We just got the fucking bus fixed, and now *this*? Can just one goddamned thing work the way it's supposed to on—"

"Connor." A.J. jumped in before he could talk himself out of it.

The lead singer's teeth snapped shut, and he turned to A.J., eyes narrow.

"I'll check with the facilities guy and the roadies." A.J. kept his voice low and even. "It's probably just the electrical hookup outside. The same thing that happened back in Charlotte, remember?"

Connor pressed his lips together, glaring at the piece-of-shit coffeepot like he was about to do them all a favor and smash the damn thing.

"There's a Starbucks half a block from here," A.J. went on calmly. "And if you go the other way, there's a café that the roadies say has really good coffee. If you'll go get us each a cup, I'll make sure the facilities guys get the hookup fixed before tonight."

Connor eyed him, but then slowly released his breath. "Okay. I'll . . . What kind do you want?"

"The usual."

Connor nodded. "All right. Thanks, man."

"Don't mention it."

Connor shoved his wallet into his pocket. "Guys, I'm going to Starbucks. Anyone else want anything?"

Thank God—situation defused.

As Connor and Shiloh headed across the empty lot, A.J.'s heartbeat gradually came down. Every time he ran interference and tried to calm Connor, even over stupid shit, he was sure this would be the time it blew up in his face, especially now that Jude's presence was making Connor extra volatile. A.J. didn't like confrontation, and he didn't like engaging someone who was ready to lose their shit, but the alternative was letting Connor flip his lid until he'd worn his voice raw. That would fuck the whole band that evening, and anyway, God knew why, Connor always seemed to settle down when A.J. intervened.

"That calming effect of yours is going to be even more crucial than ever. Trust me, A.J. You're not going anywhere."

A.J. scowled. Well, at least he was good for something.

And at least Connor was gone, and now Jude had stepped outside to have a smoke, so everyone else could finally breathe.

Vanessa rolled her eyes. "God, when the hell did Connor turn into such a diva?"

"He's always been a diva," Richie muttered.

"Not like that."

Richie huffed. "Yeah. Not until Jude came back and Connor couldn't blame anybody but himself."

"Jude played his part," Vanessa said.

"So did Connor, and you know it."

Vanessa scowled. "Well, karma's a bitch, I guess."

"Yeah, well, it'd be nice if karma bitched somewhere else. This is a fucking tour, not the rolling Connor-Jude Shit Show."

A.J. bowed out of the conversation, muttering an excuse about needing to take care of the electrical issue, and got the hell off the bus. He hadn't even had breakfast yet, and he'd already had it up to here with the drama.

Eventually, he found a roadie who had the number for the facilities manager, and made the call. With that situation resolved—or in the process of being resolved, anyway—he headed back to the bus.

He boarded it, left a note on the coffeepot for everyone to leave it off until the electrical issue was fixed, and then took out his phone to text his drum tech about setting up for tonight's show.

"Did I see you coming back with Jude last night?"

Vanessa's voice startled him, and he spun around. "Huh?"

Her eyebrow arched, silently repeating her question.

"I, uh . . ." He nodded, sliding his phone into his pocket. "Yeah. We grabbed dinner at the burger joint down the road."

The suspicion in her gaze made his skin crawl.

"What?" he asked.

Vanessa folded her arms, and he swore she had daggers in her eyes. "You're gonna want to be careful with him. He's in this and everything else for himself, and he'll use you and fuck you over just like he did the rest of us. Remember, he's the guy who almost broke all of this." She gestured at the places where their bandmates usually sat. "I mean, he *did* break us, but thank God we found you."

A.J.'s stomach knotted.

"Anyway." Vanessa faced him. "Just watch yourself with him. He's not someone you want to get buddy-buddy with."

"Buddy-buddy?" A.J. shrugged. "It was just a bite to eat."

"Mm-hmm."

He gritted his teeth. He desperately wanted to remind her that he'd had nothing to do with the band's preexisting drama, or the recent shit with Connor and Wyatt, and that he wanted nothing to do with any other shit that came up. He was here to be a musician. End of story. And if he decided to hang out with the only man within a hundred miles who he could talk to about drumming—well, when he could talk at all, since Jude seemed to evaporate his vocabulary with a look—it didn't mean he was taking sides or stirring the pot. The road was a lonelier place than he'd expected. Fucking sue him if he wanted some goddamned human interaction between shows.

But he didn't say anything, and when Vanessa gave him a slight nod and headed off the bus, he didn't stop her. Ironically, as much as he wanted to stand up for himself and defend his friendliness with Jude, it was Jude's presence that made him keep his mouth shut. Rocking the boat wasn't a good idea when there was someone around who could easily take his place.

Not that Running with Scissors seemed all that keen on keeping Jude for longer than they had to, but if A.J. started stirring up shit, they might just decide that one jackass was better than two, and they'd probably hang on to the better musician.

Might as well enjoy the ride as long as it's smooth . . .

CHAPTER 7

Holy.

Fucking.

Hell.

Jude had missed being onstage, and he'd been itching to get under the lights again, but this was nothing he'd ever experienced before. He'd played in clubs with Running with Scissors, and whatever moderately sized venues they'd been able to snag around Los Angeles. They'd even played a few outdoor festivals that allowed unsigned bands, giving them the most microscopic lines on posters and about four minutes of stage time in front of a few hundred stoners.

Nothing like this.

As the roadies set it all up, and Jude followed Richie and Vanessa onto the stage for sound check, he stared out at the empty seats. Literally *thousands* of empty seats, not to mention the floor, which would be standing-room only. The show had sold out. In a few hours, this place would be packed. There was already a line outside the gate, and he'd overheard someone commenting that the two main parking lots had been full since before noon.

Okay, so they were mostly coming to see Schadenfreude, but still. Tonight, after eighteen months of believing this was all behind him, he was getting up on *this* stage in front of *that* many people.

Goose bumps prickled beneath his guitar strap. This was going to be *amazing*.

As he tuned his bass, the strings thrumming beneath his taped fingertips, he pulled his gaze from the empty seats and scanned the stage, which was currently packed with people, gear, and boxes. Several roadies wore Schadenfreude T-shirts and helped venue employees set up equipment, tape down wires, and adjust lights.

At the rear of the stage, dead center, A.J. and his drum tech had finished setting up the drum set, and A.J. took a seat behind it. The tech was explaining something to him, and A.J. absently flipped his drumsticks over and over between his fingers, occasionally spinning them so fast they blurred.

Jude's fingers curled at his sides, the raw skin protesting sharply at the unwelcome motion. He could almost feel the unfinished wood against his palms and fingertips, and the way each beat echoed through his arms. The way the bass thumped beside his own heartbeat, and the snare and cymbals sent electricity crackling along his veins. God, he missed that.

But it wasn't just the drums or the sticks that held his attention.

Oblivious to Jude's gaze, A.J. made adjustments to his rig and directed his tech. He seemed perfectly at ease behind the instrument, like he didn't even notice all the empty seats out there in front of them. Then again, this wasn't his first rodeo.

Jude still marveled at the idea of A.J. drumming for this band. The guy was so timid, it was difficult to imagine him filling the role for any rock band, never mind Running with Scissors. The high-energy music, the aggressive percussion—it just didn't seem like *him*.

"Jude," Richie called.

Jude turned around. "Yeah?"

Richie fussed with his earpiece. "You ready?"

"Whenever you are."

Sound check took his attention away from A.J. He and Richie played a few bars from "I Never," and then the entire second verse of "By and By," pausing now and then to tune their instruments and adjust the feed on their earpieces. Vanessa joined in, and after a few clumsy verses—he wasn't used to playing alongside the house mix anymore—Jude got the hang of it. Just like riding a bike and all of that.

Once he was sure he could not only hear the house mix properly, but that he really did have a grasp on the songs they'd be playing tonight, his excitement began growing again. They were really doing this. Less than a week ago he'd been rotting in a cubicle, and now . . .

He gazed out at the empty seats, his heart pounding as he flexed his tender fingers.

Now this.

He and Vanessa started to retreat backstage while Richie stayed to play alongside A.J.

Jude paused and then backtracked, curious how A.J. would sound. While he watched, taping his fingers again with the roll he'd kept in his pocket, A.J. and Richie continued with sound check. Richie rested his foot on the platform beneath A.J.'s drum set and played the intro to "Hold Fast." After two bars, A.J. came in.

And Jude's heart sank.

Really? *That* was how he played "Hold Fast"?

Come on, A.J. Come on. Play, man! Play it hard!

He was holding back. He had to be. There was no way in hell they'd have hired him on if *that* was his style.

During his own drummer days, he had held back during sound check sometimes—well, whenever they'd *had* a sound check—to keep his wrists and hands fresh. That must be what A.J. was doing now, much like Jude had carefully manipulated the strings so he wouldn't shred his fingers quite yet.

Except A.J. still seemed . . . out of place. Like Richie or Vanessa trying to play beside a classical symphony or Connor in front of a country-western band. The technique was there, and the music was there, but the vibe was all wrong.

Presumably, the rest of the band had known what they were doing when they brought him in. As much as Jude liked the guy, though, he was dubious.

Guess we'll see how tonight plays out.

After sound check, they waited backstage for their cue to go on. Schadenfreude's sound check had been a lot longer, so everyone had to warm up again in their ready room.

It was cramped back there—the headliner probably had better digs, but Jude wasn't complaining. And at least Connor's preshow vow of silence meant no sniping or bickering. Everyone was too focused anyway.

Jude peeled the tape off his fingers and flexed them gingerly, knowing they'd be hamburger before the end of the night.

Come on, callus. You can show up anytime now.

Across the tiny room, like any drummer with half a brain, A.J. was doing some stretching to limber up his arms and shoulders. He was wearing a tank top, as Jude often had during his drumming days. Being onstage could get wicked hot, and besides, sleeves restricted movement. And damn, A.J. looked good like that. His arms were as powerful as any drummer's should be, and surprisingly free of ink—unlike anyone else's in the band.

And just as Jude had suspected he might, he'd put on eyeliner, and damn but he wore it well. It brought out the blue of his eyes and intensified his gaze. When he glanced at Jude at one point, Jude almost jumped out of his skin— A.J. may have been a church mouse, but his eyes didn't let that show tonight.

Maybe that was the purpose of the eyeliner. The slim black lines were a mask of sorts, a degree of separation between the world and who A.J. was when the lights went down. Jude knew a lot of musicians who wore makeup, costumes, sunglasses—anything to put a barrier between them and the audience so they could perform without losing their sanity. As a friend of his had once described it, stage makeup and costumes were temple garb for worshipping at the altar of stage fright.

Did A.J. have stage fright? Quite possibly, now that Jude thought about it. He struggled to hold eye contact during a one-on-one conversation. So maybe—

"You guys ready?" Someone from the venue leaned into the tiny room. "You're on in five."

The five minutes before a curtain went up always passed like five nanoseconds, and this time was no exception. The man had given them their five-minute warning, and just like that, Jude was onstage under the hot lights, the roar of the crowd vibrating beneath his feet. He couldn't see much beyond the lip of the stage, and his earpiece drowned out most of the noise, but he could feel the crowd. He could feel their collective presence extending out into the shadows and up the sides of the immense stadium. The roof didn't even seem to exist, and the crowd soared up, up, up as if they all went on forever.

That presence, the unavoidable reality that thousands of people were watching and listening, was like lightning through his veins. All the drama between him and Connor, all the side-eyes and uncertainty from the other band members—it was gone. Out here, there was nothing but music and lights, and Jude was dizzy from it all. Giddy, even. Nothing had ever made him as high as playing onstage, and this was like taking a deep toke of the strongest weed he could find after abstaining for too many years.

And goddamn, but he'd forgotten how much he loved being onstage with this group. Exchanging glances with Richie. Shiloh dancing, singing, working the crowd. Vanessa powering through riffs that gave Jude goose bumps.

And Connor. Jesus. Though Jude and most people could say a lot about him, the guy could bring a standing crowd up onto their toes. He had even more charisma to burn than Shiloh.

Yes. Yes, this was right. Whatever drama they all had offstage, they had their collective shit together here, and it was magic just like in the old days. For better or worse, Running with Scissors was back, and Jude was almost overwhelmed by adrenaline and emotion as the past simply disappeared.

Three songs into the set, the lights above them went down, and Richie and Jude backed off, playing in the background and making way for the drum solo.

Jude turned around, and his fingers slipped off the strings for a beat.

He could've sworn he'd seen A.J. on the throne behind the drum set when they'd taken the stage, and he'd heard and felt the powerful percussion since the opening number, but . . . that couldn't possibly be A.J., could it?

Beneath the blinding spotlight, A.J. was lost in the intense drum solo, his hands and drumsticks blurring as they beat and tapped and crashed. Droplets of perspiration flew. The percussion line reverberated through Jude's bones. It was like he was looking at a whole new person.

Drenched in sweat, with muddy smears of eyeliner emphasizing his blue eyes, his skin flushed and his shirt gone, A.J. wasn't the shy kid who'd waited beside Kristy back in Nebraska, or who'd blended in with the upholstery on the tour bus, or who'd nearly disappeared into his own hoodie while they ate last night.

Holy shit.

There was nothing shy or timid behind that drum set. The stage brought out a side of A.J. that made Jude's fingers fumble on the strings and his mouth go dry. Yeah, A.J.'d been holding back during sound check, but he sure as fuck wasn't holding back now.

It was like the stage was a parallel universe, one in which Connor was fun and happy, where Jude fit seamlessly into the band he'd founded, and where A.J. the church mouse exploded out of his shell and beat the crap out of that drum set like his life depended on it. Maybe the real world and all its shyness and drama would still exist when the lights went down and the instruments went back into their cases, but here on this stage, it vanished.

A.J.'s solo wound down, and as Richie, Vanessa, and Jude started playing their hearts out once again, Jude vowed to savor every moment of this other world for as long as they let him play in it.

As the set continued, he couldn't get A.J. out of his mind. Whenever possible, he stole glances over his shoulder as if to remind himself that, yes, that really was A.J. back there. That those sounds, those powerful beats, came from the hands of the kid who could barely hold eye contact.

And who was he kidding? The music held his attention, but so did the man himself. Sweaty, passionate, lost in the beat—A.J. was hot. He personified everything that could turn Jude on.

Right then, eyes locked.

The corner of A.J.'s mouth rose.

And Jude forgot what song they were playing.

The bass line completely derailed—*fuck*. He stopped, listened for the beat and the guitar, and fell back into sync with them. All told, he'd only lost two or three bars, and he doubted anyone even noticed, but damn, he sure did.

He didn't dare look at A.J. again. Not unless he wanted to fumble his way through the rest of the set. Not that he could get the hot drummer out of his head, but he'd damn sure try.

And somehow, despite A.J. playing just a few feet away from him, Jude made it through the set without fucking up again.

Barely.

After their set, the band retreated backstage while the fans chanted for Schadenfreude. Kristy shoved water bottles into everyone's hands, and despite the sweat they high-fived and even embraced. Jude knew damn well it was just the postshow buzz, but he took it, though Connor still cold-shouldered him. He was too high and happy to let his ex bring him back down.

Kristy and Richie ribbed him a little for botching that section of "Hold Fast," but considering it was his first time ever playing in a venue like that, and he'd only been playing at all for the past few days, no one seemed to hold it against him. He didn't argue—if they were willing to write it off as rusty musicianship, he could swallow his pride and agree. At any other time in his life, he'd have argued fiercely that something had distracted him, but tonight . . . yeah, he could play the rust card.

While Vanessa, Richie, and Connor watched Schadenfreude from backstage, Jude left his bass with a roadie and headed toward the ready room to retrieve the towel and clean shirt he'd left back there.

His legs barely remembered how to walk. All that energy from the stage still tingled through his body. He didn't know if he wanted to go somewhere and sleep it off, or find someone who wouldn't mind some quick, wild sex with a sweaty musician, or if he just wanted to laugh and cry and beg someone to tell him they still had another set to play tonight.

He was . . . he didn't even know. High? Horny? All of the above? His hands were still shaking, his fingers still vibrating from the strings. Sleep? Not anytime soon. He was too spun up. Too dizzy. Too . . . giddy, and crazy, and— He stepped into the ready room, and immediately ran out of breath.

Oh fuck.

A.J. was leaning back against the wall, eyes closed and chest rising and falling as he caught his breath. He was drenched now, and it wasn't just sweat. There was a mostly empty bottle of water in his trembling hand that he must've dumped over his head as he'd come off the stage, soaking his bleached blond hair, his bare torso, his jeans.

And below his belt . . .

Jude gulped. It might've been a trick of the light or maybe a fold in A.J.'s drenched jeans, but from here, it looked like the denim was clinging to one hell of a hard-on.

Before Jude could turn away and pretend he hadn't been staring, A.J.'s eyes opened, and he let his head loll to the side. Suddenly, they were looking right at each other.

Jude gulped. A.J. pushed himself off the wall, making a not-very-subtle gesture out of adjusting the front of his jeans. No, that was no trick of the light or fold of fabric.

And the look in his eyes . . . Fuck. It wasn't just the smeared eyeliner intensifying his gaze. Whatever had come alive in him onstage was still alive now. The hairs on Jude's neck stood up—the tiny room vibrated with the bass from Schadenfreude playing nearby, but that wasn't the only thing making the air crackle. As A.J. came toward him, Jude was genuinely surprised electricity didn't arc from one of them to the other. He held his breath—the closer A.J. came, the more the building energy in this room demanded release, and the drummer's blue eyes left little to the imagination about how it would be released.

Less than an arm's-length away, A.J. stopped. He didn't break eye contact. Neither did Jude. In his mind's eye, Jude imagined them pressed up against the wall, doing something about their hard-ons, kissing and panting and grinding to the beat of Schadenfreude or their own heartbeats or whatever. He didn't care. The thought alone was making him breathe harder.

A grin played at A.J.'s lips just like the one that had tripped up Jude onstage. "Nice going out there. Didn't think you'd really be able to play like that your first time out."

Jude swallowed. "Likewise. You're . . . damn good."

The grin broadened, coming completely to life and turning Jude's knees to liquid. "It's a rush, isn't it? Being out onstage like that?"

Jude nodded. "Yeah. It is." He swept his tongue across his lips, and A.J. jumped as if that electricity *had* arced between them.

He quickly cleared his throat and glanced past Jude at the door. "Where's everybody else?"

"Watching."

"Right. Forgot. They . . . they always watch Schadenfreude."

Their eyes met again, and Jude had no idea what to say. For a moment, A.J. seemed to waver between the shy kid he'd been from the start and the balls-to-the-wall drummer he'd been onstage. Then he ran a hand through his damp hair, messing up the spikes and Jude's blood pressure, and that grin came back to life. "I should go grab a shower before everyone else heads back to the bus."

His eyebrows lifted just slightly, and Jude swore there was an unspoken "Care to join me?" written in the gleam in his eyes.

And yes. Yes, he absolutely did.

But . . .

Jude dropped his gaze. "I think I might go watch with everyone else. I've never heard Schadenfreude live." He chanced a look at A.J. again, and though the disappointment was subtle—his grin fading just a little—it was there.

"Okay." A.J. nodded. "I'll see you back at the bus, then." He flashed a brief smile, and then brushed past Jude.

Almost immediately, his footsteps were gone, disappearing into the noise of the band performing onstage.

Are you stupid? You're passing up an invitation to—

Yes. Yes, he was. Because mixing sex with this band was a bad idea. He'd promised Kristy and the others that he was here to bail them out, not tangle them up any further. As much as he desperately wanted to be pressed up against A.J. while they both rinsed away the concert's sweat, none of them could afford the inevitable drama.

And yet he still felt like an idiot for letting A.J. walk. That body, that passion—a talented musician in the form of a spike-haired Adonis. If there'd been no potential fallout, he would've been hot on A.J.'s heels right then, hurrying to that cramped, barely functional tour bus shower for . . .

He shivered.

Closing his eyes, he swallowed hard. This was insane. He had no business looking at anyone else in this band, especially after the way his relationship with Connor—and Connor's relationship with Wyatt—had nearly derailed everything.

Besides, A.J. had just piqued his interest because he was the only one in the band who didn't give Jude the hairy eyeball at every turn. Combine that with his primal, animalistic musical abilities, and the adrenaline of being onstage—which clearly had similar effects on both of them—and he was bound to get Jude's attention like that. Didn't mean they needed to act on it. Didn't mean they should, in a million years, act on it.

But goddamn, he was sure as fuck going to fantasize about it.

CHAPTER 8

All the way back to the bus, A.J. hoped like hell that Jude would change his mind. Every time he heard footsteps—or *thought* he heard footsteps—his heart sped up, and he prayed that it was Jude jogging after him.

But when he reached the bus, there was no one in sight except for some roadies and venue employees moving equipment around outside. Sighing, he opened the door and climbed aboard.

In the bathroom, he stripped off his sweaty jeans and boxers and stepped into the shower. The water heater was still temperamental, and tonight it refused to offer anything hotter than lukewarm, but it felt good. And at least they had a shower. Some of the cheaper, shittier tour buses out there didn't. It was only because Schadenfreude demanded the highest quality, no-expenses-spared buses that Running with Scissors had been lucky enough to score one like this. Compared to the rest of their caravan, it was the runt of the litter—the little bus that sometimes could—but it was better than a limping RV or a 1970s throwback.

And . . . shower.

He stood under the water, eyes closed as it rushed over him and cooled him off. The shower brought the postshow adrenaline down just like it always did, but he couldn't relax completely. Not with this persistent hard-on.

He'd been imagining that look from Jude. There was no way in hell Jude had been staring at him, mouthwateringly impure thoughts etched all over his face, but A.J. couldn't shake the certainty that, yes, actually he *had* been staring at him like that.

A.J. exhaled. He pressed his forearm against the shower wall and leaned forward a bit, stretching his back as the water beat on his exhausted muscles. The buzz from the show was wearing off fast, zapping what little energy he had left, but there was no shaking off his arousal that was intensifying by the second—especially as he let his brain play out every possible thing he and Jude might've been able to do in this tiny shower stall.

Maybe they couldn't have fucked in here—not comfortably anyway—but, hell, who was he kidding? He'd fucked in cars that barely accommodated properly seated passengers, and he'd once had a threesome in his slightly-larger-than-a-futon bed back in LA. He could make this shower work if he wanted to.

And if Jude wanted to.

And if that look on his face had been any indication, he had wanted to.

A.J. swore. His cock hardened and his frustration deepened—what if he could have had Jude in here now to help him take care of this?

That was a moot point, though, and when he was less turned on, he'd remember why it was just as well they weren't hooking up. All he could think of at *this* moment was this erection that needed attention. His hands were practically numb and his arms ached from the shoulders down, but he closed his fingers around his cock and pumped it.

He pressed his forehead against his other arm. Eyes squeezed shut, he fucked into his fist and bit down on a groan just in case somebody else had come back. Just what he needed—Jude walking onto the bus, hearing him jerking off in the shower, and . . .

Joining him. Brazenly stepping into the bathroom, stripping off his clothes, and wedging himself into the stall with A.J. Pushing A.J.'s hand out of the way. Jerking his cock. Maybe rubbing both of their cocks together.

And kissing.

Fuck. He stroked himself faster. His spine tingled as he pictured himself pinned up against the wall, finally finding out what Jude's mouth tasted like and if he was the kind of kisser who'd take the lead, or if he'd turn to putty in A.J.'s arms and let him take over. Jesus. The thought of Jude surrendering, letting himself be pinned, kissed, fucked—

A moan slipped through his lips, and he no longer gave a damn if anyone heard him. His arm burned with fatigue. His knees trembled beneath him. He leaned harder against the wall, gripped himself tighter, stroked harder . . .

His orgasm knocked him off-balance as he imagined himself fucking Jude's mouth with his pulsing dick, watching Jude swallow every drop while his eyes begged for more.

He shuddered once again, and relaxed. Jesus.

After he'd rinsed off his hand and arm, he had just enough presence of mind to shut off the shower—no sense hogging all the hot water before his bandmates returned—and then stood there, trembling, panting, dripping, until his vision cleared.

His hands were shaking badly, as much from drumming as from jerking off, and toweling himself down proved to be a challenge, but he managed. He put on the clean boxers and T-shirt he'd brought into the bathroom with him, and stepped out.

No one else had returned yet. The whole world still thumped with the bass from Schadenfreude's show, so the rest of Running with Scissors was likely still watching from backstage.

Which meant he still had the bus to himself. He could breathe. Maybe read for a while. Maybe fantasize a bit more about Jude.

He climbed onto his bunk and lay back.

Read. Fantasize. His eyelids drooped. Sleep, maybe. Heavy muscles. Heavy eyelids.

Schadenfreude's bass faded away. So did his thoughts. And without the postshow adrenaline to keep him going through the postorgasm lethargy, he gave in and drifted off.

He awoke to the sounds of his bandmates riffling through duffel bags, wandering in and out of the bathroom, and chatting casually over the sounds of activity outside. Jesus. This late at night, and the roadies were still working? And the band—who were usually considerate as hell after hours—were being this noisy?

He swore and rubbed his eyes. Bright lights too.

The scent of coffee made it to his bunk. Seriously? They had all the lights on and were drinking coffee this late? *Jerks.*

Wait. He fumbled for his phone, which he kept between his mattress and the wall, and winced when the screen came to life. As his eyes focused, he squinted.

Well, shit. No, they weren't working and making noise after hours—it was almost eight in the morning.

He stumbled out of his rack, stretched, and shuffled into the living area. Vanessa and Richie were goofing off on their phones, some empty McDonald's wrappers crumpled on the table between them. Connor and Kristy were nowhere in sight, and a wisp of smoke outside the window zeroed him in on exactly where Jude was.

From one of the armchairs, Shiloh smiled over her Starbucks cup. "Morning, sunshine. I was starting to wonder if you'd gone into a coma or something."

He laughed sleepily. "Nah, I'm good. Just needed some sleep, I guess."

"Apparently so." She glanced at her watch. "Well, grab coffee if you're going to. The bus is rolling out in like twenty."

"Shit. Already?"

"Says the guy who slept in."

"Yeah, yeah." He went back to the sleeping area, quickly changed into a pair of jeans and a T-shirt, and headed out.

Near the door, Jude was finishing up his cigarette. A.J. paused, and their eyes met.

Was I imagining what I saw last night?

Jude slowly exhaled some smoke, drawing A.J.'s attention right to his lips. *Fuck.*

"We're hitting the road soon," Jude said. "If you're getting coffee—"

"Right. Right." A.J. shook himself. "I'll . . . I'll be back in a few." He was thankful for the urgency of his coffee mission—anything to distract him from staring at Jude like an idiot.

Before he went too far, though, he found the bus driver checking the tire pressure.

"Hey, Bob." When the driver turned, A.J. gestured over his shoulder with his thumb. "I'm just going to grab some coffee. Ten minutes, max. Don't leave without me, okay?"

"Thanks for the heads-up." Bob gave him a good-natured salute. "Holler when you're back, and we'll pull up anchor."

"Will do."

He was on his way back with a triple-shot espresso when he saw Connor going the same direction, struggling to carry two boxes that were apparently heavier than they looked.

"Hey, Connor. You need a hand?"

"Oh, thank God." Connor groaned and set the boxes down with a *thud* on the pavement. As he stood, he shook out his hands. "I thought I could carry both, but . . . not so much."

"No problem." A.J. took one of the boxes and carefully balanced his coffee cup on top. "Where did these come from?"

Connor flexed his fingers gingerly, then picked up the remaining box. "The ticket office. They wanted some flyers to hand out at the door, and this is what's left."

"Nice of them to give them back and not toss them."

"Right?" Connor nodded in the direction of the bus. As they started walking, he said, "You disappeared last night. You all right?"

"Yeah, yeah." A.J. adjusted his grip on the box. "Just needed to crash and burn, I guess."

Connor grimaced sympathetically and nodded. "Happens to everyone. This touring shit is brutal."

"No kidding."

Connor shifted the box onto one arm and let the other fall to his side. "How are you holding up otherwise, though?"

"I'm okay. It's draining, but it beats the hell out of a regular job."

Connor laughed. "You can say that again."

A.J. hesitated. Then, "How are *you* doing?"

Connor sobered. His gait slowed, and then he stopped. "I'm . . ." Sighing, he set the box down again. "It's weird."

"I can imagine." A.J. set the other box at his feet. "Are you okay?"

"Does it really matter?" Connor rubbed his eyes with his thumb and forefinger. "I never should've fucked things up with Wyatt."

A.J. chewed his lip. "Do you think he'd ever reconsider quitting?"

"No." Connor shook his head. "I tried calling him last night after the show, but as soon as he realized it was me . . ."

That wasn't surprising. Those two had been prone to shouting matches at the slightest provocation. Wyatt hadn't been at all above walking out before Connor could even finish screaming at him. Nothing had been more fun for the whole group than the two of them being trapped on a moving bus together when things got really ugly.

He shook himself. "What do you think we should do? As a band?"

"I don't know." Connor rubbed the back of his neck with both hands. "Shiloh seems to think everything will be fine. I guess I need to talk to Vanessa and Richie. And Kristy. Figure out if there's any possibility of auditioning someone else, or . . ." He waved his hand. "I don't know."

A.J. gritted his teeth. *Thanks for including me in that list.*

"Anyway." Connor rolled his shoulders and crouched to pick up the box. "We should get back."

"Right. Yeah." A.J. picked his up too, and they continued toward the bus. He quickly changed the subject, and they shot the shit about last night's show. This was the Connor everyone liked. When he was mellow, everyone could breathe. His short-tempered side was missing in action, and if he'd just stay like this all the time, there'd be a hell of a lot less tension on the bus. But like everyone in the band, the touring and the close confines took its toll on Connor, so A.J. could understand why his temper was so threadbare sometimes. Especially with Jude around.

That thought smacked him in the face. He chewed the inside of his cheek. Jude drove Connor insane just by being there, and he distracted the hell out of A.J. But how much worse would it be if he and A.J. indulged in temptation and then had to face each other the next day? And what if people found out? Or what if things went to shit? All they'd done last night was have a short, tense staring contest backstage, and they'd barely been able to look at each other this morning. Taking that staring contest any further would be a recipe for disaster.

He followed Connor onto the bus and quickly zeroed in on Jude, who was parked in a chair with his bass across his lap and the brim of his baseball cap casting a shadow over his eyes. Connor brushed past Jude, whose head turned slightly as he apparently followed him with his gaze.

Then he looked at A.J. Despite the tinted lenses, A.J. was pretty sure they'd made eye contact, and he broke it almost immediately, ostensibly to continue after Connor and stow the boxes of flyers.

If things were this weird after exchanging a look, and after A.J.'d jerked off to thoughts of Jude that no one knew about but him, then actually doing anything was the mother of all bad ideas.

And hopefully he'd remember that next time he and Jude were alone together.

CHAPTER 9

The bus stopped somewhere in . . . New Mexico? Jude couldn't remember where they were, or where they were heading. Every time he dozed off, he woke up to more scrubby desert or farm country. Sometimes a truck stop, sometimes a town he couldn't identify.

They weren't performing tonight or tomorrow, so that meant two easy nights in a row. The vocalists could rest their voices. The instrumentalists could rest their hands. Thank God for that—his fingers were still painfully raw. The roadies were probably all comatose on their buses. Jude swore they'd been running themselves ragged nonstop ever since he'd arrived in Omaha.

At a truck stop off Interstate 40, he stepped outside to stretch his legs and his lungs. He'd barely taken his first drag before Richie joined him.

"Hey." He gestured at Jude's cigarette. "I'm out—can I bum one?"

"Yeah, sure." Jude handed him the pack.

Richie slid one free, used Jude's lighter, and the two of them smoked quietly for a moment before Richie spoke.

"So, you and Connor." He inclined his head, exhaling smoke through his nose. "It's still pretty weird, huh?"

Jude cringed. Since that confrontation in Omaha, he and Connor had barely said more than two words to each other, and he'd hoped like hell that no one but him noticed the tension, though that had obviously been wishful thinking from the start. "I'll bet it will be for a while. Not surprising, but . . . Guess I made that bed, so now I get to lie in it."

Richie studied him. Then he shook his head. "I'm never going to get why you guys can't just let that shit go and move on. You dated. Now you're not dating, but you still can't put up with each other." He waved his free hand. "What the fuck?"

"We didn't exactly *stop* dating nicely."

"It was almost two years ago. Is it *that* bad?"

"It's . . ." Jude chuckled. "You know what? Just be glad you *don't* get it. You're fucking lucky."

"I am. Always have been." Richie laughed as he brought his cigarette back up to his mouth. All this shit between Jude and Connor—and Connor and Wyatt—probably made Richie roll his eyes until his head ached. Richie had known since he was like fifteen that he was asexual, and as he'd told Jude a few years back, part of the reason he'd figured it out so young was watching Jude and Connor as well as Shiloh with one of her high school boyfriends. They'd confused the hell out of him.

"You guys all get stupid for each other." He'd shrugged, gesturing with the joint they'd all been sharing. *"Why? So you can get naked together and then break up and hate each other? It's just dumb."*

Okay, so he'd had a point. They'd tried to explain to him why they did it, and what made them so stupid, and it had been like explaining colors to a blind man. It just did not compute, and probably still didn't. On some level Richie had eventually understood that all four of his bandmates were attracted to men, and Connor and Vanessa were sometimes attracted to women, but Richie himself didn't feel that way about anyone.

Vanessa had insisted for a long time that Richie was missing out. Then somewhere around the seventh or eighth time Connor and Jude had split up—or maybe after Shiloh and her ex had finally called it quits in catastrophic fashion—Richie had shaken his head and muttered, *"Missing out? My ass."*

To Jude's knowledge, no one had tried to talk Richie out of his asexuality after that.

Jude dropped his cigarette on the pavement and crushed it beneath his heel. "Anyway, I really am sorry about how this has jacked up the band. It's . . . it's in the past now. As much as it'll ever be, I guess."

Richie scowled, but then he shrugged. He pulled in a drag, held the smoke for a second as if it were weed instead of tobacco, and then exhaled slowly. "Well, whatever. It's between you guys. And listen, man. I know shit with you and Connor is rough, but it's good to have you back."

"It's good to be back." Jude smiled. "I missed you guys. And the music."

Richie dropped his cigarette and let it smolder on the ground. "We missed you too, man."

Jude swallowed. "Can I ask you something kind of weird?"

"Sure."

He hesitated. "You know Vanessa better than I do. How does she feel about this? Me being back?"

"I don't know." Richie slid his hands into his pockets and watched the cigarette butts on the pavement. "I mean, she was pretty freaked out when Wyatt left because we were kinda fucked."

"What'd she think when my name came up?"

Richie laughed dryly. "I don't know. I was too busy listening to Connor throw a fit about it. She's cool, though. Give her some time. I mean it was rough, when you left, but . . ." He shrugged again. "Shit happens, you know?"

"She didn't seem all that willing to give me a shot."

"Eh, she'll come around. She's speaking to Connor again."

"I guess that's promising." Relief slowly untangled the knots in Jude's muscles. He rolled his shoulders. "Well, we'll see how things go. I'm not bailing on you guys, though. Not this time."

Richie met his gaze, and he smiled. "Yeah, I know."

Well, at least someone around here still had some faith left in him.

The afternoon heat turned into a pleasantly cool evening, and after everyone had eaten, Jude slipped back outside. He didn't feel like smoking, but he'd been cooped up on that damned bus for so long, he wanted to enjoy some real air for a while.

There were some picnic tables not far away, so he sat down at one, with his back pressed against the edge of the table, and gazed out at the landscape. The air was as dry as the desert surrounding them, and it reminded him a bit of LA, minus the sour taste of smog. On either side of the endless stretch of blacktop, the landscape was desolate and scrubby—after spending his whole life in one of the biggest cities in the US, it was weird to see this much open space without so much as a building in sight. Well, aside from the greasy-spoon restaurant and the tiny hut that passed for restrooms at this truck stop. Otherwise, they were well and truly out in the middle of nowhere.

He took in a long, deep breath of the clean air and then glanced at his phone. It was a little after six, so five in California. If he'd still been at his desk job, he'd be on his way home now. Just leaving work, actually, no doubt desperately sucking down smoke and searching for some music on the radio to bring his blood pressure down. It had been just days since he'd last made his five-o'clock exodus to crawl through traffic and go back to his shitty apartment.

Funny how things could change. And how *fast* they could change. He still had to pay rent for this month and part of next month, since he'd left without giving his roommates any notice to speak of, but otherwise it seemed like he'd been away from that whole world for years now. Like it had never existed at all. No terrible apartment. No lazy roommates. No miserable job. All those arguments over dishwashing and meetings about retirement contributions seemed like someone else's memories. Something he'd seen on TV.

This was the world where he belonged. On the road, behind an instrument, under bright lights. Closing his eyes, he smiled. Even if working his way back into his band's good graces was a slow process, and even if the instrument he was playing wasn't his first love, he was glad to be here. Happy to be out on the road, living from convenience store to convenience store, with absolutely no privacy and little to no downtime, all in exchange for the thrill of performing for thousands. Thousands! As second chances went, he could have done a hell of a lot worse.

All you have to do now is not blow it.

Which would be a lot easier if he could sleep, and that was getting more difficult with each passing night. They had to play tomorrow night. When it came time for lights-out, he'd need to shut off his brain, go to sleep, and rest enough to keep from passing out onstage.

But his brain hadn't wanted to shut off the last couple of nights, and he doubted that was going to change. His mind kept flipping back and forth between the many, many moments when A.J. had caught his attention. When he'd held back during sound check. When he'd let fly onstage. Grabbing burgers in Denver. Those times when he was sweet and shy. The others when he was crazy and animalistic.

Jude rubbed his eyes. One minute, he wanted to wrap his arms around A.J. and protect him from everything. The next, he wanted to drop to his knees and do whatever that wild-eyed drummer told him to.

He shivered, barely keeping himself from gasping at the conflicting but equally intriguing images of the man who, after lights out, would be sleeping above him.

It occurred to him that he wasn't even sure if A.J. was into guys. But in his mind's eye, he saw that look A.J. had shot him backstage. Sweaty. Smeared eyeliner. Something primal. Something . . . undeniably sexual.

He swallowed. He had no idea what A.J.'s orientation was, but going by the look on the drummer's face that night, he wouldn't have been surprised if A.J. had been willing to fuck anyone who thought they could handle him.

Me. Me. Please, me.

He mouthed a string of silent profanity. Hadn't he been convinced he was going to lose his mind at his day job?

Oh, how he'd underestimated what rejoining the band would do to him. Mostly because he hadn't been aware of A.J.'s existence. He was aware of it now, though. No doubt about that.

Yep. I'm gonna lose my mind.
Hell, maybe I already have.

The tour bus door opened, and he turned his head. Immediately, his heart sped up.

Six feet of temptation in a ripped Pink Floyd tank top. And he was coming right this way.

Jude sat up. "Hey."

"Hey." A.J. smiled. "You mind if I join you?"

"Uh, no." Jude cleared his throat. "Not at all."

A.J. took a seat at the next bench, his back to the table. He stretched his arms along the sun-bleached length of wood and gazed up at the sky. "God, it's nice to get off that bus."

"Isn't it?" Now that A.J. was here, the cigarette suddenly seemed necessary, if only to give him something to do with his hands. And his mouth. He busied himself getting one out and lighting it. "I like touring so far, but yeah, it's good to be outside once in a while."

"Seriously." A.J. met his gaze. "At least this weather isn't shit. Nothing like having the choice between staying on the bus and getting out when it's subzero."

Jude scowled. "I might have to quit smoking before that happens."

A.J. laughed. "Richie and Vanessa both gave it up for a whole week while we were going through Michigan and Illinois in January."

"I don't blame them." Jude shivered. "I'm way too California for that kind of cold."

"You and me both." A.J. paused, some of the amusement leaving his expression. "Do you . . . Are you still planning to tour with us? For the next album?"

"Planning on it." Jude sucked in some smoke and blew it out. "We'll see how the next few weeks go. And if Connor and I don't kill each other while we're recording."

"Guess we'll see. For what it's worth, though, I can see why they wanted you back."

"Yeah." He laughed bitterly. "I'm the only bassist who knows the fucking music."

"But you're picking up the new stuff too. You're really good."

"Thanks. Now if we didn't have all this drama, we'd be set."

"Eh." A.J. shrugged. "Musicians are volatile as a species."

"Isn't that the truth."

"And you and Connor have a history. There's going to be some drama, and there's going to be some adjustment. You've only been back in the band like a week." He paused. "Besides, give it another week or two, and Connor and Shiloh are going to be so busy finalizing everything for the next album, he'll probably forget you're there."

Jude couldn't really argue with that. When Connor was writing music, especially when he was at the stage of perfecting it so it could be performed or recorded, he was nothing if not focused.

"You're probably right," he said quietly. "That should keep him busy for a while."

A.J. laughed. "Well, and he'll have Shiloh there too. I'm sure you know what it's like to work with her."

Chuckling, Jude nodded. "Oh, yes." He hadn't thought of that, but A.J. was right. Even if Connor wanted to be a tool and snipe at Jude, he'd have Shiloh there to keep him on task—the woman was a hell of a workaholic, and didn't have much tolerance for people slacking off while she had her nose to the grindstone. Once those two got to work, she'd have Connor burning the midnight oil whether he liked it or not. He wouldn't have *time* to deal with Jude.

"Well, anyway. Thanks for the pep talk."

"Don't mention it." A shy hint of a smile flickered across A.J.'s face. Neither of them said anything for a while, but they stayed where they were. As Jude finished his cigarette, A.J. finally broke the silence. "I'm curious about something."

"Shoot."

A.J. turned to him. "Where'd the name of the band come from?"

He laughed. "No one's ever told you?"

"Nope. I've asked a few times, but I always get blown off." He paused. "Honestly, when I auditioned, I thought it was from the movie or that book that came out a few years ago."

"There's a movie?"

"Yeah. The one about the kid who has to go live with his mom's psychiatrist?"

Jude arched his eyebrow. "I . . . can tell you without a doubt that isn't where the name came from. Is it any good?"

"Don't know. Never saw it."

"Huh. Well, obviously I haven't either."

"So where *did* the name come from? I've been dying of curiosity since I signed."

"It comes from someone literally running with scissors." Jude absently pulled out his cigarettes, but decided not to smoke another one after all, and pocketed them again. "We've known each other since we were kids. Shiloh and I went to kindergarten together. Connor moved to the area in first grade. Richie, Wyatt, and Vanessa came along in middle school."

"Wow. You guys have a long history."

"Yeah." He sighed, tamping down most of the memories that tried to surface. "Anyway, so when we were in . . . second grade, I think, we had one of those teachers who was super strict about everything, and freaked the fuck out over safety. And I don't know if you've noticed, but rules and warnings are the fastest way to make Connor rebel."

A laugh burst out of A.J. "Oh my God. You don't say."

Jude chuckled. "So you *have* noticed, eh?"

"Ya think?"

They exchanged glances, and both laughed.

A.J. smirked. "So you're serious. The name is literal."

"It's literal. You ever seen Connor without his shirt on?"

A.J. quickly sobered. "Uh . . . is that a trick question?"

"No, no. But, I mean, he takes it off onstage sometimes, and you guys have roomed together, so . . ."

"Right. Yeah, I've seen him. But not like—"

"It's okay." Jude smiled. "Relax. I wasn't making any accusations." Though now he was suddenly imagining Connor and A.J. together, and that mental image was definitely one he'd have to save for later. He cleared his throat. "Have you seen his scar?" He tapped just below his rib cage on the left side. "Right there?"

A.J. snorted. "Oh my God."

"He was being a little shit in class one day, just to mess with our teacher, and grabbed a pair of those huge scissors off her desk. He started running around the room and taunting her."

"Let me guess—he tripped?"

"Twelve stitches later . . ."

A.J. grimaced. "Ouch."

"It was pretty nasty. So from then on, anytime one of us thought about doing something stupid, the rest would warn them against running with scissors. Drove Connor crazy for a while, but . . ." He shrugged. "He got in on it too. Then in high school, when we started the band, we couldn't think of a name, but one night, Vanessa did . . . something. I don't even remember now. And Richie was like, 'Damn it, Vanessa. Stop running with scissors.' And we all just kind of paused and looked at each other, and we started laughing, and that was that. We never even considered another name."

"What did Connor think?"

"He thought it was hilarious. And I guess it was until it . . ." His humor faded. "Until it kind of became a self-fulfilling prophecy. Connor and I are both especially good at doing stupid shit and, well . . ."

"You know this doesn't even count as running with scissors, right?" Shiloh's voice echoed in the back of his mind from the night he'd walked out. *"This is taking the fucking scissors and straight up stabbing yourself in the foot."*

"Or stabbing the rest of us," Vanessa had added coldly.

He shook himself. "Anyway. Yeah. That's where we got our name."

A.J. watched him for a moment, as if he could see through to the guilty conscience and those memories. "Well, everybody grows up eventually, right?"

Jude pulled out another cigarette. "One can hope."

CHAPTER 10

A.J. was somewhere between asleep and awake when movement beneath his bunk brought him all the way back into reality.

Directly below him, Jude's mattress creaked softly. A.J. heard a crinkle, and then bare feet padding on the fake linoleum. A moment later, the bus door opened, and the change in air pressure jolted him.

That was weird. Aside from that first night in the motel back in whatever city Jude had joined them in, he didn't usually get up in the middle of the night to smoke. Not unless he and Connor had been at each other's throats or something.

The evening had been pretty peaceful, but Jude had been quiet ever since their conversation about the band name and his past with Connor. Shit. Maybe A.J. had touched a nerve or two.

He eased himself down onto the floor, careful not to wake Richie or Connor.

As he made his way out of the sleeping area, he told himself he only wanted to make sure Jude was all right.

On some level, he might've even believed that was why he was heading out, and that it wasn't an excuse to have another moment alone with Jude. Because God knew he needed to tempt himself like that.

Before he could talk himself out of it—not that he really tried—he slipped on his shoes and stepped off the bus.

As A.J. quietly shut the door behind him, Jude looked up. Eyes fixed on A.J., he turned his head and blew out a cloud of smoke. "Oh, hey. Coming to keep me company again?"

Wishing we could keep each other company in—

"Just couldn't sleep."

"I didn't wake you up, did I?"

"Not really." He hugged himself against the desert chill. "I don't sleep very well on the road."

"I know the feeling." Jude put the cigarette between his lips, and the end glowed orange as he took a drag. Goose bumps prickled A.J.'s neck. God, those lips . . .

He shook himself and looked away. This was definitely a bad idea. Jude was nothing but walking temptation, and indulging in these stolen moments alone and staring at Jude's mouth or his hands or his eyes did nothing to keep him from wanting to take that temptation further.

He cleared his throat. "I just needed some air anyway, I guess." As soon as he said it, he cringed. "Sorry . . ."

Jude laughed. "Don't worry about it. Connor isn't the only one who needs some fresh air once in a while." He held up his cigarette. "Maybe not as fresh as you'd hoped, right?"

"It's all right. I'm upwind."

"Fair enough." Jude put the cigarette between his lips again. "I really should give these things up, but . . ."

"Easier said than done?"

"When you're in a bus full of people who can't stand you?" Jude held up the cigarette like he was offering a toast. "You'd better believe it."

A.J. shifted his weight. "That's a bit of a stretch, don't you think?"

"Not really, no." He tapped the cigarette and watched the glowing coals drift down toward the pavement. "It'll get better, though. Hopefully." He glanced at A.J. "I'm doing what I can."

"It's not you that's the problem."

Jude held his gaze and then chuckled as he brought his cigarette back up. "Let me guess—Connor?"

"Ya think?"

"Surprise, surprise." Bitterness laced Jude's tone.

A.J. cocked his head. "It's hard to picture the two of you dating."

Jude took a long drag, and as he let out the smoke, he shrugged. "Tell me about it. But we did, off and on. And off. And on." He waved his hand, sending a few sparks flying from the cigarette. "And off again."

"That must've been tough. Any time I've seen you two in the same room, you look like you're ready to kill each other." *You look like you wouldn't mind going in there and choking him right now.* "It's just hard to imagine you ever even liked each other."

Jude laughed bitterly. "I'd show you some pictures from the old days, but it'd be about as depressing as looking at a divorced couple's wedding album."

A.J. winced.

Jude's eyebrows rose. "Sorry. Did I . . . I mean, was that . . ."

"Nothing." A.J. gestured dismissively. "Don't worry about it." He cleared his throat. "I don't know. I'm the one who brought it up anyway. Sorry."

"It's okay. You know how dating in high school is nonstop drama? And everything's a crisis?"

A.J. nodded.

"Connor and I just . . . didn't stop with that after graduation." Jude's eyes grew distant. "He's a good guy. He really is. And I'm sure he's not happy to see me every damned day. I just hope it'll get easier as we go. For everyone."

"Me too." A.J. wasn't as optimistic about that as he wanted to be. This thing between Connor and Jude seemed like a powder keg. Or like one of those bombs that had fallen during World War II and sat there festering for decades until something came along and inadvertently set it off.

As the streetlights illuminated Jude's dark eyes, and as the cigarette smoldered between his long fingers, A.J. swallowed hard. Something told him that sneaking out in the middle of the night to spend a moment with Jude, exchanging those looks backstage, letting his mind quietly entertain the not-so-quiet things he'd like to do—well, he might as well drive a bulldozer through a minefield and hope nothing blew up.

He knew this was a bad idea. And yet, here he was. *Again.*

And as Jude put out his cigarette and lit up another, A.J. made no move to go back inside, not even to get away from the chilly night.

Apparently he was a better fit in this band than he'd previously thought.

Because standing out here, letting himself indulge in fantasies he had no business having, knowing he risked upsetting the tenuous peace within the band . . .

So this is what running with scissors feels like.

CHAPTER 11

The New Mexico scenery whipped past. Jude sat in one of the armchairs, staring out the window and wondering why the hell he couldn't relax. He should've been asleep, snoring away like Richie and Vanessa, who were racked out on the couch. Even Connor had dozed off after they'd stopped for lunch.

For as little sleep as Jude had gotten, and with three people sleeping nearby, he should not have been this wide-awake. But he was. He was restless, just like he'd been when he'd gone out for a smoke because lying under A.J. like that had been driving him insane. And then A.J. had *come outside* with him, and the nicotine had stopped doing a damn bit of good. Two cigarettes later, they'd gone back inside, and he still hadn't been able to sleep.

Good thing they weren't playing tonight, but he'd better be well rested tomorrow, or he was liable to nod off while they were onstage or—

Tap. Tap. Tap-tap.

Jude's head snapped up.

Tap. Tap. Tap-tap.

His gaze slid toward A.J.'s fingers, which were tapping out the rhythm on the armrest. Their eyes met, and a subtle vibration buzzed in Jude's fingertips.

Because they weren't tapping.

Anymore.

He glanced down at his hand, wondering how long he must've been drumming without realizing it. Before he'd stopped, anyway.

Tap. Tap. Tap-tap.

Jude relaxed, and he started tapping his fingers again, falling back into a rhythm that felt familiar. Had he been drumming this cadence before? He couldn't remember—it was usually an unconscious thing. Nervous energy always seemed to come out as percussion.

Fuck. A.J. had interrupted his stress-relief cigarette last night—clueless to the fact that he'd been the reason Jude had needed to smoke it in the first place—and now that he'd driven Jude to this outlet, he was joining in too.

And yet, it didn't feel intrusive. In its own way, it was a relief.

You're here. You're fucking with my blood pressure, but I can breathe now. What the hell?

A.J. grinned. He sped up, and Jude's rhythm adapted naturally. Then Jude added a crescendo, tapping harder, and A.J. complemented him effortlessly. This was one of the things Jude loved about music—the wordless dance, the way two musicians fed off each other, responded to each other, built on each other's sound with nothing to guide them but the music itself and some sort of innate telepathy.

A.J.'s head bobbed slightly in time with the beat, and Jude realized he was doing the same thing. They were completely in sync, shutting out the world around them and focusing on sound, on tempo, on each other.

A thought nearly froze his hands in place—would he and A.J. be this responsive and adaptable if they were in bed together?

Oh God.

He shuddered, breaking his rhythm for a split second. A.J. gave him such a wicked grin, Jude wondered for a second if he'd spoken his thoughts aloud. Maybe A.J. could just read him that well—hearing his sexual fantasies as clearly as he heard his finger-tapping.

He changed the rhythm slightly, turning the first three beats into a triplet and adding a couple of longer beats at the end. A.J. grinned again—*challenge accepted*—and met him tap for tap. Jude couldn't help grinning himself. Their eyes locked, and their fingers moved in perfect time, and—

"For *fuck's* sake," Connor grumbled, shifting on the couch. "Is that *really* necessary?"

A.J.'s hand stopped immediately, and he jerked it back as if the armrest had suddenly turned hot. "Sorry."

Connor muttered something Jude didn't understand.

Jude rolled his eyes. Connor was always doing that, talking shit under his breath as if he hoped somebody would call him out. He'd been doing it since he was a little kid, and like everyone else in the band, Jude knew better than to take the bait. Instead, he met A.J.'s gaze, and they both shrugged. *What can you do?*

His fingertips still vibrated, and his muscles itched to start moving again, but the moment had passed. A.J. looked out the window. So did Jude. He folded his hands on the table and watched the scenery go by, but he couldn't get that exchange out of his mind. It had been just like a real jam session, when everything lined up and the music was playing itself. When everyone was on the same wavelength, as if they could predict every beat and chord before it was played, and the music just . . . happened.

Right up until Connor had shushed them like a pissy coworker.

Jude scowled out the window. Maybe he and A.J. could give it another shot when Connor wasn't there. Hell, maybe when they were alone. After all, A.J. seemed to like joining him whenever he went out for a smoke, and there usually wasn't anyone else around.

But things like impromptu jam sessions on tables and armrests, those weren't something he could plan any more than a couple of musicians could plan what would happen during a real jam session. Moments like that either happened or they didn't.

He just hoped A.J. wanted it to happen again as much as he did.

As he always did during sound check, A.J. held back, but he no longer gave Jude the impression of a passive, shy kid who didn't belong there. He was halfway between—he was shy and uneasy, and he was a fearless rock star ready to unleash the inner beast. The tank top he wore tonight was loose and ragged, with a tear in the collar that brought to mind Bruce Banner's tattered clothes after shifting back from the Hulk.

Jude turned away. He needed to . . . What was he doing?

He absently strummed the bass's strings and snapped back into reality. Right. Tuning. Sound check. Idiot.

He adjusted his earpiece and concentrated on the task at hand, even though every tap of drumstick to snare echoed through his bones and distracted the fuck out of him. Fortunately, if there was anything in the world that could pull most of his focus away from A.J., it was the music, and he made it through sound check without making a complete ass of himself.

Now he just had to get through the show. Knowing how A.J. let loose and went full-on Hulk during a show . . .

Fuck.

But there was no bailing tonight—especially not on the grounds of how much he wanted to fuck the drummer—so with a prayer for strength and restraint, he went onstage with his bass and his bandmates.

Show time. I've got this.

He managed to keep himself focused on the music and not tripping over cords or equipment, at least until "Hold Fast." As it did every night during this piece, the spotlight shifted to A.J. for the drum solo, and Jude . . .

Jude stared.

The air itself seemed to vibrate with every smack and crash. Sweat flew off A.J.'s arms. He played like a man possessed, oblivious to what that did to Jude's pulse. Or his dick, for that matter—watching someone play like that, especially someone as smoking hot as A.J., was more of a turn-on than it had any right to be.

Jude tore his gaze away again, which was about as effective as having his back to a man who was fucking him. He couldn't see A.J.'s face, couldn't see the hunger and sweat, but he could feel every impact and the feverish frenzy that drove A.J. and made all the fans go crazy.

Bass. Play the bass. Get your head out of your ass and do your job!

He took a swig of cold water from the bottle he kept behind his amp. This was madness. He wasn't a fifteen-year-old boy who got turned on if the wind changed direction. Or got distracted at the memory of their middle-of-the-night conversation. And the way the streetlights had played on A.J.'s features, highlighting his cheekbones and picking out the blue in his eyes. And how a failed attempt to go to sleep had mussed A.J.'s spiky hair, leaving it somewhere between stage-ready and bedhead.

Jude. Focus.

By the grace of God, he made it through the show. After everyone had cooled down and put instruments in their cases, the rest of the band headed back toward the stage to watch Schadenfreude for the billionth time, but Jude stayed in the ready room. He needed a minute to catch his breath and pull himself together.

He ran a hand through his wet hair. Even pouring a bottle of cold water on himself hadn't done a damned thing to snap him out of this. He could barely see straight. This was getting out of control. Even Connor had never had this effect on him, not even in the early days when they were fucking every chance they had and could barely finish a conversation without making out.

I'm losing my mind. That's all there is to it.

Maybe I just need to get laid.

How long has it been?

Something raised the hairs on the back of his neck.

He turned around.

A.J. stood in the doorway, a pair of drumsticks in his hand. His precisely applied eyeliner was smeared now, and his gaze was fixed right on Jude. He hadn't accidentally happened by. He'd come here on purpose. He'd come looking for Jude.

As the thumping bass of Schadenfreude's set reverberated down the walls and across the floor beneath their feet, A.J. came closer, eyes still locked on his. He wasn't flinching away from this eye contact like he often did, but silently daring Jude to look away.

Jude couldn't have looked away if he'd wanted to. He stared back, feet planted and mouth watering.

Please let me be reading him right.

He couldn't hear anything over that bass. Couldn't even hear his own beating heart, but God, he felt it, and it beat harder and harder as they stared each other down like this.

Less than an arm's length from him, A.J. tossed his drumsticks on the heap of gear by the wall. A drop of sweat rolled down his temple, and Jude followed it with his eyes, watching it trace a muddy line through the smeared makeup over his cheekbone and down to his jaw. It hovered there for a second, clinging to the faint hint of five-o'clock shadow, and then fell to A.J.'s collarbone before it slid beneath his ripped collar.

Jude's eyes flicked up again, and met A.J.'s.

A.J. grinned. Jude ran his tongue along the inside of his lower lip.

And God in heaven, A.J. came closer.

"Thought I'd find you back here," he whispered, his voice nearly disappearing into Schadenfreude's sound.

"You did." Jude swallowed. "Now what?"

"Don't know yet." The distance between them narrowed farther, body heat and energy crackling in the remaining space.

Heart thumping against his ribs, he put a hand on A.J.'s waist. A.J. pulled in a breath, but didn't pull away. In fact, he reached up, and his callused fingers curved around the back of Jude's neck, sending electricity straight down to his curling toes and right back up to his balls.

"So you were looking for me." He moistened his lips again as A.J. drew him closer. "You must've had something on your mind."

Even closer.

"Yeah. I did."

Their lips brushed. Jude shivered. "You know this is a bad idea, right?"

"Yeah. I do." A.J. pushed him up against the wall and kissed him.

Jude mirrored A.J. and gripped the back of his neck. All that passiveness and shyness had gone out the window, and this side of A.J. . . . God, it was hot. He was cautious bordering on timid most of the time, but put him onstage or turn him on, and he was a beast. Jude could only imagine what he was like in bed—naked, with privacy and lube and *please don't stop*, and Jude prayed like hell they made it that far.

He slid his hands down and into A.J.'s back pockets, and A.J. groaned, pressing his hips and that thick erection against him, and kissed him even harder. His chest rubbed Jude's nipple piercings through his shirt, turning his knees and spine to liquid.

Oh fuck. This was even better than he'd fantasized about. The onstage beast was nothing compared to this turned-on, demanding, trembling A.J. who had him pinned to the cinderblock wall. His fingers dug into Jude's skin, and when he slid his hand up into Jude's hair, he gripped it tight enough to hurt, which almost dropped Jude to his knees right then and there.

Above them, the music dimmed and then stopped, and though the whole place still vibrated with the roar of the crowd, other sounds made themselves known. Roadies moving equipment around.

And voices. Familiar voices. *Nearby* voices.

Shit!

He broke the kiss. "We shouldn't." He held A.J.'s shoulders, not sure if he was pushing him away or keeping himself from going back in for more. "This is . . ."

"I know." A.J. looked over his shoulder, oblivious to how much of his throat he was baring, and how much Jude wanted to kiss and taste every inch of skin from his torn collar to his jaw. As A.J. faced Jude again, his expression was quickly edging toward the uneasy kid, leaving the "who the fuck cares?" drummer behind.

Jude took his hands off A.J.'s shoulders.

"Yeah. We . . ." A.J. stepped back. "What now?"

"I'm . . . We really . . ."

"I should go."

Jude nodded, curling and uncurling his fingers at his sides as he fought the urge to grab A.J. and reel him back in. He bit his tongue because the only thing he wanted to say was *No, you shouldn't leave*, and he knew damn well that one of them needed to go before this went too far. Which it already had.

Without another word, A.J. walked out, and Jude sagged against the wall. He wasn't terribly well acquainted with that thing called restraint, and he fought hard to keep himself from running after A.J.

That kiss was everything he'd fantasized about. Aggressive. Frantic. There'd been no sign of shy A.J., and every sign of that primal beast of a drummer, and for the life of him, Jude couldn't understand why they weren't pounding each other into the ground right then. He should've been bent over that stack of amp cases, taking every inch of the hard-on he'd had pressed against his hip, but he wasn't.

Because that would get us booted out of the band. Because Kristy would kill us. Because—

"Jude?" Shiloh startled the hell out of him, and his eyes flew open. "You okay?"

Oh shit. What if A.J. hadn't left? Or she'd walked in like two minutes ago? Fuck!

He cleared his throat. "Yeah. Yeah. Just, uh, tired." He rubbed a hand over his face. "Needed a few minutes to decompress."

She eyed him, then shrugged. "Back-to-back shows can get pretty draining. You'll get used to it." She nodded toward the stack of black and silver boxes beside him. "Could you hand me my makeup kit?"

"Yeah. No problem. Here." He handed it to her, and a moment later she was gone.

He pushed himself up against the wall again. Shit, that was closer than it should've been.

And not nearly as close as he'd needed it to be.

CHAPTER 12

Surprise, surprise—A.J. couldn't focus on *anything*.

There was no going back after that kiss. What had been tasted could not be untasted, but that didn't mean they dared take it any further, and at least they both had the good sense to stay away from each other after that show. They didn't look at each other when A.J. returned to the bus and found Jude smoking outside. They were careful to stay as far apart as possible while they were on the road next day. When Jude started idly tapping his fingers, A.J. folded his own just to keep from joining in. The minute the bus was parked at the next venue, Jude hurried outside for a smoke and A.J. took off to find food.

He wasn't even sure what city they were in. Not that he needed to know. The only ones who had to know that for sure were Shiloh and Connor, and that was just so they didn't shout out "How's it going, Minneapolis?" while they were onstage in Chicago. All he needed to know was that there was always food near a venue, and tonight, finding that food gave him a reason to stay away from Jude.

Except it would only be a temporary reprieve. Tomorrow, the next day, the day after that—sooner or later, they'd have to be in the same space again. The bus. The stage. Their sleeping area. Maybe in time, it would get easier. Maybe once the novelty wore off and he found someone else to lust after.

Today, though, an hour or two away from Jude didn't do him a damned bit of good, because every time his vitals started leveling out again, he and Jude would be in the same room again, and he'd be all over the place. Again. By the time they were wrapping up sound check, A.J. was on the verge of losing his fucking mind.

Thank God he could drum in his sleep. They'd be onstage shortly, and at least he could trust muscle memory to carry him through the show when his brain was all *Jude, Jude, Jude.*

From the corner of his eye, he watched Jude in the ready room. Despite all the backstage noise, and the roar of the excited crowd, A.J. was irrationally certain the rest of the band could hear his pulse pounding.

It was just a kiss. What the hell?

Okay, a look. And then a kiss. And then another look.

But still, just a kiss.

He was no virgin, not by any means, but no one he'd ever touched—male or female—had turned him on like Jude did. He had no idea what it was about him, why Jude lit up nerves in him that no one else did, but it didn't matter why. He did. And A.J. wanted more. Needed more.

And couldn't have any.

Get a fucking grip. It's show time.

He followed his bandmates out onto the stage, and thank God he had the music now to keep his mind out of Jude's pants.

He shivered as he took his place behind the drums. Oh, he'd be able to concentrate until the end of the show, that much he was sure about. It was after that was the problem. That was when he was high, trembling with the lingering thrill of performing for thousands of people, his bones still vibrating and his heart still racing. That was the most dangerous time to be anywhere near Jude. Sex after a performance was always the best, so a kiss like that while their hearts were still pumping from being onstage was bound to be hot. It didn't mean anything. It didn't mean that A.J. had met his match, or that sex with Jude would be as spectacular as that kiss had promised. That deep, relentless kiss.

Oh fuck. He was never going to get him out of his mind. Now that A.J. had felt him sweaty and out of breath, he wanted to feel him naked, sweaty, and out of breath. Not just turned on, but satisfied, shaking from an orgasm, his skin slick with not just sweat, but cum.

A.J. shook himself. This was insane. Where Running with Scissors was concerned, band members sleeping with band members had proven to be an epic disaster; both times had ended with someone leaving the group and the remaining bandmates scrambling to replace him.

But . . . Jude.

He was intriguing as hell, and talented. Nothing attracted A.J. to a man more than raw musical talent. Someone who seemed to get it—that music was more than numbers, notes, measures, and technical bullshit. Someone who played like he felt it.

As the show kicked off, A.J. stole a few glances at Jude, catching little glimpses of the gorgeous tattooed bassist as he rocked one song after another. All the stories he'd heard about Jude so far had created an image of a cool-as-ice guy with unrivaled musical talent. He seemed confident most of the time, but damn, those moments when he was alone with his thoughts and cigarettes, or when he was facing down the band he'd walked away from, there was another side to him that A.J. hadn't expected. It was almost like realizing a seasoned performer had a crippling case of stage fright—it brought him down to earth and made him human, and yet made him seem even larger than life if he could still perform that well despite that much fear.

No wonder A.J. hadn't been able to keep his hands off him. No wonder he was still struggling to keep his hands off him.

An image flickered through his mind of bending Jude over his amp and fucking him into the ground, and A.J. almost lost the beat.

Focus, idiot!

He scrubbed that image from his brain and concentrated on the music. Well, no. He never "concentrated" on it—it just took over, and he let it. He glanced occasionally at the other band members, but carefully kept his gaze away from Jude. No point in distracting himself more than he already was.

Movement to his left caught his eye. Without thinking twice, he turned his head.

Richie, Vanessa, and Jude jumped in unison, bouncing to the beat he was providing, and right when A.J. looked, Richie and Jude exchanged glances. They were both smiling, almost laughing—having the time of their lives.

Jude was sweaty. Disheveled. The muscles and tendons stood out from his bare arms, fingers moving effortlessly on the strings, and every time he bobbed his head, sweat flew from his hair.

Dude, focus, you're—

A.J. misjudged a stroke, and hit the snare's rim just right to send the stick flying out of his hand. He quickly snatched another from the can he kept beside his seat, and recovered as fast as he could—people probably didn't even notice anything, aside from the stick spinning up into the air and disappearing into the shadows—but onstage fuckups mortified him.

He pulled his shit together and didn't let Jude distract him again. Eventually, though, he had a momentary break between songs. While Connor worked the crowd and Richie switched out instruments, A.J. gazed at everything he could see from his perch at the rear of the stage. The band. The enormous crowd that was barely visible now thanks to the lights.

And Jude. Hovering between Vanessa and Richie, throwing back a few gulps of water while he had a chance.

A.J. swallowed. He shifted his attention from Jude to everything else—the band, the crowd, the lights.

This was what he'd dreamed about since the first time he'd picked up an instrument. As hot as Jude was, and as much as A.J. loved the way he kissed, there was no way to make this work without risking everything they both wanted as musicians. There was just too much on the line to even consider it.

Jude turned, and they locked eyes for a split second, but A.J. quickly looked away.

This had to stop.

Though, technically it had stopped when they'd pulled apart the other night. They'd both agreed not to continue, and they'd gone their separate ways as much as anyone could in a shared sardine can.

Oh, but it hadn't stopped, had it? He couldn't focus around Jude. Jude kept shooting him looks that sometimes said *I can't believe we did that*, and sometimes seemed to say *I can't believe that's as far as we got*. Every glance was loaded. Every time A.J. heard Jude tapping—and God, did that man constantly tap and fidget and tap some more—he wanted to join in, but he didn't because then Connor might get pissed off. And besides, if they started that tapping again, he was pretty sure it might turn into erotic Morse code or something—rhythmically undressing each other from across the bus, every beat painting a picture of messed-up hair and rumpled sheets.

At the front of the stage, Connor turned around and gave A.J. a subtle nod—his cue to start the intro to "Peripheral."

Time to focus. Sorry, Jude . . .

A.J. didn't know why he bothered trying to stay away from Jude. It was only a matter of time, and it didn't take long. After their set, while their bandmates were probably off watching Schadenfreude again, he returned to the bus to avoid another ready room incident—and suddenly found himself facing down the bassist.

Jude cleared his throat. "Hey."

"Hey." A.J.'s heart sped up and his stomach started doing somersaults. "What's . . . what's up?"

Jude hesitated, gnawing his lip. "Can I talk to you for a minute?"

A.J. squared his shoulders. "Yeah. Sure."

"We, uh . . ." He paused, and then nodded toward the door. "Shit. I need a smoke."

A.J. nodded. "Okay."

Silently, they stepped outside, and A.J. tried to ignore it when they stood conspicuously farther apart than they usually did.

He stayed quiet while Jude lit a cigarette, and gave him a minute to get some nicotine into his system before he asked again, "What's up?"

Jude watched himself tap his cigarette. "Listen, um . . ." He rubbed the back of his neck and kept his gaze down. "About what happened . . ."

"You don't have to say it."

His eyes flicked up and met A.J.'s.

A.J. exhaled. "I get it. And I'm just glad you had the balls to even bring it up. I know— We can't let the other night happen again."

Jude sighed. "No, we can't. Look, I'm sorry. I guess I just got caught up in—"

"We both did. It's okay." Little by little, his heart sank—though he knew this was the right thing, it was disappointing as hell. "We are supposed to be professionals, right?"

"As much as anyone in a rock band ever is."

Their eyes met, and they both managed quiet, uncomfortable laughs.

Jude kept smoking, and A.J. kept standing there like an idiot with no idea what to say or do next. After a moment, though, he realized Jude was still watching him—head tilted, brow furrowed just slightly, those dark eyes studying him through the thin cloud of smoke.

"What?" A.J. asked.

"Hmm?" Jude shook his head and stared at the ground. "Nothing. Sorry."

"Oh." A mix of disappointment and relief twisted in his stomach. So that was that, wasn't it? They were both professionals. Or at least, they were both going to behave like professionals. Too much on the line, too many reasons to stay away from each other, and too many places on Jude's body that A.J. would've sold his soul to taste.

He blew out a breath and raked a hand through his hair. "So, um. Was there anything else you wanted to talk about?"

Jude met his gaze again, and shook his head. "No, I think we just needed to clear the air." He dropped his cigarette on the pavement and crushed it with his heel. Then he picked up the butt and dropped it in the ashtray. "I'm going to go find something to eat while places are still open. You, um, want anything?"

Just you.

A.J. cleared his throat. "No, I'm okay. I think I'm just going to grab a shower and turn in."

"Okay." Jude slid his hands into his pockets, and A.J. tried not to think about those same hands sliding into his own back pockets the other night. "Well, um." Jude met his eyes, but only for a second this time. "I'll see you around?"

"Yeah. See you around."

With that, Jude headed out, and A.J. went into the deserted bus. Alone, he rested his hands on the back of one of the chairs and released a long, heavy breath. This was how it needed to be. They were on the same page about it, and they'd keep a safe, professional distance. They were doing the right thing. Bullet dodged, crisis averted.

And the relief would kick in *any*time now.

CHAPTER 13

No matter how hard he tried, Jude couldn't get that goddamned kiss out of his mind, but that didn't surprise him too much. Between his desk job and all the time he'd wasted generally feeling sorry for himself, not to mention wallowing in his guilt over cheating on Connor, he hadn't been laid in longer than he cared to remember.

And he'd *never* been kissed like *that*.

As the bus wound its way through the Rockies, taking them from show to show in cities he couldn't tell apart, his desire for A.J. intensified with every passing night. Every time he watched A.J. on the stage, he wanted him more. Every time they passed each other, especially after a show when they were both sweaty and shaking with adrenaline, he had to fight even harder not to drag him into a dark corner somewhere and throw caution to the wind.

It didn't help that A.J. kept shooting him looks that weakened his knees. Not just because his blue eyes were hypnotic in their own right, but because every glance seemed as loaded as the one he'd given him the night he'd *almost* suggested showering together.

And there were how many weeks left on this tour?

Fuck.

He tried like hell to think about anything besides A.J., but . . . not a chance. The man who'd kissed him backstage hadn't been the timid kid who hung around the band. It was like he'd been sitting next to Clark Kent this whole time, thinking the soft-spoken guy was nice and hot in a cute kind of way, and then he'd blinked and found himself pinned up against the wall by Superman. A sweaty, disheveled, eyelinered Superman who'd just torn up the stage like he was born to rock the drums. And every time the shy kid tore off the veil and became the sexually charged rock star, Jude went a little further out of his mind.

Lying on his rack after a show in . . . hell, whatever town they were in, he couldn't sleep. His bone-deep exhaustion didn't hold a candle to the things A.J. did to him. Or rather, the things he kept fantasizing about A.J. doing to him.

One night. Just one night. That couldn't be too much to ask, could it? Some privacy, a flat surface, enough lube and condoms to get all this out of their systems? Except there'd be no getting this out of his system. One kiss had him hooked. Spending the night together would be a point of no return.

But, God, it would be worth it. He wanted to see what happened when A.J. was turned loose in bed like he was turned loose onstage.

In the darkness, he stared up at the rack above him. A.J.'s rack. Sleeping this close to him fucked with Jude's brain anyway, and tonight it was unbearable. He could hear A.J.'s slow, steady breathing, imagined him sprawled

136

on his side, maybe with his face buried in the pillow and an arm tucked beneath it. Peaceful, relaxed—a sleeping dragon Jude wanted to wake up and rile up.

He shivered. Then he mouthed a curse into the stillness—another night beneath A.J., another night of wondering if it would be worth the risk of jerking off to relieve the hard-on swelling beneath his shorts. What no one heard wouldn't hurt him, right? And it was better than waking up with blue balls. Again.

He squirmed beneath the covers, trying to think of anything that might distract his dick long enough to go to sleep. Not a chance. Not this time. Every night was worse than the last—harder in every way—and tonight, he wasn't sleeping it off.

A.J. was right above him. A few feet away, Connor and Richie. On the other side of a partition, Shiloh, Vanessa, and Kristy. Privacy? Not here.

But he also wasn't going to sleep with an erection this hard and the object of his horniness snoring softly overhead.

To hell with it. Moving as quietly as he could, he slipped his hand beneath his boxers, and as his fingertips brushed his cock, he clenched his teeth to keep from gasping.

In his mind, he'd taken A.J. up on that silent offer after the first show. The bus's shower stall was barely big enough for one, but had plenty of space for two bodies pressed close enough together. He couldn't even hold on to one thought—making out under the water, jerking each other off, fucking A.J. until he cried, A.J. fucking him until *he* cried—and his head spun as his cock got even harder. He barely remembered where he was or why he had to stay quiet, and damn near let a moan slip free.

He froze, listening, but no one else's breathing changed. Nobody stirred. Slowly, he started again, and this time, he pressed his lips together and held his breath, using every last scrap of concentration he had left to focus on staying silent. When he absolutely needed air, he forced himself to exhale as silently as possible, and to pull in a slow, stealthy breath.

In his mind, he wasn't being quiet, and he sure as fuck wasn't holding his breath. Not while A.J. pounded him against the shower wall, strained groans turning into curses in Jude's ear. If A.J. fucked like he kissed, Jude wouldn't be able to walk the next day, especially since he hadn't been fucked in ages. Taking it as roughly as he imagined A.J. giving it would undoubtedly hurt, and that thought made his spine tingle.

Make it hurt, A.J., just don't stop . . .

His eyes rolled back, and his toes curled beneath the covers. Still holding his breath, still keeping absolutely silent, he came . . . and nearly fucking passed out from the intensity and the lack of oxygen as hot semen coated his fingers. Everything went white for a few seconds, but somehow—God only knew how—he didn't make a sound.

As his orgasm tapered, he exhaled as slowly and quietly as he could. Catching his breath was a challenge when he didn't dare pant, but after a few minutes, his pulse came down, his lungs stopped screaming for oxygen, and his head stopped spinning. He waited another minute or two and then got up to use the communal bathroom— at least that wouldn't raise any suspicions, since just about everyone got up to take a piss at some point during the night.

In the bathroom, he cleaned himself off and washed his hands. Then he went back to his rack, pulled the covers up, and fell asleep to the sound of A.J. breathing above him.

The next morning, Jude couldn't even loo
eye. Or at least, he didn't imagine he'd be abl
up and got the hell off the bus for the f
cigarettes before A.J. had even stirred.

The nicotine didn't help, but smoking gave him
something to do while he was alone with his thoughts.
And alone was the best place for him to be right now,
since the place he wanted to be would be disastrous to the
band.

The tension was still palpable anytime he was in the
room with one of his bandmates. He was getting along
with Shiloh and Richie, but he hadn't made any headway
with Vanessa, not to mention Connor.

Which meant he still had to tread carefully. Though
he was the one bailing them out, *he* owed *them* for the
second chance. And above all, he owed it to them not to
listen to his impulsive side and sabotage the success they'd
busted their asses to achieve. No walking away when
emotions ran too hot. No getting involved with bandmates
who were too hot to ignore.

Easier said than done, of course. Everyone had called
him a musical prodigy since he was in kindergarten, but
days like this, he wished he'd been born with mediocre
musical talent and prodigy-level skill at relationships.
Because goddamn, whatever blessings he had when it
came to music had apparently been balanced out by his
failures in *that* department.

He sighed and pulled out another cigarette.

The bus door opened, and Kristy stepped outside.
"Morning, sunshine."

"Morning," he muttered.

She watched him smoke for a few seconds. "You
okay?"

"Yeah, why?"

"Because I've seen that look before." Kristy folded
her arms and arched an eyebrow. "You're about twenty
seconds away from booking a ticket home, aren't you?"

Jude stared at his cigarette, and he was pretty sure the heat in his cheeks was visible. Quitting hadn't really occurred to him, but now that she mentioned it, the idea had a certain appeal. He wouldn't *do* it, but . . . "Well, I doubt anyone on the bus would mind if I did." And it sure would get him away from that blond-haired temptation who was probably taking a shower at this very moment, naked under the water and—

He cleared his throat and then took a deep drag. *You're insane. You know that, right?*

"Jude. Honey." She stepped closer. "What's going on? Seems like you and everyone have been getting along lately. Better than I expected you to. I mean, you and Connor have been staying out of each other's way, the shows have been great, and—what gives?"

"I . . . yeah, we've all been getting along, but . . ." *But I want to get along even better with the drummer, and we all know that'd be a fucking disaster.* He turned his head and exhaled a cloud of smoke. Then he faced her again. "I don't know. I guess I've just been wondering if it was a mistake to come back."

"A mistake?" She laughed. "Are you insane? You guys are doing great onstage, and you're not killing each other backstage. It's less of a catastrophe than I expected."

He sucked in some more smoke, but didn't speak.

"Look," she said. "I know this is an adjustment for everyone. And even when you guys aren't fighting, I know it's hard being around Connor."

"Isn't just Connor."

"You've gotten along pretty well with the band since you came back, especially considering how and why you left." She added just enough emphasis to that last part to make it clear the barb was absolutely intentional.

He stared at the ground. "I know. And you're right." He shook his head. "I'm just overthinking everything, that's all."

"Good. Because if you up and leave this time—"

"I won't. I promise."

She eyed him skeptically. "From anyone else, I'd believe that."

He took another drag. "So I fucked up before, and now I'm a liar?"

"No, but I know you." Her voice was oddly gentle. "I don't think you're a liar, but I think you get scared and frustrated, and when you do, you run. That has always been how you handle things, Jude, and it's going to keep blowing up in your face every fucking time. I promise you that."

He couldn't argue. His impulse to run for the hills had never served him well beyond the short term. Sighing, he nodded. "I know. And you're right. I . . . Sometimes I don't know what else to do."

"The same thing the rest of us do, sweetie." She grimaced. "You face the music, no matter how much you don't want to."

Jude nodded, but didn't speak.

"I'm going to get some coffee." She gestured over her shoulder toward the row of shops and restaurants at the other end of the parking lot. "You want to come?"

He dropped his cigarette and crushed it beneath his heel. "Sure. Why not?"

Together, they headed across the parking lot, chatting about the previous night's show and tomorrow night's. All the while, though, Jude's mind stayed firmly in that smoky space beside the bus where they'd had their conversation.

Kristy was right. When he was backed into a corner or pushed to his limit, he did stupid shit without thinking about it. Cheating on Connor. Walking away from the band. Quitting his job to join the tour. And hadn't it always blown up in his face?

Walking away wasn't an option this time. What little money he had was already dwindling, and there'd be no more coming in if he dropped this gig. Right now he was being paid like a contractor—a set amount per show, and not a penny more. It wasn't much, either, just what the band could cobble together from what little they'd actually made from their record deal. Hell, the band was actually in debt to the record company—what band wasn't?—so God knew where the money was even coming from. All he knew was that it might as well have been a per diem to keep him stocked with food, smokes, and Band-Aids for his healing fingers.

If he walked, though, there would be nothing else. He'd screwed himself out of finding a job in Los Angeles. Employers weren't exactly hurting for applicants, and answering yes to the "have you ever left a job without giving two weeks' notice" question would virtually guarantee he couldn't score so much as an interview for anything outside of a sweat shop or one of the more dehumanizing gigs on a shady porn set.

Jude shuddered as he followed Kristy into a coffee shop. Okay, maybe the job market wasn't that bad. He could probably find some form of employment out there that didn't involve mopping up cum or coaxing hard-ons out of exhausted porn stars, but he was pretty sure he'd screwed himself out of anything as cushy as his last job. As miserable as that place had been, at least it'd had halfway decent benefits and paid above minimum wage.

Way to burn that *bridge, genius.*

What was done was done, though, and he was out of second chances. He had to focus on the music this time. Not on Connor. Not on A.J. The music, the music, and nothing but the music.

As hard as it was, he needed to keep everyone—including A.J.—at arm's length.

CHAPTER 14

Show after show, city after city, A.J. kept his hands to himself—but damn, it wasn't easy. Jude was the closest thing to a friend he'd made since joining the band. He wanted to keep that going since it beat the hell out of feeling like an outsider, but getting closer to Jude didn't bode well for staying *away* from Jude.

Not that it was easy to stay away from anyone on this tour. They were, for all intents and purposes, half a dozen roommates living in an overcrowded rolling studio apartment with a semifunctional shower and a temperamental coffeepot. Though things had been peaceful—as peaceful as they ever were with Connor around—everyone was wearing thin, itching to have some space and be in a familiar town. Rumor had it, even Schadenfreude's members were at each other's throats. It was definitely time to go home.

Eventually the band made its way back to LA, and after one hell of a final show at the Hollywood Bowl—one of the places A.J. had dreamed of playing—the tour came to an end.

Now it was time to get to work. They had two weeks to polish the edges off their new songs, and then start recording.

But first, they had a much-needed week-long break. Jude made a comment about spending time with his family in Sherman Oaks, and the band had barely finished the Hollywood Bowl show before he disappeared. Connor took off to Florida to visit his parents. Shiloh vowed to spend every waking hour on a beach. Vanessa and Richie joked about hitting up a dealer and spending the whole week stoned—A.J. wasn't sure if that was entirely a joke, and he couldn't say he blamed them either way.

A.J. went back to his studio apartment in one of the shadier areas of Culver City.

The tour had stretched his finances almost to a breaking point, and several times he'd considered dropping the apartment, but he'd hung on to it. The rent wasn't that bad by LA standards, and having his own place meant he wouldn't have to crash at his mom's or dad's house—and face the inevitable bitching over whose house he'd chosen—when he returned.

He keyed himself into the little shoebox, and as soon as he'd stepped inside and closed the door he was glad he'd kept the place. He let his bag slide off his shoulder and onto the floor with a heavy thud, and he sagged against the door. This apartment had seemed obscenely tiny when he first rented it, but now, it might as well have been a stadium. All this . . . *space*. Vast, empty space occupied only by his few possessions and cheap furniture, with no one to leave empty soda cans on his milk-crate table or stuff empty potato chip bags between his mismatched couch cushions.

For a solid five minutes he just stood there, taking in the silence and the elbow room, breathing in familiar air that he didn't have to share with anyone else. It was peaceful in here, and there was no one around to fuck that up. If any of his bandmates wanted to argue with each other over the next week, they were welcome to do so—it wasn't his problem. For seven whole days, he would be nobody's peacekeeper.

Eventually he pushed himself off the door and shuffled across the room to the kitchenette. Of course the fridge was empty. So were the cupboards. The takeout menus on the freezer door were probably still good; maybe he'd order something. Somehow that seemed like more work than it was worth, though.

Instead, he wandered from the kitchenette to the twin bed pushed up against the wall a few feet away. He toed off his shoes and pulled off his shirt, intending to take a shower, but suddenly that bed looked awfully tempting. It was barely bigger than a futon but, compared to his rack on the bus, might as well have been a California king.

So he lay back across it, limbs stretched out in all directions, and passed the fuck out.

When he opened his eyes again, daylight was pouring in through the windows.

There were voices outside. Neighbors, he guessed. He didn't recognize any of them, though. This complex had a revolving door of tenants, so he was probably surrounded by strangers now. Fine. As long as they stayed out there and he stayed in here, he didn't care.

He stumbled out of bed and into a bathroom that he didn't have to share with anyone. If California hadn't been ass-deep in a drought, he'd have taken the longest, hottest shower in the history of mankind just to savor the fact that no one was waiting impatiently outside the door.

After a brief shower, he dressed and tried to figure out what to do next. The mere thought of settling into his routine was weird. Not that he'd had much of a routine before, but whatever it was, it hadn't involved living in close confines with several other people, dividing his time between the road and the stage, and . . .

Jude.

He shivered. It was definitely weird to feel any kind of relief over being this far away from Jude, but damn it, he needed to catch his breath. For the last few weeks, he hadn't been able to turn around without bumping into the man he desperately wanted, and now he could finally chill.

In fact, there wasn't a whole lot else *to* do. When this week was over, they'd start rehearsing again, playing the new music they'd all been practicing when time and space had permitted. Then they'd start recording, and once that was done, they'd be rehearsing for the tour. The headlining tour. The real thing. *Holy shit.*

But that was next week. He couldn't exactly practice here in his thin-walled studio apartment. That was probably a good thing—his joints and muscles had been getting achier after each show. A week wouldn't make him rusty, and it would do wonders on the fatigue.

No bus. No shows. No drums. One week of blissful solitude and breathing room. And now that he had some time and space to himself, there were two things he wanted more than anything: a damn good meal and a damn good lay.

The first one was easy. There was a grocery store up the street, and he had money in his checking account for once in his life.

The second . . .

He hadn't set foot in a club in ages unless it was to perform. He was terrible at approaching guys, even online. And the more he thought about it, the less he was sure that a random guy could scratch this itch. Then again, maybe they would. Something casual with someone who wouldn't stick around might just be the distraction he needed. That wasn't usually his cup of tea—he'd never been particularly promiscuous, and usually only slept with boyfriends—but after sleeping *right above* a man he *really* wanted to fool around with, the idea of jumping into bed with anyone sounded pretty damn good. He couldn't have Jude, but he could find someone to distract him for a night.

Yeah, right. Jude could melt him with a kiss. A.J. could find the hottest single gay man in Los Angeles, grab a second one for good measure, and have a four-alarm threesome, and he'd still be thinking about Jude the whole time.

He rubbed his eyes with the heels of his hands. There was only one man in all of Southern California who was going to satisfy him.

More than that, though, while he had felt like an outsider since the start, and had fully expected a turf war with Jude, it was Jude who'd made him feel like a permanent part of the band. It was hardly Jude's decision whether A.J. stayed, but he seemed to accept A.J.'s presence without question.

Slowly, the pieces fell into place. Jude had given him what no one else in the band had—the feeling that he belonged. That he was *wanted*.

He sighed. That was all it was. Yeah, Jude would be attractive to any red-blooded gay man, but that wasn't why A.J. was this hung up on him. The road was a lonely place, and he was clinging hard to the one person who hadn't made him feel like they wouldn't notice if the bus left without him.

It wasn't infatuation, it was insecurity. Plain and simple.

He rolled his tense, tired shoulders.

It was disappointing, realizing that what he'd called chemistry was really something else, but a relief in its own right too. Now that it had a name, and that name wasn't "uncontrollable lust," he stood a better chance of ignoring it.

And now he had a full week to sell himself that oceanfront property in Arizona.

After their one-week reprieve, the band came together again in a producer's studio. Recording wouldn't start quite yet, not until they'd had a chance to iron out the kinks in the new songs. This was their rehearsal space until then.

Shiloh was tanned and smiling, so she must've made good on her plan to stay at the beach all week. Connor looked more refreshed and relaxed than A.J. had ever seen him. The ever-present tension in his lips and between his eyebrows was gone, and he and Kristy were chatting and laughing as they sipped their coffee. Richie and Vanessa were both extra mellow as they set up their amps and tuned their guitars, so they probably hadn't been joking about their plans for the week. Seemed like it had done them both some good—like Connor, they were in good spirits. Vanessa's cheekbones were a little smoother, the shadows beneath them not quite so heavy, so she must've had a decent meal or two. Maybe the munchies, maybe just enjoying the opportunity to eat something that didn't come from a convenience store, but either way, she looked healthier already.

And Jude . . .

Well, he always looked good. And A.J. couldn't put his finger on anything that was different about him, just that every time he glanced Jude's way, his pulse went crazy. He focused as best he could on setting up his instrument for the rehearsal, but he was so fucking distracted by the quiet bassist sitting beneath the window that he damn near dropped the high hat while he was adjusting it.

Because he doesn't make you feel like an outsider. It's that simple. Get over it.

He shook himself and focused on adjusting his rig while his bandmates warmed up. Once everyone was ready to start, Connor held up the list of tracks. "Okay, so we're in agreement for the songs we want to record, right? No one wants to make any changes?"

"No, we're good," Shiloh said. "I think so, anyway."

The rest of the band nodded in agreement.

"And Jude's recording with us?" Vanessa's tone was flat, her eyes narrowing just enough to hint at her displeasure.

"Yes," Connor ground out. "That was the deal."

Richie glanced back and forth from Vanessa to Jude. "Well, as long as he's here, maybe we should put Jude on the drums for a song or two. You know, for old time's sake."

A.J.'s gut clenched.

Jude's eyes darted toward A.J., and then he turned to Richie and shook his head. "Nah. I, um . . . better stick with the bass. My wrists are a little tender as it is." He paused, flicking his gaze toward A.J. once more. "He's the drummer."

Richie shrugged. "All right, man. Whatever you say."

Slowly, A.J. released his breath. Yep, that was it—Jude didn't question his place in the band, and that was why A.J. kept gravitating toward him. The only reason. Otherwise, Jude was just another hot guy in a city full of hot guys, and A.J. made a mental note to give Grindr another look tonight. Anything to remind himself that Jude was not the only fish in this particular sea.

As the rehearsal went on, most of the songs were smooth enough—still rough, but coming together.

One song, though—"Sanguine"—refused to cooperate. Connor's vocals were fine, but every time another instrument came in, the whole thing fell apart. A.J. couldn't figure out why, and nobody else seemed to have a clue either. Neither Jude nor A.J. could find the rhythm. Richie and Vanessa could play a few bars alongside Connor, but it just didn't mesh. Nothing worked.

Connor swore, rubbing his neck with both hands. "I don't get it. I . . . Fuck. It sounded good in my head."

Jude cleared his throat. "What if we slowed it way down?"

Connor turned to him, his expression as neutral as it ever was. "Slow it down?"

"Yeah. Maybe this one isn't meant to be so upbeat. Maybe it wants to be a ballad."

A.J. held his breath—Connor was usually willing to take criticism, but how willing was he to take it from Jude?

Connor's eyes lost focus. His lips moved soundlessly, and he bobbed his head slightly in time with a beat no one heard but him. Then he stopped and met Jude's gaze. "I think you might be right."

A.J. exhaled. So did the others. Apparently he hadn't been the only one worried that personal might trump professional here.

"Okay," Connor said. "A.J., can you give us a beat?"

Sure enough, the piece was born to be a ballad. With a slower tempo, each part found its way in. A.J. and Jude fed off each other until they'd created a rock-steady rhythm, and Connor adapted the vocals to match. Richie strummed a gentle guitar line, and Vanessa harmonized. Each time they went through the first verse and the chorus, the music blended together until it was almost seamless. More rehearsing would perfect the piece, but it was finally working.

They went through that one a few more times before moving on to the next song. This piece was, thank God, a hell of a lot more cooperative. The guitarists added a few flourishes here and there, and A.J. and Jude found a badass rhythm that upped the energy, and it probably would have been ready to record right then and there if the vocals had been stronger.

Shiloh gingerly swallowed some tea.

Connor rubbed his throat. "Damn, I need a break. Voice is getting a little raw."

"I could use one too." Vanessa shook out her hands. "Lunch?"

"Lunch sounds good to me." Richie put his guitar aside.

"I'm fine for now." Jude chuckled. "My mom made enough breakfast to overstuff an army."

"Damn, can we stay at your place?" Richie clapped his arm as he got up. "Or tell your mom to send food to rehearsal. Does she still make that tater tot casserole?"

"I can ask her."

"Yes," Shiloh said, her voice scratchy. "*Please.*"

"Okay, okay." Jude chuckled. "I'll have her make up a bunch."

"Awesome. Thank you." She picked up her purse. "I need to eat something now, though. I could go for a burger."

"Isn't there an In-N-Out up the road?" Connor asked.

"I think so. You guys coming?"

"Absolutely," Vanessa said.

"There's food." Richie rolled his shoulders as he headed for the door. "Duh, I'm coming."

"Of course you are." Shiloh smacked him playfully. They all started for the door, but she paused. "What about you, A.J.?"

He shrugged. "I'm okay for now. I've been grazing all morning." He pointed a drumstick at the half-empty can of cashews he'd balanced on a music stand beside his kit.

Shiloh adjusted her purse strap on her shoulder. "Suit yourself."

Connor threw A.J. a weird look, and Jude a weirder one, but he didn't say anything.

As their bandmates filed out of the room, Jude clasped his fingers above his head and stretched. A.J. sat straighter, working a crick out of his back.

"I think I will step out for a smoke." Jude put his bass aside. "Be back in a minute."

"I'll, uh, babysit the instruments."

Jude laughed. "Just make sure mine stays out of the cookies and doesn't watch too much TV."

A.J. offered a two-fingered salute. "You got it."

While Jude was gone, A.J. sat back and stretched again. He skimmed over the list of songs Connor had printed out. This album was going to be amazing, even better than their first, and he still couldn't quite believe he was going to be a part of it. With any luck, he'd be around for the third album. There were rumors of a world tour for that one, depending on the success of the one they were working on now.

What I wouldn't give . . .

A few minutes later Jude came back in, snapping him out of his fantasies of playing Wembley Stadium and one of those huge festivals in Eastern Europe.

Jude took his seat. "All the instruments behave themselves?"

"The guitars are in time-out, but—"

Their eyes met, and they both laughed. Jude left his bass where it was, leaning against another chair, and released his breath as he sat back.

"So how's it feel?" A.J. asked. "Working on an album?"

Jude grinned. "Been waiting my whole life for this. I can't wait until we're actually recording."

"Hmm, so I shouldn't shoot down your dreams yet and tell you how tedious the recording process is?"

"You can try." Jude lowered his hands and rested his forearms on his thighs as he stretched his back. "And then I can tell you about the year and a half I spent holding down a desk. Tedious recording beats that bullshit any day."

A.J. wrinkled his nose. "I'll take your word for it."

"You never had one of those jobs?"

"Not in an office, no. But I did whatever retail and fast-food gigs I could get my hands on and still perform with my bands."

"Sucked?"

"Sucked."

"I don't doubt it. I worked at a sunglass kiosk for a few months in high school." Jude grimaced. "If I never have to do that again . . ."

"You got to be one of those assholes? I'm sorry."

"Yeah, it didn't last long." Jude laughed. "I'm pretty good at getting myself fired when I'm miserable, so . . ."

"Do I even want to know?"

Jude sat up again, and his smile was a little sheepish. "Let's just say you should check the freeways before you tell your boss you'll be two hours late because of traffic." He clicked his tongue and rolled his eyes. "The one time the I-5 was actually clear at that time of day."

A.J. laughed. "Uh, yeah. Helps to check out your own alibis."

"Believe me, I know. But hopefully, I won't have to do one of those stupid jobs again." He wasn't looking at A.J. anymore, and after a moment A.J. realized Jude was gazing longingly at the drums.

"Miss it?"

Jude jumped like he hadn't realized A.J. was watching. "What? Shitty retail jobs?"

"No, the drums." He gestured with his drumsticks. "You miss playing?"

"Oh yeah. Definitely." Jude eyed the drum set, and A.J. wouldn't have been surprised if the man's mouth was watering. "Nothing like drumming, you know?"

A.J. fidgeted. While Jude could move between instruments, A.J.'s only place in this band or any other was behind the drums. It was hard not to get territorial, especially when he'd been wringing his hands over his job security since well before Jude showed up.

Still, he couldn't imagine being this close to a drum set and staying hands-off, so it must've been torture for Jude.

Tentatively, he held out the drumsticks. "You, um, want to give it a shot?"

Jude's gaze darted back and forth from the sticks to A.J.'s eyes. "Really?"

"Sure." A.J. shrugged. "Everyone says you're really good. I'm kind of curious to hear you play."

Jude still didn't move. "But you're . . . I mean . . ."

"One time. Just for the hell of it."

Jude eyed him, but finally smiled. "Well, if you insist."

"Have at it." A.J. forced a laugh. "Just don't tell the rest of the band."

"Secret's safe with me." He took the drumsticks, and they switched places. While A.J. stood by the seat Jude had vacated, Jude sat on the throne behind the drums and exhaled slowly, spinning a drumstick between his fingers as he gazed at A.J.'s rig. He seemed to be scrutinizing every inch of it—the height of the high hats, the angle of the snare. A.J.'s gut clenched—what did he think of the setup? Was it all wrong?

Oh for God's sake. It doesn't matter if it's all wrong for him. This is my *rig. If he doesn't like it, his bass is over there.*

He rolled his eyes at his own thoughts. Every drummer had to acquaint himself with a new setup. Jude wasn't judging. He was just figuring out where everything was.

Then he started playing.

A.J. had no idea how long it had been since Jude had touched a drum, but he took to it like it hadn't been any time at all. A.J. could've watched him for hours. The man was a god behind the drums. Or on any instrument, really.

It was impossible to look at him while he was playing and not believe—not be wholly convinced—that he felt every beat and every nuance like it was a part of him. He was exactly the kind of musician who made A.J.'s pulse race even when he *hadn't* kissed him, jerked off to him in the bus's cramped shower, tripped over his own feet while imagining himself balls-deep in him.

Jude glanced at A.J.'s leg, then up at him. Puzzled, A.J. looked down and realized he'd been tapping his fingers on his thigh in time with Jude's beat. He didn't know when he'd started, only that Jude had noticed before he did, and now they were both playing—bobbing their heads in time with each other while A.J. tapped out the same rhythm on his thigh that Jude was banging on the drums.

They both grinned. Jude kept playing. A.J. kept tapping. There was no way in hell Jude could hear the soft percussion of fingertips on denim-covered skin, but A.J. sure could. He felt it as surely as he felt the impact of stick to snare, and as he held Jude's gaze, he wasn't sure who was leading whom. If one of them was leading, or if they were both pulling the same cadence from the ether and following that. Jude sped up. So did A.J. Then A.J. slowed down, and Jude followed.

So much for this crush being about insecurity—Jude was like walking, talking catnip, and playing one-on-one with him like this, drumming together the way some people danced together, brought all those dirty fantasies back to the forefront of his mind.

There were so many reasons to keep those fantasies in his head where they belonged, but every move Jude made gave him another reason to wish they could have one night together. Just one night.

Abruptly, Jude stopped. "Ah, that was fun." He smiled as he stood. "Thanks for letting me . . ."

"Yeah, don't mention it."

Jude held out the drumsticks. A.J. closed his fingers around them.

But Jude didn't let go.

Their eyes met.

Though it must've been his imagination, A.J. was sure he could feel Jude's pulse echoing down the wooden sticks and into his own palm. He and Jude were practically touching, and yet Jude might as well have been all the way across the room. Too far away. Much too far.

Spine tingling with nerves, A.J. tightened his grip and pulled.

Jude stumbled, apparently caught off guard, and when he righted himself they were toe to toe. Damn near nose to nose.

A.J.'s pulse shot skyward.

His fingers twitched on the drumsticks. Jude's must've done the same—the sticks subtly ground together in A.J.'s hand. Any other time, he might've let go or backed off, and that was exactly what he should've done this time, but he remembered all too well what Jude's kiss tasted like. So many reasons to stop this before it started. One damned-hot reason to see where it could go.

But before he could make a move in any direction, Jude let go of the drumsticks, grabbed the back of A.J.'s neck in both hands, and kissed him.

CHAPTER 15

By the time they came up for air, Jude's head was spinning.

Their eyes met.

Before a single synapse in Jude's brain could fire, A.J. shoved him back a step. Jude's shoulders hit the wall, and A.J. was against him, and then they were kissing again, and Jude forgot which way was up.

Walk away? Stop this before it starts? Don't jeopardize your place in the band by getting involved with a bandmate? Any of that ring a bell?

Not while he was pinned between A.J. and a wall, it didn't. Reason and logic and common sense had gone right out the window. He had no idea what to do next, but pulling back and walking away didn't even factor into the equation. He'd been fighting this for too damn long. The hammer was as good as dropped now. Might as well—

A.J.'s hard-on brushed his, and Jude's mind went blank. He wrapped his arms around A.J., grabbing handfuls of his T-shirt as they explored each other's mouths. His fingers slid up into Jude's hair and pulled enough to make his scalp burn right as he nipped Jude's lower lip, the sharp sting sending a shiver down Jude's spine. He moaned into A.J.'s kiss and pulled him closer, thankful for the wall to hold him upright.

He slipped a hand under the back of A.J.'s shirt, and when his fingertips met hot skin, they both gasped. A.J. broke the kiss. He touched his forehead to Jude's, panting hard against Jude's lips. "I've been . . . wanting . . ."

"Me too." Jude swallowed. "Why the fuck are we stop—"

A.J. kissed him again. Jude slid his hand higher. A.J. pressed harder against him. God in heaven, how had they made it so long without doing this? Jerking off had nothing on being pinned to a wall, kissing like their lives depended on it, hot flesh beneath fingertips and cool breath on skin.

Voices and footsteps jarred him back to reality. A.J. too—they jumped apart, heads snapping toward the door. His heart was pounding for an entirely different reason now as their bandmates came down the hall, and he and A.J. quickly adjusted themselves and separated. A.J. sat behind the drum set, not so casually pulling his loose T-shirt over the front of his pants. Jude took his seat too, and thanked God for the bass across his lap as everyone filed into the room, coffee cups in hand and laughing about something.

Pulse thumping and stomach fluttering, he absently strummed his bass as he cleared his throat. "Hey guys."

Their bandmates murmured hello and sat down beside their own instruments. As the guitarists got situated and the vocalists looked over lyric sheets, Jude and A.J. exchanged glances.

That was close.

But it was hot.
Too close.
Too hot.

"Okay." Richie rolled his shoulders. "We ready?"

"Yeah." Connor took a swallow of something—probably tea, since his voice still sounded raw—and set the cup aside. "We can start on 'Fanatic' if you guys are down."

Shiloh grimaced. "Dude, you sound like shit. Why don't we work on 'Delirium' while you give your voice a break?"

Connor scowled but shrugged. "Works for me." He sat back, sipping his tea quietly while everyone else warmed up and jumped into the music.

As the minutes passed by and the group focused on their rehearsal, Jude still hovered in that postkiss trance, too caught up in the taste of A.J.'s mouth and the way his fingers had pulled and dug. That kiss had left him reeling just like it had when they'd made out backstage, and there was no postshow adrenaline to take the blame this time. And A.J. hadn't disappeared to take a shower—he was right here, less than six feet away at the drum set.

The rehearsal went on, their bandmates apparently oblivious to his distraction and unaware of the kiss that had ended way too soon. Muscle memory was the only thing keeping him from making an ass of himself; A.J. had grabbed his attention and wasn't letting go for anything.

Fuck. What now? After a kiss like that, he wasn't just going to jerk off and move on. That would require being able to ignore A.J., and that wasn't possible. Especially not now. The man who'd kissed him here was an entirely different animal from the one sitting behind the drum set now. That didn't surprise him all that much anymore. After all, at every turn, A.J. had caught him off guard. Onstage, he transformed from shy bordering on passive to a powerful, violent drummer. Here, he shifted—effortlessly, it seemed—back and forth from soft-spoken and apologetic to the kind of aggressive that brought to mind sex that left marks.

When they'd first met, if he'd had to guess, Jude would've suspected A.J. was the type who would need to be coaxed at every step in bed. He hadn't seemed to have an assertive bone in his body. Now, with Jude's lip still throbbing ever so slightly from getting pinched between teeth, he was pretty fucking sure that a night with A.J. would end with broken furniture and pissed-off neighbors. Maybe even lights and sirens.

Want. Now.

While Shiloh and Vanessa talked through a troublesome section, he sat back and stretched a crick out of his neck. As he did, he glanced at Connor and realized his ex was watching him over the rim of his cup.

It was impossible to read Connor's expression. There was definitely some scrutiny and plenty of hostility, but was it just his usual contempt? Or did he suspect something?

That was crazy. Of course he didn't suspect anything. He and A.J. had separated completely by the time the band had wandered back in, and they'd been far enough from the third-floor window that no one could have seen a thing. He was just being paranoid. Not that he had a guilty conscience or anything.

The rehearsal went on. They'd been practicing these songs in between shows during the last few weeks of the tour, and thank God for that, since the record label had them on a balls-to-the-wall timeline for finishing this album. One by one, they sanded the rough edges off most of the songs that had been dog-eared for the album. The producer would certainly have more feedback for them, but after a few grueling hours, each piece was beginning to sound like an actual song instead of something coughed up by a fledgling garage band. Despite his absent brain, he felt great about the progress they'd made. This was going to be a kickass album, especially if the band could really put the past aside during recording and work together like they had today.

"I think we're good to go. I'm ready to call it a night." Shiloh's voice was getting almost as scratchy as Connor's, so no one argued.

Connor cleared his throat. "I want to try some of the other songs tomorrow, just to see if we want any for the album." He tapped the list they'd been working from today. "But we've definitely got a good list to get us started. The label's schedule is still going to be a bitch, but I think we can swing it."

"Which songs do you want to look at tomorrow, then?" Richie picked up his copy of the "maybe" songs. "So I know which ones to practice tonight?"

While the band debated the list, Jude rubbed his hands with callused fingers. He was about to suggest one of the songs they'd played but never released way back in the day, but right then, his phone buzzed.

It was a text from A.J., and it was short and to the point:

Tonight?

After that, an address. One that included an apartment number.

He gulped. He met A.J.'s gaze from across the room, and thank God the drummer had a convincing poker face. Jude probably didn't—not when he was this close to openly drooling over A.J.—but A.J.'s expression was neutral, not giving away a single thing despite locking eyes with him.

Jude dropped his gaze and stared at the text message. At the one-word invitation and the address.

Lead me not into temptation, for I know the way myself . . .

He slowly released his breath.

Well, Jude. What's your priority?

The drummer you jerked off to last night?

Or the band you've always regretted walking away from?

CHAPTER 16

A.J. paced in his cramped studio apartment. What the hell was he *thinking*? It didn't matter how hot Jude's body was, or how good his kiss tasted, or how many different ways A.J. could imagine them getting each other off, this was a *horrible* idea.

Jude hadn't actually given him a "yeah" or a "no." Not even a "maybe" or a "probably not." Just a look, and another look, and a look that had lasted conspicuously long considering they'd been surrounded by their bandmates.

Then the rehearsal had ended, and Jude had gotten the hell out of there. A.J. hadn't been far behind, hoping he'd run into him in the studio's parking lot, but Jude and his car had both been long gone by the time he made it outside.

Now he was home, jittery and freaking out, and he didn't know if he hoped Jude showed up or if he wanted him to stay the fuck away. All he knew was that this was such a bad idea on so many levels. The awkwardness if things got weird. The backlash if they got caught. Shit, if he was going to get naked with anyone in the band, he'd picked the absolute worst person besides *maybe* Connor. If anyone found out, he and Jude would have their walking papers by dawn, assuming Vanessa and Connor didn't literally shred both of them to ribbons.

A knock at the door almost gave him a heart attack.

Oh God. He came.

He took a deep breath, and then he went to the door and pulled it open.

From across the threshold, Jude met his gaze.

His stomach flipped. Blood pounded in his ears. He wondered if Jude was freaking out beneath the surface, even though he looked calm and cool.

Without a word, A.J. stepped aside, and Jude came in. A.J. hadn't noticed the door hinges making a sound before, but as he closed the door now they creaked softly, just enough to emphasize how silent the room was otherwise. The lock clicked, and his shoe squeaked as he turned around. And then nothing. God, yes, it was dead quiet in here. Two people, no one breathing—if not for the distant growl of freeway traffic and the heavy thumping of his heart, he might've thought he'd lost his hearing altogether.

He stepped closer to Jude, who tensed but kept his feet planted.

Their eyes met, and A.J. couldn't read Jude's to save his life.

If one of us is going to be the adult and call this thing off, now would be the time.

Jude reached for A.J.'s waist. A.J. grabbed his shirt in one hand, the back of his neck in the other, and kissed him, and the "call this thing off" ship sailed away, sank, and was never heard from again.

He let go of Jude's shirt and wrapped his arms around him, and Jude did the same. With no one else here, no chance of getting caught, they didn't hold back anymore. They kissed like they were hell-bent on making up for lost time—deeply, frantically, breathlessly, bodies rubbing together and hands all over each other.

He pulled Jude back a step, then another, until they'd stumbled and shuffled their way to the other side of his tiny apartment. There, he dragged Jude down onto his sad excuse for a bed. It was small, but it would do—all he needed was enough room to get as close to Jude as possible, and the tiny mattress gave him an excuse to do exactly that. As if he needed one. And as if Jude wasn't trying to do the same thing.

Jude pushed him onto his back and sat up over him. He peeled off his T-shirt. Christ. He'd been slim to begin with, and the road had still managed to shave off a pound or two, bringing out the mouthwatering contours of his muscles. His tattoo sleeve continued over his shoulder and down his rib cage, and he wore shining black barbells through each nipple. Holy fuck, he was gorgeous.

And entirely too far away.

A.J. dragged him back down, and as he kissed Jude's neck and ran his thumb over one of the piercings, Jude sucked in a breath. He pushed his hands under A.J.'s shirt, and with some effort on his part and some wriggling on A.J.'s, they managed to get it up, off, and onto the floor where it belonged.

They pulled each other close again, kissing and panting, and though A.J. had been skin to skin with plenty of men before, the heat of Jude's body against his made him dizzy. This was all a fantasy, right? He was lying alone in his bed, jerking off to thoughts of a half-naked Jude and a crazy kiss, wasn't he?

He drew in a deep breath through his nose, and a low groan thrummed against his lips as Jude kissed him harder. He was so caught up in how Jude kissed when he was this turned on, he barely noticed Jude's hand moving until the other left the back of his neck.

And suddenly both hands were between them.

On A.J.'s belt buckle.

Fumbling with his belt buckle.

A.J.'s lips and tongue moved of their own volition because his brain had gone completely blank. He couldn't remember how to kiss. All he could think of were Jude's hands on him. *Holy fuck.*

Jude broke the kiss and started down A.J.'s neck. A.J. squirmed under him, coming unglued from hot breath and soft lips on his skin. His cock pushed hard against the inside of his zipper, and no, this was no fantasy. In his fantasies, he was articulate enough to tell Jude exactly what he wanted—clothes off, condom on—but now he was no more able to speak than he would've been if his tongue were still tangled up with Jude's.

Fuck. He really was in bed with Jude. *Oh God.*

Jude trailed light kisses down A.J.'s stomach, and every time he exhaled, the warmth of his breath made A.J.'s head spin faster.

When Jude pushed himself up and slid his hand over the front of A.J.'s jeans, A.J. thought he was going to lose his mind. He pressed against Jude's palm, wishing like hell there were some magic word that would make clothes evaporate.

But then Jude started unbuttoning A.J.'s jeans, and maybe that magic word wasn't necessary after all. The sight, the sound, the feel of Jude undoing the button and zipper—waiting a few more seconds to be naked was well worth it now.

Jude managed to get A.J.'s belt apart and his zipper down, and slid his hand into A.J.'s boxers and—

Fuck. Holy fuck.

His hand was a little rough, and his grip was *strong*. Not painfully so, but the way he stroked A.J.'s dick was just . . . *fuck*. He stroked him and kissed his neck, nearly reducing him to tears.

Jude tugged at his waistband, and A.J. lifted his hips enough for him to slide jeans and boxers down over his hips. Jude didn't bother taking them all the way off—apparently he just needed them out of the way, and now that they were, he leaned down, and his lips closed around A.J.'s cock, and . . . *holy fuck*.

Squeezing his eyes shut, A.J. arched off the bed. Just like when he was onstage and didn't think about the music, when he just went with it, he didn't think and didn't analyze and didn't care what Jude was doing with that amazing mouth as long as he didn't stop. A.J. struggled to breathe, kneading Jude's hair and moaning things even he didn't understand.

"Gonna . . ." He gasped for breath. "Gonna come if you . . . keep . . ."

Jude stopped. A.J. ground out a curse, not sure if he was frustrated that Jude had quit, or relieved that this wasn't over yet.

"Can't come yet," Jude murmured. "We still have clothes on." He got up, and when he went for his own belt, A.J. took the hint. They both kicked off the last of their clothes, and as soon as they came back together in another deep kiss, A.J. shoved Jude onto his back and pinned him there, kissing him hard and grinding against him. Jude whimpered, clawing at A.J.'s shoulders. He squirmed beneath him. Fuck. He was too . . . This was so . . . He wanted . . . He needed . . .

A.J. had a million fantasies he wanted to live out tonight, and he wanted to make this thing last as long as he could before they both came to their senses, but he was too turned on to worry about time management or consequences or coming sooner than later. He wanted to fuck Jude, and he wanted to fuck him *right now*.

He reached for the condoms he'd left on the nightstand, but Jude stopped him with a hand on his hip.

He tugged gently, as if to draw him back, and then guided him up so A.J. was straddling his chest. He lifted his head and started sucking A.J.'s cock again, enthusiastically teasing him with his lips and tongue.

A.J. steadied himself with a hand on the headboard and rocked his hips, sliding his cock in and out of Jude's mouth. Shit. This was amazing—the talented mouth working its magic on his dick, the view of himself slowly fucking Jude's mouth . . .

He groaned. If he'd known Jude loved sucking cock this much, he'd have given in to this a long, *long* time ago.

Jude stopped again. He grinned up at A.J., and this time he was the one to reach for the condoms. A.J.'s heart skipped—they hadn't even talked about who'd be on top, or if they'd switch, or . . . well, anything. And as much as A.J. preferred being on top, he had no objection whatsoever to taking Jude's cock. He just wanted to fuck. Soon. *Now*.

Though Jude's hands were usually rock steady, they were trembling as he tore the wrapper. A.J. hadn't been fucked in a long time, but at this point, he couldn't think of anything he wouldn't let Jude do. As long as they were fucking soon, he didn't care whose cock was in whose ass. *Just . . . now . . . please . . .*

Jude moved closer, and when he rolled the condom over A.J.'s cock instead of his own, A.J. thought he was going to black out. *Yes. Oh God, yes.*

As A.J. put some lube on his hand, he was about to tell Jude to get on his knees, but Jude grabbed him and kissed him. He pushed him onto his back. A.J. instinctively wanted to fight him—*oh, you think* you're *getting on top?*—but Jude's kiss melted his resolve. He didn't care who was on top, what position they were in, who was fucking who, as long as Jude kept kissing him like that.

Jude broke the kiss enough to murmur, "Fuck, I can't wait." He kissed him again, and then slurred, "Been waiting too long for you to fuck me."

"Then what're you waiting for?"

Jude brushed his lips across A.J.'s one more time, and then he sat up. He lifted himself, and A.J. reached between his legs with his lubed fingers, but Jude stopped him. Grinning, he pinned both of A.J.'s wrists above his head. A.J. tightened his fists and gritted his teeth, ready to wrench himself free, put Jude on his back, and fuck him senseless, but the gleam in Jude's eyes gave him pause.

He relaxed. Jude grinned. He released one wrist. Then the other. A.J. kept his arms where they were—they were free to move, but that look in Jude's eye kept him still and restrained even more than a sharp *Don't move!* would have.

Jude put some lube on A.J.'s cock, steadied it, and lowered himself onto it. There was resistance at first, and A.J. fought the urge to lift his hips and press against him. He lay there, holding his breath, wondering if he could even handle being inside him—and then Jude relaxed, and they both groaned as he sank down onto A.J.

A.J.'s vision blurred. Despite the condom, with a man as tight as Jude, that first shallow stroke was mind-blowing. Jude had only taken the head of his cock, and he was already out of breath.

"Oh Jesus . . ." Jude let his head fall back. He lifted up, then came back down, but he was still too tight.

He took a breath. Released it slowly.

And . . .

Oh God.

As A.J. blinked his eyes into focus, Jude lifted up and came down again, taking a little at a time. Just as A.J. expected, Jude relaxed more and more. Moaning, gasping, shaking—he took him deeper, and before long at all, they were moving easily together.

A.J. slid his hands over Jude's thighs, up to his narrow hips, and Jude didn't protest. When A.J. started rolling his own hips, meeting him thrust for thrust, Jude swore softly and shuddered. So did A.J. Even with the lube, a certain amount of friction was inevitable, and it made his head spin. Jesus, Jude felt amazing. He tried to tell him that—to murmur *Fuck, you feel good* or *I've been waiting forever for this* or, hell, he didn't even know what he wanted to say—but all he could do was moan again.

"Fuck . . ." Jude gasped for breath. He dropped onto his hands and sped up, and A.J. quickly fell into sync with him. Every time one of them changed speeds, the other did too, their bodies moving together like they were completely in tune, on the same wavelength while their minds were just along for the ride.

A.J. couldn't get enough. He ran his hands all over Jude's body—his tattooed arms, his pierced nipples, his gorgeous broad shoulders.

Faster, he wanted to . . . beg? Order? Plead? Every time he met Jude's gaze, though, he forgot what speech was. And though he loved the way Jude fucked him— slowly, fluidly—he was going to lose his mind if he didn't find out what it felt like to slam himself into Jude until they both fell apart.

To hell with it. He grabbed Jude's hips and thrust upward.

"Oh fuck!" Jude's eyes widened. A.J. thrust into him again, and Jude shivered. For a second, A.J. was sure Jude was going to grab his wrists and pin him again, but he didn't. Instead, he leaned on one hand and, with the other, stroked his own cock as A.J. fucked him from beneath.

Oh. God. *Yes.* Every time A.J. bottomed out, Jude moaned, and the harder they fucked, the more Jude trembled. A.J. would've given anything to have Jude bent over or flat on his back, but this? This was insanely hot. Jude might have been on top, but there was no mistaking who was in control, and if those blissful little whimpers were any indication, Jude loved it as much as he did.

A.J. thought he heard himself cursing but didn't care one way or the other. He was inside Jude, thrusting deep and hard while Jude jerked himself off, and holy fuck, this was hot. Every time Jude took him, he was sure he was going to lose it, but somehow he kept going. He was out of breath, falling to pieces from the inside out, but he wasn't coming yet, and thank God because he wanted to enjoy this ride as long as he possibly could.

Jude whimpered. His hand faltered, and he swore softly. Still struggling to catch his breath, A.J. pushed Jude's hand out of the way and took over stroking his thick, rock-hard dick.

"Fuck . . ." Jude squeezed his eyes shut. His abs tightened. His rhythm fell apart, but it didn't matter because they were still moving together—erratically, with no regard for anything except what felt good, and it all felt good. "Fuck, A.J. . . ."

Jude rode him faster. A.J. stroked him harder. Jude sucked in a breath, and he clenched around A.J., and then he was coming, his hips jerking as his cock shot cum all over A.J.'s stomach.

A.J. moaned and fucked Jude even harder as his own orgasm started to take over. Back arching, vision blurring, he ground out a whispered curse and pulled Jude down so his cock was buried as far as he could take him.

"Jesus . . ." He shuddered one last time, and his hands slipped off Jude's hips. Jude slumped over A.J. His arms trembled like his elbows might collapse, so A.J. pulled him the rest of the way down.

And they were both still. As it had been almost the entire time since Jude had arrived, the apartment was silent except for their breathing—faster now, and sharper—and the marcato of A.J.'s pounding heart.

After a minute or two, Jude lifted his head and met A.J.'s gaze. Slowly, he ran his tongue along his lips. "All the way here," he whispered, "I was sure we shouldn't do this."

"I'm pretty sure we shouldn't have."

"Probably not." Jude ran his fingers through A.J.'s hair. "But now that we're in bed like this, all I can think is, how the hell did it take us so fucking long to get here?"

A.J.'s skin broke out in goose bumps. He ran a hand up Jude's chest. "I don't know. I'm just glad we finally did."

"Yeah. Me too."

CHAPTER 17

A.J. took care of the condom, and then they collapsed in bed. Despite the narrow confines, they fit comfortably together, and for a while they just lay there, A.J.'s head resting on Jude's chest, Jude's arm around A.J.'s shoulders. A.J. was awake as near as Jude could tell—his breathing wasn't slow enough for someone who'd drifted off.

Eventually, Jude turned on his side and met A.J.'s blue eyes. "So I have to know something."

"Hmm?"

"Who are you and what have you done with A.J.?"

A.J. burst out laughing. "What are you talking about?"

"I mean . . ." Jude hesitated. "It's like there's two sides of you. You're such a different person onstage."

A.J. laughed again, this time uncertainly. "Aren't we all?"

"Yeah, but . . ." Jude trailed his fingers along A.J.'s sculpted forearm. "You're . . ."

A.J. lowered his gaze. "I guess the stage is the one place where I'm not afraid to be that guy."

Jude arched his eyebrow. "I don't think the stage is the only place."

"What do you mean?"

He grinned, curving his hand around the back of A.J.'s neck. "I've seen that side of you when we're alone. I just saw it a few minutes ago."

A.J. shifted a little, and a shy smile formed as his cheeks colored.

Jude's fingertip traced a line up the middle of A.J.'s abs, his own muscles contracting when A.J.'s did. "It's like you're kind of shy, maybe even a bit passive most of the time, but there's this side of you that comes out onstage. And apparently it comes out in the bedroom too."

Sighing, A.J. shifted onto his back and stared up at the ceiling. "I don't know. I guess I don't have to walk on eggshells on the stage. Or in the bedroom."

Jude pushed himself up onto his elbow. "Why would you have to walk on eggshells?"

A.J. eyed him like he'd lost his mind. "Why do you think?"

"I don't know. That's why I'm asking."

"The band. Obviously."

"Okay, *I* have to walk on eggshells with the band, but . . ." Jude cocked his head. "They like you. And you're an amazing musician. Why the hell . . . What are you so afraid of?"

A.J. shook his head. "I'm not even sure. Rocking the boat, I guess. I'm so used to playing the peacekeeper, and trying to keep people from killing each other . . ."

Jude grimaced. "The band has fucked with you that much?"

"No, no. I mean, yes. Kind of." A.J. swept his tongue across his lips. "Yeah, I do the peacekeeper thing with the band, and it's irritating, but it's always been that way. I was the one who kept my siblings from fighting so we wouldn't get in trouble, and so my parents wouldn't fight because they couldn't agree on how to discipline us for it, and . . ." He sighed. "That was pretty much my childhood—keeping people from fighting."

Jude slipped his fingers between A.J.'s. "But when you're onstage . . ."

"No one's fighting. No one's really even there." A.J.'s gaze turned distant. "It's just me and the beat." He paused for a long moment. "I guess it's the same way in bed. Approaching guys has never really been my strong point either. Once I know we're on the same wavelength, though, and we both want the same thing . . ." He looked at Jude, and that grin made Jude's pulse jump. "Why hold back, right?"

"But why hold back the rest of the time?"

"I guess . . ." A.J. exhaled and stared up at the ceiling. "Ever since I joined the band, I've been waiting for the other shoe to drop. Like I'm one bad step away from someone changing their mind and replacing me."

"I don't think that's going to happen. You're an amazing drummer."

He laughed quietly. "I think the only time I believe that is when we're onstage. That's the only time I'm sure no one's going to come along and say 'You—out.' I'm there until the end of the show, and I'm not holding back for anything. But I've . . . I mean, I've been in Running with Scissors for a year and a half, and I still feel like the new kid. I'm not really part of the group, you know?" He sighed. "Except as the peacekeeper, I guess."

"That has to be exhausting. Trying to toe the line and keep the peace."

"Yeah. Tell me about it. And between you and me, there are definitely times when I wish that one time, someone else could be the adult, you know?"

"Yeah. Especially with this bunch."

"Eh, they're not so bad. Keeping them from killing each other beats the hell out of trying to keep my *parents* from killing each other." He pursed his lips.

Jude kept quiet, sensing A.J. wasn't finished.

"I'm the oldest of four," A.J. went on, "and my parents were on the rocks for a long time before they finally split up."

"You got caught in the middle?"

"Oh yeah. So I guess I kind of learned to defuse situations and not rock the boat myself."

"Wow. I mean, it's bullshit that your parents put you in that position, but I have to admit, that peacekeeping thing . . . I kind of envy that about you."

"Envy it? Why?"

"Because you've got a cool head. It's fucked up that people take advantage of it and leave all the diplomacy shit on you instead of, you know, being adults." He slid a hand over the top of A.J.'s. "But when idiots like me lose control and do stupid shit, a guy like you still has his head together. That's . . . I mean, I admire that. I'm a hothead. Connor's a hothead. Put us together and we're a hot mess." He brought A.J.'s hand up and kissed his fingers. "But yeah, you're right—you shouldn't have to be the adult all the time."

"Shouldn't. But . . ." A.J. shrugged. "There it is."

Jude studied him. Then he draped his arm over A.J.'s chest and leaned in to kiss him. "Well, feel free to let this A.J. come out whenever you want to."

A.J. flashed him a toothy grin. "Careful what you wish for. Someone might get hurt." He snapped his teeth, and when Jude jumped, they both laughed.

"I can handle a few scratches." Jude kissed him again gently and then settled back onto his elbow. "You're a handful, but I like it that way."

"Just don't tell the rest of the band."

"That you're a handful? Or . . ." He hesitated. Their eyes met, and they both tensed. "Right. They don't need to know about any of this."

"No. Definitely not."

Silence descended, and it threatened to get awkward, so Jude quickly cleared his throat. "So what does 'A.J.' stand for, anyway?"

A.J. groaned. "It stands for 'my dad's a hard-core rock fan who didn't stop to think about how naming his kid "Axl" might make middle school a living hell.'"

Jude snorted. "Are you serious?"

"Yep. I thought about going by James, which is my middle name, but that's also my dad's first name. And I just didn't feel like answering to the same thing as some guy who'd give his kid a name like mine."

Jude was curious, but wanted to tread carefully. "Am I to assume you and your dad don't have a great relationship?"

"No, no. We have a good one. I just don't think he quite thought it through when he came up with my name." A.J. shrugged. "And as for going with A.J.: both of my names came from someone else, and I guess . . . I don't know. I wanted my own name."

"Your own identity?"

A.J. nodded.

"So, if your dad's that into rock, he must be especially proud of you being a musician."

"There was no avoiding music in my family, but yeah, he was pretty happy that one of us decided to go this way." Chuckling, he shook his head. "How many people do you run into in this business who say their parents wanted them to go this route?"

"Not many."

A.J. sobered, avoiding his gaze. "He probably thinks the joke's on him. I became a musician and got involved in the kind of music he'd always dreamed about, and I fucking made it, but had to wreck it all by being gay."

Jude exhaled. "Seriously? They have a problem with that?"

"Yep."

Jude rolled his eyes. "For fuck's sake. It isn't the 1950s anymore."

"Tell me about it. I mean, he's gotten better about it, and we still get along, but he definitely wishes I was straight."

"Ironic. My parents never batted an eye over me being gay, but I doubt they'll ever forgive me for going into rock instead of becoming a proper musician."

Their eyes met, and A.J. laughed quietly as he slipped his hand into Jude's. "It is ironic, isn't it?"

"Yeah, it is." They held each other's gazes, and that uncomfortable silence elbowed its way back in. They could make small talk and snark about backward parents all they wanted, but reality was still there, waiting for them to stop and acknowledge it.

A.J. swallowed. "We're being idiots, aren't we?"

"Probably."

A.J. shifted, and his hair fell onto his forehead, casting one of his eyes into shadow. Jude ran his fingers through the disheveled hair, smoothing it out of the way so he could see A.J.'s face.

"We really shouldn't do this," he said. "I know we shouldn't do this. But damn . . . I really, really want to." He paused. "The last time I dated someone in the band, it fucked everything up. And I'm scared to death that's going to happen again. It could ruin everything for us, and for the rest of the band."

"Yeah, I know. It's a huge risk, and it's probably a stupid thing to even think about." A.J. brought Jude's hand up and pressed a soft kiss on his palm. "But every time I look at you . . ."

His eyes flicked up.

Jude swallowed.

Then A.J. moved in, and when their lips met, Jude's skin tingled, as if every place they'd touched earlier was a cooled ember suddenly glowing back to life. As they pulled each other closer, letting a languid kiss go on and on, A.J.'s cock brushed Jude's thigh. They were both quickly getting hard again, but A.J. didn't seem to be in any hurry, and Jude sure as hell wasn't.

Of all the things he'd missed about having a partner, this was one of the biggest—just lying in bed, making out and touching in no rush at all, even when they were still in that early stage when sex with each other was a shiny novelty. There'd be time for that. For now, they just held each other and kissed, and even the guilty knot in Jude's stomach couldn't take away from how right and perfect this felt.

Fingertips skated over skin. Lips and tongues moved together like they'd long ago memorized every nuance of each other. Body heat mingled with body heat until they were both getting too hot, so they kicked the sheet out of the way and then kept making out without missing a single beat.

A.J. touched his forehead to Jude's. "I want to fuck you again," he breathed. "Slower this time."

Jude shivered. "Please do."

"Turn over." A.J. kissed him lightly and then reached for the condoms. "I want you on your stomach."

Jude's body was already obeying before his mind had caught up. A.J. put on the condom and lube, arranged himself over Jude, and they both sighed as A.J. slid into him. Though they'd already fucked once, he was careful, inching his way in until his hips met Jude's ass.

And God, he wasn't kidding about fucking him slowly. Every stroke took forever, especially when he was sliding in.

Jude curled his fingers over the edge of the mattress and pressed his forehead into the sheet. A.J. felt so damned good, but Jude was losing it. He wanted to be fucked. Hard. Deep. Until there was no doubt in his mind he'd still feel this a week from now.

"F-faster."

A.J. chuckled, and he sounded . . . almost sadistic. "Faster? Don't you like this?"

"Yes, I—" Jude shuddered, squeezing his eyes shut. "But I want . . . I want you to . . ."

A.J. slowed his hips, taking his sweet goddamned time sliding back in.

Jude cursed. "How do you have . . . that much . . ." He shivered. *"Control?"*

A.J. laughed, his warm breath giving Jude goose bumps all the way down to his toes.

"How do I have this much control?" A.J. leaned down, wrapped his arm around Jude's waist, and kissed the side of his neck. "It's easy when the reward is hearing you *lose* control."

"Fucking sadist."

A.J. laughed, his breath hot on Jude's skin, and whispered, "Not a sadist. Just like watching you squirm." He slid all the way in and stopped. "Unless you want to stop and argue semantics?"

"You son of a . . ." Jude trailed off into a growl and rocked beneath A.J., trying to encourage him into motion. "Fuck me, damn it."

He fully expected another quiet denial, but instead, A.J. pulled out and *slammed* back into him. Jude cried out with a mix of surprise, pain, and pleasure, and A.J. did it again. He fucked him harder, faster, exactly the way Jude wanted him to, and Jude clawed at the bed to anchor himself.

"Oh God," he moaned. "So good. So . . ."

"You feel amazing," A.J. slurred. His teeth grazed Jude's shoulder. "Fucking . . ." He trailed off into a moan. Teeth brushed skin again, making Jude shiver, and then A.J. bit down in the same moment he thrust, and Jude would've collapsed if he hadn't already been on his stomach. A.J. thrust again, and Jude moaned as he crossed that point of no return, and he was at the mercy of A.J. and a second powerful orgasm.

A.J.'s chin scraped across Jude's shoulder, and then came teeth again, and he bit down even harder, driving a whimper out of Jude. A.J. grunted as his hips jerked and his cock pulsed.

With a long sigh, A.J.'s whole body went slack. Jude's fingers loosened on the edge of the mattress.

A.J. pulled out but didn't move. "You're more than welcome to stay tonight." He kissed the back of Jude's shoulder where he'd bitten him a moment ago. "I've got plenty of condoms left."

Stay tonight? Plenty of condoms left?

Good God. This guy was going to be the death of him.

Oh well. What a way to go.

"Don't think I'm going anywhere."

A.J. laughed and kissed the side of his neck. "Mission accomplished. I'll be right back."

Jude still didn't move. A.J. got up and rustled around beside the bed—taking the condom off, probably—before collapsing beside him.

A shower was in order, but Jude wasn't even sure he remembered all the intricate motions required to stand up, and anyway, that assumed he still had bones. Right now, that was debatable. Good thing he had an invitation to stay the night, because he didn't trust himself to walk out to the car, never mind drive himself home.

Note to self—sex with A.J. requires a designated driver.

Despite his limbs suddenly being made out of chewing gum, he turned onto his side. As they faced each other on the narrow mattress, he gnawed his lip. "So what happens next?"

A.J. swallowed hard. "What happens next? I'll let you know tomorrow if I'm still breathing."

"That's . . ." All the air rushed out of Jude's lungs. He hesitated but then reached for A.J., and when his fingertips landed on A.J.'s waist, he found his breath again. They drew each other back in, closing the unnerving distance they'd put between them, and just before their lips met Jude said, "That's good enough for me."

This was so fucking stupid. There was way too much at stake, way too many ways this could blow up in their faces in spectacular fashion.

But lying here with A.J.'s sweat on his skin, kissing lazily while a bite still throbbed on his shoulder and the aftershocks of his orgasm still tingled along his spine . . .

We're doing this, aren't we?

A.J. met his gaze, eyelids heavy and a sleepy smile on his lips.

Oh yeah. We're doing this.

CHAPTER 18

Clinging to his coffee cup, A.J. winced and swore as he got out of his car in the recording studio parking lot. He was exhausted, dragging his feet and struggling to keep his eyes open, and sore in places he'd forgotten he had. How many times had they fucked last night? Hell, he didn't know. They'd made a valiant effort at sleeping so they'd be refreshed and presentable today, but that hadn't lasted long. By the time he had fully woken up in the middle of the night, he was already tangled up with Jude, kissing and rubbing and hard. Neither of them had come, and they'd drifted off again eventually, but they'd sleepily fooled around a few more times after that. Or maybe he'd dreamed it. He had no idea.

His legs and back ached as he walked toward the gleaming building. If he was this sore, he could only imagine how Jude felt. They hadn't even been able to finish the last round because, as Jude had put it, the spirit was willing, but the body was weak.

Well, he'd find out in a moment if Jude was still in one piece. Jude had left his apartment to change clothes at home, and they'd agreed to arrive separately. A.J. had been afraid to even park beside Jude's car, as if that might somehow tip everyone else off about last night's "sleeping" arrangements.

At the door, he paused to twist a crick out of his back. This was going to be one long rehearsal. Good thing they weren't recording yet. And a damn good thing they weren't performing.

He took a deep swallow of coffee, then continued into the building.

As he stepped off the elevator on the third floor, his heart dropped into his feet. He was still four doors down from where the band would be rehearsing, and he could already hear shouting. Perfect way to start the day.

"Christ," he muttered into his coffee cup. "What now?"

As he neared the open door, the shouting became actual words instead of indistinct, angry noise.

"If it's not a fucking priority, then just say so," Connor snarled.

"Don't put words in my mouth," Jude threw back. "And it's not just my schedule that's the problem. You and Kristy have booked all of us within an inch of our lives after we've all been out on the road, so—"

"You weren't even on the road with us that long!" Connor's sharp sigh was audible even from out in the hall. "What the hell do you have to bitch about?"

"Connor, for fuck's sake—"

Right then, Shiloh stepped out of the studio and closed the door behind her, cutting off most of the shouting. She exhaled hard, and rolled her eyes.

"Sounds like the day's off to a good start."

She jumped as she turned to him. "Oh, hey. Morning." Glancing over her shoulder, she frowned. "They've been at it for the last hour. Somehow I don't think Connor will be rehearsing much today."

A.J. scowled. "What's going on?"

"Oh, who knows?" She rubbed her temples. "He was okay earlier, but the minute Jude walked in . . ."

His blood turned cold. "What? Why?"

"Why?" Shiloh laughed. "Honey, you've been around them long enough. This"—she gestured over her shoulder—"has been a spat waiting to happen ever since Jude came back. Now let's go get some breakfast while they get it out of their systems."

She started down the hall. His stomach knotted as the shouting continued behind the closed door. The acoustics swallowed up most of the words, but the fury was palpable even from here.

"A.J.?"

He turned.

Shiloh raised her eyebrows. "You coming?"

"Yeah. Yeah. I—" He threw the door one last look, then followed her down the hall. If the fur was flying between Jude and Connor, he didn't want to be anywhere nearby.

As they waited for the elevator, he asked, "What are they arguing about, anyway?"

Shiloh groaned. "Connor booked a photographer for the album artwork." The elevator doors opened, and they stepped inside. She stabbed the button with her thumb. "Jude said something about having a possible scheduling conflict, and . . . well, there they went."

The doors closed, and A.J.'s stomach dropped faster than the elevator.

"These guys. I just . . ." Shiloh kneaded the back of her neck. "They were exhausting back then, and now . . . Fuck."

A.J. chewed the inside of his cheek. "So it's just schedule bullshit?"

"This time," she muttered. "I mean, you know Connor. He's got that tendency to commit us to things like this without making sure everyone's free. And yeah, it's annoying, but hey, at least someone's getting shit done. Kristy's got so much on her plate, and I'm not very good at . . ." She waved her hand. "Anyway. So Jude asked him about the dates, and if it was written in blood or if there was a possibility of rescheduling, and off they went."

He could see Connor flying off the handle like that, but Jude? "Really? That's it?"

She laughed humorlessly as the elevator lurched to a stop. "Here's the thing with those two." They stepped out and headed toward the ground-floor café. "If they're screaming at each other, you can almost guarantee that whatever they're screaming about is not what they're actually fighting about."

"Why's that?"

"Because neither of them can communicate for shit. You've got Connor and his insane temper. Then you've got Jude and that damned impulsive streak. The minute one pisses the other off, Connor blows up and Jude goes off and does something stupid." She shook her head and clicked her tongue. "Sunrise, sunset."

His stomach twisted. "Any idea what they *are* fighting about this time?"

She shrugged. "Your guess is as good as mine."

Let's hope my guess is wrong, and Connor doesn't have a clue.

In the café they grabbed some food, paid, and took the table by the window. He sat down gingerly, wincing as every ache and twinge reminded him of that long, long night.

As he sipped his coffee, Shiloh picked at the muffin she'd bought. "So you and Jude go out partying last night or something?"

A.J. nearly spat coffee all over her, but managed to choke it down. "What?"

She laughed. "He came limping in this morning like he'd been run over by a truck. And now you're—" Abruptly, her expression hardened. "A.J. . . ."

He cleared his throat, struggling to hold her gaze.

She narrowed her eyes. "Where were you last night?"

I'm guessing "inside Jude" is not the right answer here . . .

He coughed again to get his breath moving. "Am I suddenly—"

"Cut the crap." She set her jaw. "If something happened between you and Jude, I would suggest—"

"What the hell, Shiloh?" He threw up his hands, nearly unloading his coffee in the process. "I'm moving a little slow this morning, and suddenly you think I was screwing around with Jude?"

The corner of her mouth twitched. Folding her arms, she asked coolly, "Were you?"

"What makes you think I was?"

She chewed her lip, her eyes darting down for a moment before meeting his again. Then she pushed her muffin away. "I'm sorry. That was out of line. It . . . I shouldn't have . . ." She showed her palms. "I'm sorry, A.J."

"Don't worry about it," he muttered. As he replayed the conversation in his head, though, his tone made him cringe. "I'm sorry too, by the way. For getting so defensive. I . . . didn't mean . . ."

"It's okay." She faced him and smiled. "I deserved it."

"No, you didn't."

"Honey, I accused you of sleeping with a bandmate." She covered her face with her hands for a moment, then dropped them and looked him in the eye. "I'm so sorry. I'm just . . . I'm so worried about the band."

A.J. swallowed. "You think history's going to repeat itself?"

She nodded. "The band has almost fallen apart twice thanks to members screwing around with each other, and I guess with as volatile as those two have been all morning, I'm . . ." She slouched in her chair. "God, I don't even know. The thing is, when Wyatt quit, I was scared things would fall apart. It was even worse when Jude left because we thought we'd missed our shot at a record deal. And now, I mean, ever since Jude came back, I've been waiting for . . . something to happen. Like he's just here temporarily, and right when we need him the most, shit's going to hit the fan somehow and send him packing again." She leaned forward, pressing her fingers into her temples. "How many more times will this band survive that kind of thing, you know?"

He absently turned his coffee cup between his fingers and shifted in his chair, the twinges in his hips reminding him how right Shiloh was about his whereabouts last night.

She lowered her hands, and when she met his gaze, her eyes looked exhausted. "We've all worked so hard for this. It just pisses me off how it can be built up by half a dozen people, and completely wrecked by one. Or two, I guess."

"Yeah, I get that." He sipped his coffee and didn't taste it. "Maybe a year and a half was long enough for both of them to mature though."

She snorted. "You heard them. They haven't changed." She picked at her muffin again. "All I can do is hope they don't start fucking again."

His mouth went dry. "Hypothetically, if they did—"

"I would choke the shit out of both of them." The hard edge of her tone left him wondering if she was exaggerating at all.

"Well." He muffled a cough. "Let's hope they don't."

"Yeah. Let's hope."

By the time Shiloh and A.J. returned to the studio, the shouting had ceased. Connor was nursing a cup of hot tea, probably to soothe his throat, and the guitarists were tuning their instruments.

"Feel better?" Shiloh asked through clenched teeth.

Connor shot her a glare. "Let it go."

"I could say the same to you," she growled. "You're going to kill your voice and—"

"Guys," A.J. said, quietly and cautiously. "We only have the room for a few more hours. Where's Jude?"

"Smoking," Connor muttered.

"Should I go get him?" A.J. asked. "So we can get started?"

Shiloh's eyes darted toward Connor, but then she sighed and rolled her shoulders. "Yeah. You know where the smoke pit is?"

He nodded. "I'll be back in a minute." He left the studio and headed out to the balcony that the smokers used. Sure enough, Jude was standing out there, gazing at the hills with a cigarette between his fingers.

As A.J. shut the door behind him, Jude turned around. They both tensed. Jude took a deep drag, lowered his gaze, and then faced the hills again.

A.J. stopped beside him. "Sounded like things got pretty rough with Connor."

"Sorry you had to hear that."

"It's okay. You all right?"

Jude nodded. The hand holding his cigarette shook slightly. Nicotine? Adrenaline? Nerves? Hard to say. "Just needed a minute."

"Did you guys sort out the schedule?"

Jude half shrugged. "As much as we ever will. Just annoys the shit out of me that he expects the whole band to be at his beck and call without so much as checking."

189

He brought the cigarette up but lowered it again without taking a drag. "Richie and Vanessa both told him three times last week that they had shit going on, and now they'll have to shuffle it around so they can be at that photo shoot, which is a pain in the ass for both of them. I mean, we only get a little bit of time at home before we're back out on the road again. Anything we need to get done, we have to do it now. Richie's trying to get some dental work done; Vanessa's . . . I'm not even sure what she's doing, but you get the idea."

A.J. nodded. "Yeah, I get it."

"Anyway." Jude finally took a drag. "I called him out, he lost his temper, and . . ."

"So I saw."

Jude deflated. "I'm sorry. I know you're not a fan of conflict."

"Can't really be avoided." A.J. paused. "And, uh, speaking of which . . ."

Jude faced him, eyebrows up.

"While you two were fighting, Shiloh and I had an interesting conversation."

"Oh yeah? What about?"

"Us. Kind of."

Jude's eyes widened. "Does she . . . You didn't tell her, did you?"

"No. But she suspected it."

"Why?"

"Because she noticed that neither of us was walking very comfortably this morning."

"Oh." Jude looked out at the hills again. "Shit. But you shot it down? Told her we—"

"Yeah, I took care of that part." He swallowed. "The thing is, she was really stressed about you and Connor fighting."

Jude sighed. "I know. We shouldn't have done it in front of the rest of the band."

"Well, there's, I mean, there's that. But she's worried about the band falling apart again. And I got the feeling she's not just worried about you and Connor causing it."

Jude turned to him. "You think she's really onto us?"

"Who knows? I think she's just edgy about anyone hooking up or breaking up." A.J. folded his arms loosely, just trying to give his hands something to do. "Are we being idiots? Getting—" He glanced at the door. "Getting involved with each other?"

"Probably. We knew that going into it." Jude shook his head. "I don't want to put the band at risk any more than you do. And I think me and you can be a bit more levelheaded about things than me and Connor could."

"Still . . . shit happens."

"Yeah. It does." Jude pulled in a breath and pushed his shoulders back. "What do you think we should do?"

A.J. knew damn well what the answer was, but Jude locked eyes with him and things like *We shouldn't repeat last night* or *We should cool it* stopped making sense. So did *Last night was just sex* and whatever other bullshit he'd tried to feed himself on his way here this morning.

The man looking back at him was more than the sum total of aches, twinges, and regrets. They'd been circling each other for weeks, and now that they'd finally given into the physical temptation . . .

Goddamn. That wasn't a one-night stand, was it?

They'd been avoiding each other physically, keeping each other at arm's length to avoid what they both knew they wanted, but what A.J. had really missed most was that period when they'd found every excuse imaginable to hang out and talk. He hadn't realized until now that he'd looked forward to Jude's smoke breaks almost as much as Jude probably had, and he missed that even more than he itched for physical contact.

In his mind, he heard Jude and Connor shouting.

"If they're screaming at each other about something," Shiloh had said, *"you can almost guarantee that whatever they're screaming about is not what they're actually fighting about."*

He swallowed. That was what they'd done too, wasn't it? They'd avoided each other under the pretense of not giving into sexual temptation. They'd kept their distance, and he realized now that while he thought they'd been circling each other, they'd been spiraling closer. And closer. And closer. Until yesterday. And last night. And now.

Jude gulped. A.J. couldn't read his mind, but that wasn't just a blank, inquisitive stare. This wasn't in A.J.'s imagination, was it?

And when had he started drumming his fingers on the railing? He drew his hand back, folding his arms again. "What do we do now?"

"Well." Jude crushed his cigarette in the ashtray. "I guess we've got two choices."

A.J. raised his eyebrows.

Jude mirrored him, arms folded loosely across his chest. "We either keep this thing going and be discreet about it, or we pretend it never happened and be adults about it."

"I probably don't have to tell you which option I want to take."

"Yeah. Same here."

"What happens if things don't work out?"

Jude's eyes lost focus. After a moment, he shook his head. "I don't know."

A.J. opened his mouth to speak, but the balcony door opened.

They both turned as Vanessa leaned outside. "You guys coming?" She jerked her thumb over her shoulder. "Everyone's ready to rehearse whenever you are."

"Yeah." Jude gestured with his cigarette. "I was just finishing up my smoke. We'll be there in a minute."

She eyed them both, then went back inside.

Jude faced A.J. again. "Look, I know we're taking a huge chance. And I'm not thrilled about that part, but I . . ." He took a deep breath. "To be perfectly blunt, I want to see where this goes."

A.J.'s stomach twisted and his heart fluttered. "I do too. But . . . the band . . ."

"I know. But we already know we suck at staying away from each other. We'll just have to keep it on the down-low, and no matter what happens, keep it separate from the band."

"You really think we can do that, even if things go to shit?"

Jude's Adam's apple bobbed. "I have no idea. But I can't think of any other option that'll let me keep my sanity."

"You and me both," A.J. whispered. "So I guess that's what we do—keep it quiet, and keep it away from the band."

Jude nodded. Some of the apprehension in his expression softened, and his lips pulled into a subtle but spine-tingling smile. "I won't tell if you don't."

Despite his nerves, A.J. couldn't help grinning. "Secret's safe with me."

"Good." Jude nodded toward the building. "So. Back to rehearsal?"

"Yeah. Back to rehearsal."

As they headed inside, excitement coiled behind A.J.'s ribs, but so did a hell of a bundle of nerves. It was easy to say they'd keep this on the DL and, if things went to shit, keep it separate from the band. Except he was pretty sure Connor and Wyatt had had a similar arrangement, considering how pissed off the band had been after their relationship had come to light. And that had been *before* everything went up in flames.

But every alternative included "not doing this with Jude."

And no matter how risky it was, no matter how downright fucking *stupid* it was, A.J. just couldn't resist.

CHAPTER 19

By the time they'd finished their first day of recording, Jude was exhausted. His fingers were as raw as they'd been when he'd rejoined the band. His wrists, elbows, and neck ached.

And now, lying beside A.J. on that narrow futon, his whole body ached, and he felt great. A day of nothing but music and sex—he couldn't ask for much more than that.

A.J. yawned. "What time is it?"

"Almost one."

"Already?"

"Time flies." Jude kissed his forehead. "And it was damn near ten when we got here."

"Still." A.J. lifted his chin and kissed him gently. "We should probably get some sleep. Early morning tomorrow."

"Yeah." Jude's heart sank. Sighing, he rubbed his forehead. "At the risk of sounding like a selfish asshole, I'd much rather just stay here with you tomorrow."

"Me too. I love working on an album, but . . ." A.J. grinned. "I'm getting hooked on this."

Jude met his gaze. *I'm getting hooked on you.* He touched A.J.'s scruffy cheek. "Yeah. And this is a hell of lot less stressful than . . ." He winced. "I'm sorry. I shouldn't bring that shit up in here."

"It's okay." A.J. brought his hand up and kissed his fingers. "We're either in bed or in the studio these days. If you can't talk about it here, where can you?"

"Good point." Jude sighed. "And it's not that bad, I guess. It's just tough."

"Which part?"

"Connor, mostly. There's only so many hours you can spend around someone you used to love while he's probably wishing looks really could kill."

A.J. grimaced. "Yeah, that must be hard." He paused. "If . . . if you don't mind my asking, were you guys ever happy together?"

Jude let out a long breath. "That's the part that makes it so hard. It wasn't always bad between us. The thing is, I never want to go back to him because I know we can't make it work, but it hurts being this fucked up with him. We made a shitty couple, but I miss my friend."

A.J. nodded, lacing his fingers between Jude's. "That's usually the worst part. Losing the good when you have to cut away the bad."

"Yeah. Exactly. And it . . . I mean, for all me and Connor hiss and spit at each other, we did have good times. We had—" Jude hesitated, his throat aching a little at the memories. "We had a lot of good times, actually. It's just hard to focus on those when things were so bad there towards the end." He swallowed. "So being around him . . ." He met A.J.'s eyes, and shook himself. "It's for the better." He smiled and moved in for another kiss. "I'll get over it."

A.J. returned his kiss. "Well, if you need help keeping your mind off him, you know where to find me."

Jude laughed, gathering A.J. in his arms. "You keep my mind off everything. I'm lucky I can play when you're there."

"Pfft. You're a prodigy." A.J. brushed his lips across Jude's. "You could play in your sleep."

"And yet you still distract the hell out of me."

"Sorry."

"Bullshit, you are." They both laughed this time, and Jude let another kiss linger for a moment before he sobered a bit and drew back. "To be honest, sometimes I work myself up about all this being a bad idea. Us being together. Me being in the band again." He smoothed A.J.'s bleached blond spikes. "But the second I look at you . . ."

"I know the feeling." A.J. clasped Jude's hand in his. "And for the record, it's totally worth it when *we* can be alone together."

"Yeah, it is." Jude kissed him, and this time it was A.J. who drew it out. Arms around each other. Tighter. Closer. Despite his mind and body being exhausted as hell, he couldn't help getting hard when he made out with A.J. like this. Sleep? Eventually. But they only had so much time together, and only so much of that time could be spent between the sheets.

God knew how long this would last, or how much opportunity they'd have once the band was on the road. But for now, in between the secrecy and the tension with their bandmates, Jude fully intended to seize every chance he had to be as close to A.J. as possible.

We'll sleep when we're dead. He gently rolled A.J. onto his back. *Tonight, you're the only thing that matters . . .*

They were barely a week into recording the new album, and somehow Jude and Connor hadn't killed each other yet. Between pressure from the label to wrap the record within the next two weeks and Connor's usual sunny demeanor, Jude was nearly at a breaking point. It didn't help that he wasn't getting a whole lot of sleep—though staying up until dawn with A.J. was certainly worth the extra fatigue—but it mostly came down to the natural consequences of putting Connor and him in the same room and adding pressure. The tour bus hadn't been as bad, since they hadn't had to interact much, and onstage their only contact had been the music.

But working on an album meant that from dawn till dusk, they were in each other's faces, under each other's feet, and on each other's nerves. Connor was being too pushy. Jude couldn't get the tempo exactly right. They couldn't agree if he was in or out of tune, and nobody else wanted to get involved. Every single fucking time, it ended one of two ways—Connor storming out for some air, or Jude storming out for some smoke.

Standing out on the balcony, Jude took a long drag. He closed his eyes and held the smoke in for a moment before slowly releasing it.

Connor's voice still echoed along his frayed nerves. *"So you gonna half-ass the album just to be a dick?"*

"Hey. Hey." Jude had put up his hands, but hadn't bothered keeping his voice even. *"I have bad days just like everybody else. Back the fuck off."*

"We don't have time for off days. If you're not gonna focus, why don't we just bring in someone who—"

"The deal was, I tour with you and I record on this album."

"Yeah?" Connor had narrowed his eyes. *"Then how about actually playing the piece instead of whatever the fuck that was?"*

Jude cursed around his cigarette. The nicotine wasn't even helping today. It never really did—it just gave him an excuse to get away from Connor before the cops had to get involved.

As frustrated as he was, he reminded himself over and over that this was temporary. That everyone was stretched thin and stressed out because of the long hours they were logging in order to meet the label's tight deadline. If he did something stupid like throwing up his hands and walking out for more than a smoke, he'd be fucked.

As it was, there were no guarantees he'd still have a place in the band after the tour. There'd be no more second chances after this. The band had worked too long and hard—with and without him—to let him waltz in and out whenever he got pissed off. Or, for that matter, to put up with him and Connor arguing at every turn. If things went to shit—if one of these sniping matches got out of control as it inevitably would—Jude would be the one sent packing, not Connor. If he decided to walk out himself, the consensus would be "Don't let the door hit you on the way out, asshole."

He'd already impulsively walked away from so many things, and that had gotten him precisely *where*? Right here, with a thick wall of ice *slowly* thawing between him and the lifelong friends he'd fucked over once before, and some very thin ice cracking beneath his feet thanks to his own stupid, impulsive decisions.

He pulled in a long drag. After he'd released the smoke, he took a few slow, deep breaths and willed the tension in his neck and shoulders to melt away. He was just pissed off. It was a bullshit spat with Connor. No reason to make a rash, career-altering decision.

Another deep breath. Then another. He crushed his cigarette in the ashtray while he mentally strangled Connor, and that thought made him laugh softly. He'd be all right. He'd go back in there, go with the flow, and get this album done.

For good measure, just in case that overactive flight instinct tried to send him running for the door again, he thought back to those eighteen miserable months spent in a cubicle farm, encased in bland pastel walls beneath obnoxious fluorescent lights while he and his coworkers drove each other insane. That was what waited for him if he went back now. Assuming, of course, he could even find a job.

Walk away now, and you might as well start practicing your burger flip.

No. Not a fucking chance. He was not walking away from Running with Scissors again. He'd cool down, smoke one more cigarette, and then go back in there and get that bass line right. Connor was a pain in the ass and always would be, but the band was too important to let himself be pushed away. And so was A.J.

His chest tightened.

A.J.

If there was one thing left in the world he *should* walk away from, it was A.J. It was a weird paradox—A.J. was the last person in the world he should be involved with, but their involvement was keeping him on an even keel. Their relationship—whatever the hell it was—put the band at risk, and yet at the same time leveled Jude out and kept him calm and focused, just the way the band needed him. Tonight, like every night, they'd disappear to A.J.'s apartment, pull each other close beneath the sheets, and A.J. would remind him with every kiss why this was worth the gamble. And tomorrow, like every day, they'd come back to the studio, and Jude's conscience would nag at him while Connor picked at him, and he'd be out here again, smoking and talking himself out of leaving.

Leaving who? The band? Or A.J.?

He sighed. Neither. No way in hell was he walking away from this band again, and A.J.? Not a chance.

But he was going to get kicked out of the band if he didn't get his ass down to the studio and back to work, so he put his smokes and lighter in his pocket and headed inside.

When he returned to the studio, Richie was in the box recording part of "Fanatic." Shiloh and Vanessa stood behind the producer, gesturing at the whiteboard listing the album's tracks.

"I think 'Unseen' would work better after 'Eagle Eyes,'" Vanessa said. "'Unseen' and 'Delirium' just . . . I don't know. They don't really go together."

"Hmm." Shiloh tapped her chin with the capped end of a marker. "But 'Delirium' isn't a good opening number. Maybe if we flipped 'Delirium' and 'Convicted'?"

"Oh, that could work."

"Okay. I'll play through all the preliminary recordings tonight and see how they flow together. If it works, we can run it by the band tomorrow and go from there."

"Cool. Could you send me the recordings too?"

"Will do." Shiloh made a note on the board, and as she turned around and put the cap back on the pen, she saw Jude. "Oh, hey. Didn't realize you'd come back." Her cheerful expression faltered. "You okay?"

"Yeah. Yeah." He cleared his throat. "Where's Connor?"

"Where do you think?" Vanessa muttered.

Shiloh gestured at the door. "He and A.J. went to get coffee."

Jude's chest tightened. He was with *A.J.*? But he quickly pushed that pang of jealousy aside—odds were A.J. was taking one for the team and calming Connor down. No wonder he hated being the peacekeeper.

Shiloh studied him. "Everything okay? I heard Connor grumbling on his way out, and now you're quiet, so . . ." Her eyebrows rose.

"Yeah. Everything's good." He rolled some stiffness out of his shoulders and absently pulled his cigarettes from his pocket but then slid them back in. "Just . . . still finding my footing with Connor, I guess."

She laughed, a note of hoarseness sharpening the edges. "I don't think anyone ever really finds their footing with him."

"True fact."

"It seems to be working out, though."

Vanessa snorted. "You didn't hear them fighting earlier."

Shiloh groaned. "Really? Again?"

Jude's cheeks burned. "Yeah. It . . ." He shook his head. "It was stupid."

"Always is," Vanessa muttered.

"She's got a point," Shiloh said. "But, honestly, even all the head-butting this week, I'll take it, because things could've been worse between you two."

"Yeah, I know." *And if Connor finds out about A.J., they'll get a lot worse.* "To be honest, sometimes I really wish he and I could go back to the way things were. Not . . . not dating, I mean. But . . ."

"Friends?"

He nodded. "Probably a tall fucking order, but a guy can dream."

"Give it time. It's an adjustment for both of you. Just keep doing what you're doing. Play the music, be a member of the band, and let Connor come around on his own." She smiled and squeezed his arm. "He really will come around eventually."

"If I keep playing my cards right, right?"

Withdrawing her hand, she shrugged. "One of you has to be the adult."

Jude laughed dryly. "Guess I owe everyone that much."

"Yeah, you do." There were no barbs attached to the words, and when she went on, she looked him in the eye. "Hang in there. You're doing a pretty damn good job of making up for what happened in the past. The rest will work itself out."

"We'll see."

"It'll be fine."

The studio door opened. As Jude turned, Connor walked back in, and though there was still poison in his eyes, he was obviously calmer now. The tension between his eyebrows had loosened, and his shoulders weren't drawn up like he was about to take a swing at someone. He and Jude made eye contact, and Jude tightened his jaw.

Connor muttered something in that way of his and brushed past Jude. Then, more clearly, he said, "We need to get to work on 'Eagle Eyes.' We are way behind on that one."

Jude nearly fired something back but then turned as A.J. came into the studio, casually sipping a cup of coffee.

One look at A.J., and all the knots from Connor's presence seemed to unwind at once.

There you are. Now I can concentrate. And breathe. And not commit murder.

"You doing okay?" A.J. asked.

Now that you're here . . .

Jude nodded. "Yeah. Just needed to cool off for a minute. How is . . ." He nodded toward Connor.

A.J. rolled his eyes, and as he brought his coffee up to his lips, quietly said, "Same. He just needed to vent and bitch."

"Thanks for giving him an ear. Sorry you had to—"

"It's okay." A.J. took a sip. "We all have to work together, so if listening to him bitch means he calms the fuck down, then . . ." He half shrugged.

"Still, I hate putting you in that position. I definitely owe you one."

A.J. glanced around. Then he winked. "You're damn right you do."

Jude gulped and broke eye contact, certain someone had not only heard, but could read between the lines. And even if they hadn't, well, there went his concentration. No matter how frustrating today was—and it probably would be—he knew what was waiting for him tonight.

He turned to A.J. again.

Just a few more hours, and I am all yours.

A hint of a grin played at A.J.'s lips. *I know you are. And I can't wait.*

From the moment they'd started recording, the pace had been grueling and the process had been fast. More and more, it looked like they'd meet the label's tight deadline after all.

With every track they wrapped, the tension between the bandmates came down a notch. Even Connor started calming down, especially once they were in the homestretch, when there was little left to do except record two more tracks and clean up the previous three.

The effect wasn't the same for Jude, though. Every track they wrapped made him sweat a little more. The album would be finished soon. Then the tour planning would go from something Kristy ran in the background to something they'd all be thinking about constantly.

It meant his time would no longer be divided into days with the band and nights with A.J. Privacy and personal space were about to go on indefinite hiatus. Sex would become a luxury like hot showers and home-cooked meals.

As much as he prayed for a few extra nights, there was no stopping the inevitable, and before he knew it, the day had come. The album was complete, and it was amazing—everything he had ever dreamed of in a record. The music was quintessential Running with Scissors—a solid mix of ballads and more upbeat tracks, Connor and Shiloh's songwriting blending with the rest of the band's instrumental support, and topped off with the producer's magic refining the sound quality to near perfection.

Even the artwork was sublime. They'd gone out to a beach near Santa Monica with a photographer, and in between individual shots of each bandmate standing on rocks or in the surf, he'd managed to get a shot of everyone—even Connor and Jude—laughing at something. Nobody needed to know that after everyone had left, once the camera and prying eyes were long gone, A.J. and Jude had stolen a long kiss on the sand, surrounded by their bandmates' footprints. There were no photos of that, but it was burned into Jude's memory, and every time he saw the album artwork, his mind went right back to that moment.

Especially since moments like that were probably all he and A.J. were going to have for a while. Being able to sneak quickies and handjobs at the studio and spend nights together at A.J.'s apartment—that was great. Awesome, in fact.

But now the time had come to hit the road again.

The label was promoting the album all over God's green earth. The tour was mapped out, choreographed at every level from the stage to the highway.

Jude had dreamed about a headlining tour since he was a kid. That night, lying beside A.J. for the last time before they'd head out on the road, his feelings were decidedly mixed.

"You ready for this?" A.J. asked.

"Yes and no."

"Yeah. Same here."

"I'm looking forward to playing shows again, but . . ." He kissed A.J.'s temple. "Some parts of it are going to be hell."

"Nah. We'll make it work."

"We will." He stroked A.J.'s hair. "But not being able to touch you is going to drive me insane."

"Tell me about it." A.J. met his eyes, and his smile made Jude's heart beat faster. "We'll be okay, though. It beats the hell out of one of us going on tour while the other stays home."

"Good point. We'll get to see each other." He couldn't help smiling too. "We'll get to see each other a lot."

A.J. kissed him lightly. "See? We'll be fine."

"Mm-hmm." Jude pulled him closer and slid his hand beneath the covers. "But maybe we should get a head start on making up for lost time."

"You think?"

"Yes, I do."

Not being able to touch A.J. would definitely be frustrating, but he was oddly at peace with the idea. They could have all the sex they wanted after the tour. On the road, though he'd always be at least an arm's-length away, A.J. would be *there*. Although he was disappointed at the thought of not spending every night with A.J., he was also content with the idea of just being with him, which was weird. He'd never had that feeling with anyone. Even during the good times with Connor, once they'd moved from friends to lovers, it had been all about sex, music, and finding opportunities for sex or music. Any time they spent alone, they were either in bed or working out new music for the band. Half the excitement of that relationship had been the stolen moments for kisses or quickies.

With A.J., it was different. Completely different. He turned Jude on like crazy, but they could also just . . . be together. Exchanging glances. Little smiles that no one else understood. Casual conversations while Jude smoked.

Months on end of touring, with little to no sex? He was okay with that as long as it meant he could be with A.J.

And he had no idea what to make of that.

CHAPTER 20

When they arrived in the record company's parking lot the next morning, A.J. couldn't help gawking at the immense diesel-powered beast idling in front of them.

Since they were headlining, they weren't relegated to the reject buses, but he hadn't expected something this big. The sleek, black battleship of a vehicle could've fit their old bus inside it and left room for all of them to sleep comfortably. Oh yes, this bad boy would definitely do.

One by one, the band members climbed aboard, and it was even better on the inside.

Connor whistled as he looked around. "Shit. We must be moving up in the world."

"No kidding." A.J. dropped his bag on the sofa as he, too, gazed at their surroundings. "They didn't give us the wrong bus, did they?"

"Don't anybody say anything," Connor said. "Maybe they won't notice."

The other guys—even Jude—laughed, and they went about stashing their personal gear as well as loading up the cabinets with everything Shiloh and Richie had picked up at Costco. By the time they were finished, every storage compartment on the bus was stuffed with supplies: food, extra toiletries, clothes, about seven hundred extra strings for Richie's guitar since he was obsessive about having backups in case one broke in a town without a music store. The bus wasn't exactly home, but it definitely felt like something they could all survive in for the foreseeable future.

By noon, the buses were ready and everyone was accounted for, and the caravan moved out—destination: Flagstaff. Their tour didn't actually kick off for a few days, with the opening show in Houston, so everyone just relaxed and settled into their new digs.

Since A.J. hadn't had much sleep the previous night, he dozed most of the way, and that turned out to be a mistake—when it came time for everyone to turn in, he was wide awake.

Wide awake, and lying right above Jude's rack.

He closed his eyes and sighed. Funny how sharing a bed that barely qualified as a twin had been fine, but lying alone on this rack was uncomfortable and irritating. He and Jude would never fit on here, not even one right on top of the other, but God, he missed having Jude next to him instead of below him on another bunk.

He'd learn to live with it. He had to.

To his surprise, it didn't take as long as he expected it to. That first night of traveling was rough. The second wasn't great. But then suddenly they were on the cusp of their opening performance, and then that performance came and went, and the next one was in the next city, and sleeping at night was no longer optional.

This tour was even more of an insane blur than the last one. Now that they were on the road again, time moved at breakneck speed—bed, road, stage, repeat. He rode one performance high to the next, sleeping it off on the bus and waking up ready for more.

And though he couldn't touch Jude, watching him was even hotter than it had been last time around. Seeing him play had been hot since day one, but now that A.J. knew what he looked like without that sweaty shirt on, and with those ripped jeans lying in a rumpled heap on the floor, and what he felt like when he kissed and when he came, watching him play was almost unbearable.

Especially now that getting time alone—*truly* alone— was nearly impossible. It was frustrating, but A.J. loved it. He'd so carefully toed the line from the day he'd started with the band, and every secret touch with Jude was like a delicious, sexy, long-overdue form of rebellion. And he was learning to love Jude's smoke breaks all over again. The other band members typically stayed away.

That was just fine by A.J. Nobody had to know.

By the time two weeks had passed, A.J. had readjusted to the rhythm of life on tour. Play. Sleep. Practice on the bus while endless miles of highway flashed by the windows. And enjoy the rare times when two venues were close enough together that they didn't have to be on the road before the sun came up. Like tonight, as they chilled in a venue parking lot, somewhere in Ohio.

The next night they'd play Toledo. After that it was on to Cleveland. Since it wasn't a terribly long drive tomorrow, they were all up late, hanging out on the bus and winding down after another kickass performance, while A.J. tried to anticipate when Jude might take his next smoke break. Connor set his steaming mug of tea on the counter. "So, as long as we're all here," he said, a note of irritation tinging his voice, "I think we need to talk about a few things. Specifically, a few things that need rejigging."

Shiloh sat up, stretching gingerly. "Like what? Everything seems fine to me."

"Yeah, not me. For starters, I think we need to drop 'Unseen' from the set list." Connor's eyes flicked toward A.J. "I'm not too thrilled with the percussion."

A.J.'s stomach flipped. "What's—what's wrong with it?"

"I don't know, man." Connor shook his head. "It's just not there."

"It was fine when we were recording. Wasn't it?"

Connor laughed dryly. "We had a sound engineer to pick up the slack."

Richie brushed a few strands of hair out of his face. "Should we try it with Jude on drums?"

"That might not be a bad idea," Connor said.

A.J.'s mouth went dry, and a sick feeling grew in the pit of his stomach. He wanted to jump in and get territorial, but he bit his tongue. No point in risking his place in the band over his place in one song.

It's just one piece, idiot. Relax.

Vanessa eyed Connor. "You want to put Jude on drums? This from the guy who didn't even want him here?"

Jude bristled, glancing at A.J.

Connor shrugged. "Jude left, so as far as I'm concerned, he should stay gone. But if he *is* gonna be back in the band, then we might as well put him where he's strongest. At least part of the time."

Vanessa cocked her head. "What about A.J., though?"

Connor glanced at him and then shrugged, but didn't add anything.

210

"We need a bassist," Shiloh said. "Even if we put Jude on drums for a song or two, we still need someone to play bass."

"'Eagle Eyes' and 'Unseen' don't need—"

"A.J. is the band's drummer," Jude said sharply. "If you've got a problem with how he's playing, then let's address the musical and technical issues before we start giving people the boot."

Connor's nostrils flared. Jude's lips tightened.

A.J.'s heart shifted into overdrive—*C'mon you two, don't blow up. Not tonight.* "Listen, we—"

"Let's keep this civil, guys." Shiloh gestured for both of them to calm down, and then turned to Connor. "What exactly is the problem with 'Unseen'?"

"It just feels, I don't know, off to me. Like the beat isn't consistent, and it's just weak all the way through."

Shiloh glanced at A.J. "Okay, well, maybe we can all set up a little early for sound check tomorrow, and we'll put in some rehearsal time on that one. It doesn't sound like it's anything that can't be fixed. I mean, I haven't heard it."

"Eh, I have." Vanessa sat back, tucking her feet up under her on the sofa. "It's not bad, but whatever."

"Then I say an extra rehearsal is the way to go. Can everyone be at sound check an hour early?"

Everyone nodded and murmured affirmatives.

A.J. didn't know how to feel. Part of him knew this was just one of those things that came with being a musician. You either developed a thick skin to criticism or you played alone in your own garage for the rest of your life. But he still couldn't help thinking there was an ultimatum attached to tomorrow's extra rehearsal. Like the whole band was counting on him to get his shit together, and if he didn't, well, his replacement was already on the payroll.

Stop it. You're being paranoid.

Connor picked up his tea. "I still think we should talk about switching them around."

Shiloh gave an exasperated sigh. She opened her mouth like she was about to speak, but Jude beat her to it: "I think I'm going to grab a smoke. A.J., you want to come with me?"

Cold panic knifed through A.J.—was Jude insane? But no one seemed to raise an eyebrow over it, and he did want to step away from this conversation for a moment.

Silently, he followed Jude off the bus, and he tried not to listen to their bandmates talking as he walked away. He didn't like being in this position. He didn't like it at all. Keeping the fans happy was important, as was keeping his bandmates happy, and he also wanted to keep Jude happy—but he wanted to keep this job too. And he supposed he wasn't terribly shocked that this had come up again. Jude was an amazing drummer. A.J. was . . . A.J. And at least it wasn't the whole set. It wasn't the end of the world or his career. Hopefully.

Outside, Jude lit a cigarette. "You're not happy about this, are you?"

"Would you be?"

"I'm not, and I'm the one they're talking about putting on the drums." He turned his head to blow out some smoke. "Why don't you say something?"

A.J. eyed him. "And piss Connor off?"

"Why not? We all do."

"I'm . . . I guess I'm worried about being elbowed out of the band."

Jude's brow pinched. "By me?"

A.J. lowered his gaze. "I guess. Yeah. Not deliberately, but . . . let's face it, I suck at confrontation, and since you've been back . . ." He made himself meet Jude's eyes. "You're a way better drummer than I am. You know it, I know it, and the rest of the band knows it. So I guess I'm just afraid to rock the boat and give them another reason to replace me."

"A.J." Jude touched his face. "You didn't get this gig because you're a 'decent enough' drummer. I know this band. They're picky as fuck. And you're an absolutely amazing drummer. Believe me, that is not something I throw around casually."

A.J. sighed. "So what do I do when they talk about switching us out on a song?"

"Put your foot down. *You* are the drummer in this band. Not me."

"Put my foot down?" A.J. laughed uncomfortably. "That's almost as much of a stretch as me telling Connor to stop being a temperamental dick."

"Yeah, I know, but the thing is, even if you *were* just here for the tour, which you're not, you don't have to be a doormat. I know it's hard, but stand up for yourself."

A.J. rolled his eyes. "Are you forgetting who you're talking to?"

"No, not at all. And I'm not saying it's easy. But my God, nobody needs to be walking all over you like that."

A.J. rubbed the back of his neck with both hands. "I've heard you and Connor fighting. I've heard you all fighting. Can't say I've noticed this group being all that receptive to pushback."

"They're not." Jude shrugged. "But that doesn't mean they shouldn't *get* it." He glanced up at the bus and then squeezed A.J.'s arm briefly before withdrawing his hand. "Don't let Connor or anyone else push you around. And I'll have your back. I promise."

Exhaling slowly, A.J. nodded. "Thanks. I really do appreciate it."

Their eyes met in the low light. Damn, but he really wanted Jude to kiss him right then. He could just feel the reassurance that would come from a gentle embrace and a soft kiss, but . . . not out here. Not this close to their bandmates, and especially not with the Sword of Damocles tickling the back of his neck.

"Let's go back inside." Jude dropped his cigarette and crushed it beneath his foot. "Whatever you say to them, like I said, I've got your back. I promise."

A.J. nodded, pulling in a deep breath. "Okay. Let's do this."

As they boarded the bus again, he caught the conversation in progress, and his blood turned cold.

"As long as we're talking about putting Jude on the drums," Richie was right in the middle of saying, "we should really have him play 'Eagle Eyes' too. Kind of like a showcase of our old drummer or something."

"So we've settled who's drumming on 'Unseen,' then?" Vanessa asked. "Jude's taking over for A.J.?"

A.J. cleared his throat. "No."

Every head turned toward him. Cheeks burning and stomach twisting, he gritted his teeth and didn't back down.

Connor bristled. "Is that right?"

A.J. didn't dare look at Jude, not even for reassurance as he spoke. "Yes. It is. You want me to fix the percussion line, then tell me what's wrong, but I'm not getting shuffled off the stage."

"So, what?" Connor asked through his teeth. "You don't think we should go with the absolute best on each piece?"

"I think if you want Jude on percussion instead of me, you need to just come out and say it." He kept his voice firm despite the certainty that he was talking his way right out of the band. "You guys didn't hire me on because I was just good enough to hold my own until you could eventually find someone better, or you'd have kicked me out ages ago. So make a goddamn decision—either I'm the drummer, or I'm out, but I'm not going to be slowly pushed off the fucking stage."

Vanessa and Shiloh exchanged wide-eyed glances.

Connor straightened. "You really want to give the band ultimatums just to satisfy your fucking ego?"

"No. I want the band to treat me like I'm part of it instead of a stand-in until something better comes along. If that's what I am, fine. But if I'm not, then how about we fucking act like it?"

Connor's lips parted. A.J.'s heart went into overdrive. There was no backing down now, and Lord, he wanted to back down.

"He's right, Connor." Shiloh stood, folding her arms loosely. "A.J.'s been with us since the first album. He's as much a part of this band as any of us." She nodded past him. "Jude made his decision. And we made a decision to bring A.J. in to take his place. So I say we stick to the plan to rehearse early tomorrow, and—"

"We shouldn't have to rehearse like that this late in the game," Connor snapped. "You've been practicing it for how long? We've fucking recorded it, and now you can't—"

"It's a complicated piece," A.J. threw back. "I'll work on it, but how about mentioning it to me and giving me a shot at working it out before you start threatening to switch me out with Jude?" Now that he'd started, he couldn't stop. "I mean, as long as we're on the subject, maybe while Jude fills in on drums, I can try my hand at vocals. You're replaceable, aren't you?"

Connor's eyebrows climbed his forehead. "Excuse me?"

"What? So we're all replaceable and can get shuffled around, but you can't? Or is it just me?"

"Okay, okay. Guys. Take it easy." Shiloh stepped in between them, holding out her hands as if to push them apart. "Both of you."

"Take it easy? Do you hear—?"

"Back off, Connor. He's right." She shot him a look that Kristy would've been proud of. "Every one of us, yourself included, struggles with a song now and then, and we all have off days. A.J.'s an awesome drummer, and we're not switching him out every time he isn't perfect

215

unless we're also going to replace *you* every time your voice gets scratchy."

Connor's eyes darted back and forth from her to A.J. No one made a sound, and A.J.'s heart thumped as much from nerves as frustration.

Then Connor exhaled and threw up his hands. "Fine. Whatever." Connor's lips pulled tight as he turned to A.J., and then he shrugged. "We'll rehearse tomorrow, and if we have to, we'll cut the song from the set list until he gets it right."

A.J. swallowed. He could have done without the barb—as if Connor never struggled with any of their music—but this was close enough to a win. His knees wobbled. He'd never been good at standing up for himself, and the aftermath was always a shaking *Oh my God, what the fuck did I just do?* full-body panic. He needed to walk it off, especially since he really didn't want the band to see it.

"I, um . . ." He cleared his throat. "I think *I* need some air this time."

He didn't wait for a response, and nobody tried to stop him, thank God. He hurried off the bus, picked a direction, and started walking, and he kept going until he was well out of earshot because the shouting had started before he'd even shut the door, and he didn't want to hear anything more.

At the edge of the parking lot, he found a low chain-link fence dividing the venue property from another lot. There he stopped, and rested his hands on top of the fence as he tried to convince his knees to stop shaking. It was entirely possible the group would change their minds, and the next person he spoke to would be the one they'd elected to gently send him packing. Or not so gently.

As the conversation repeated in his head on an infinite loop, he stood by everything he'd said. It had just been so damn long since he'd stood up for himself like that, since he'd put his foot down and taken a risk in the name of not being a doormat, he didn't know how to deal with it. How to come down afterward. How to do anything except stand here and imagine himself going back in there and begging all of them to pretend none of that had happened, and that he was still happy quietly sitting in the back even if it meant being reduced to Jude's drum tech or a "remember that guy?" roadie.

But even if he had fucked up his place in Running with Scissors, he had to admit—it had felt good. Connor had pushed. A.J. had pushed back. And to his surprise, he'd had support. Maybe Jude was right. Though it would still be a while before he felt completely secure in the band, he wasn't as disposable as he'd convinced himself he was.

After almost two years, it was about damn time.

CHAPTER 21

While Connor and Shiloh kept bitching at each other about his superiority complex and her siding with A.J., Jude slipped out and went to find A.J. He'd been gone for a while now, and Jude was starting to get worried.

The lot was deserted aside from a few security guys strolling around and the roadies who never seemed to sleep.

He stopped one of the roadies. "Hey, did you guys see A.J. come through here?"

"Oh yeah." The roadie pointed toward the south end of the lot. "He went that way."

"Great, thanks." Jude resisted the urge to break into a run. A.J. hadn't been gone that long, and he could certainly take care of himself. But considering how much he'd struggled with the idea of standing up to Connor, and how much he'd let fly once he'd done it, he was probably rattled as fuck.

The roadie was right, and Jude found A.J. at the end of the parking lot. He was pacing beside a chain-link fence, cupping one elbow and scrolling through his phone with his free hand.

"*There* you are," Jude said.

A.J. startled, turning toward him, and then exhaled. He slid his phone into his back pocket. "Hey. I, uh . . ." He folded his arms. "I guess everyone's done arguing?"

"Who knows?" Jude halted when he could nearly touch him. "They can keep arguing all they want, but I wanted to check on you."

"I'm okay. I'm fine." A.J. started pacing again. "Fuck. I can't believe I said all that."

"Neither could Connor, but he needed to hear it."

A.J. laughed dryly. "Maybe from someone with a little more clout than me."

"To be honest, he could go running to Kristy, and she'd tell him you were right on the money."

"Yeah. We'll see about that." A.J. stopped pacing and rubbed his neck with both hands. Now that he was stopped, Jude realized his knees were shaking.

"Hey, take it easy." Jude put a hand on A.J.'s shoulder. "You all right?"

"Yeah, I'm . . ." A.J. shook his head. "Fuck. I shouldn't have gotten in his face like that."

"What? Why?" Jude squeezed A.J.'s shoulder. "Anybody else probably would've hauled off and smacked him."

"Anybody else isn't quite as afraid as I am of getting kicked out."

"Kicked out? Of the band?"

"Uh, yeah?"

"A.J. My God." Jude pulled him into a gentle hug. "I promise, you will not get kicked out for standing up to

Connor. I guarantee you everyone on that bus has done it or wanted to do it at some point or another."

"Can't imagine why." A.J. scrubbed a hand over his face. "Jesus. I could seriously just choke that guy sometimes."

Jude laughed. "You and everybody else. Trust me." He wrapped his arms around A.J. and kissed his forehead.

A.J. leaned against him. "It's not even that I don't like the guy. I actually do like him most of the time. But goddamn, when he starts acting like that . . ."

"Believe me. I know." He tipped A.J.'s chin up, and when their eyes met, they both smiled. "Don't sweat over it, though. Even if Connor decided he wanted to throw you out of the band over it, the rest of us have your back."

A.J. closed his eyes and slowly released a breath. "Thanks. For talking me down and for talking me into standing up to him."

"Anytime." Jude kissed him gently. "I don't want to see you putting up with—"

A shoe scraped on pavement. A split second too late, Jude realized neither of them had moved.

Which meant . . .

Oh shit.

A.J. drew back. His eyes darted to the side and past Jude, and the way he tensed didn't help the panic that was inching up Jude's spine.

Jude cringed. "Please tell me it's—"

"You have got to be kidding me." Connor's voice sent that panic skittering all the way up to Jude's hairline.

He let go of A.J. and turned around as Connor stepped out of the shadows and into the glow of the streetlight.

"Seriously?" Connor glared at them. "You guys just couldn't—"

"Connor, we—"

"Don't even try to tell me it's not what it looks like. Because I know what I just saw."

221

Jude's heart sank. Shit. "All right. There's no point in lying. Yes, we're—"

"You sons of bitches!" Connor came closer, lips pulled tight across his teeth. "What the fuck? After everything that happened before, you're . . . What did you . . . *Fuck*, guys!"

A.J. jumped. Jude resisted the urge to put a hand on his shoulder because God knew that would only make things worse.

Connor wasn't finished, either. "What the hell was all that bullshit about being devoted to the band now? Not bringing in any more problems? Christ. I knew it was a fucking mistake bringing you back, Jude. I fucking knew it. I even told Kristy it would blow up in our faces. You can play bass, but you've never given two shits about this band, so—"

"Don't even go there, Connor," Jude threw back. "Yes, I fucked up. I know I fucked up. This time and last time. But don't you dare tell me I don't care about this band."

"You expect any of us to believe you *do*?" Connor locked eyes with him, and the surprise and anger faded in favor of something that cut much deeper. He wasn't quite on the verge of tears—not enough to be visible along the edge of his dark eyes—but the hurt was there. His clenched teeth couldn't hide the hint of unsteadiness as he ground out, "Because your track record isn't looking so good."

Before Jude could reply, Kristy's voice snapped his teeth shut: "What the fuck is going on out here?"

He cursed as she appeared behind Connor, along with Shiloh.

Connor looked over his shoulder and gestured sharply at A.J. and Jude. "Did you two know they were hooking up?"

"Hooking—" Kristy's features slowly hardened, barely contained fury materializing in her eyes and her tightening lips, but it was Shiloh's expression that cut Jude right to the bone. Her jaw dropped and her brow creased as she held his gaze, her eyes full of pure, unmistakable hurt just like Connor's.

"No way," she whispered. "You didn't. Please tell me . . ."

He cringed, avoiding her eyes, but he couldn't avoid that heavy sigh.

"Jude . . ."

"Spell this out for me," Kristy growled. "Because I'm about this close to losing my shit."

"Remember that rule about bandmates keeping their dicks out of other bandmates?" Connor gestured sharply at Jude and A.J. "Might want to give those two a refresher."

Shiloh shook her head. "Seriously? You're being serious right now?"

Jude swallowed. "I'm sorry. We—"

"How did you guys . . . How did this . . .?" Shiloh pressed her fingers onto her temples and squeezed her eyes shut. "I mean, after all the shit this band has been through, what in God's name possessed either of you—"

"We got to know each other, and it happened," A.J. said. "It just . . . happened."

"No, I don't fucking buy that." Shiloh lowered her hands and glared at him. "You're both grown-ass adults. You *knew* what would happen." She stabbed a finger at A.J. "You and I even talked about this. Did you . . . did you lie to me?"

A.J. flinched. "It was . . . We . . ."

"You son of a bitch. Both of you! You *both* knew damn well we'd eventually be standing here and hashing all this shit out, and you still slept together like you didn't give—" Her voice cracked. Then she threw up her hands, said something Jude didn't understand, and turned on her heel. As she disappeared into the night, Connor shot Jude and A.J. a poisonous glare, and then he jogged after her.

Eyes locked on Jude, Kristy said, "A.J., get out of here. I don't care where you go, but stay away from the rest of the band until I can defuse this shit. First, I want to talk to him."

Jude gulped.

A.J. didn't say a word and didn't even look at Jude. He wisely got the hell out of here, leaving Jude alone with the band's royally pissed-off manager.

He took a breath. "Kristy, I'm—"

"Don't you dare fucking apologize." Kristy's voice was calm and even, but had that dangerous undercurrent that meant she really was about to lose her shit. She came closer, and Jude fought the urge to take a step back. "Did I not make it perfectly fucking clear that you were coming back into the band on the condition that you and Connor kept your dicks out of your goddamned bandmates? Did I fucking *stutter* when I said that?"

"No. You didn't." He put up his hands. "Listen, it—"

"I don't want any explanations. I don't want any apologies." She narrowed her eyes. "Didn't you learn anything from what happened with Connor? Or with Wyatt?"

He nodded. "I did. Yes."

"Then why the fuck—"

"Because . . ." He shook his head. "Does it even matter? You said you didn't want an explanation, so—"

"Because there's no explanation you could possibly give that would justify this, Jude. For God's sake, I don't care if you two are some sort of magical soul mates who've been searching for each other for millennia or some stupid shit like that." She waved a hand toward the bus where the rest of the band was no doubt hearing about this. "You've both got other people depending on you. Every member of this band is depending on every other, and you and A.J. both know damn well what happens when one person lets the whole group down. Do you understand what's on the line right now?"

She looked at him with more hurt than anger, and her voice wavered slightly. "Everyone's worked so fucking hard to get here. You guys have made it, Jude. *You've made it.*" She shook her head, and he swore there was a tear in her voice as she added, "What is it going to take for you to stop getting a good thing and fucking it up?"

He avoided her eyes. Particularly when she was this pissed off, there was no way he could make her understand why A.J. had made him abandon good sense and caution. He wasn't sure he could explain it anyway—not to her, not to himself. There was nothing *to* explain. A.J. was just . . . A.J.

Kristy raked a hand through her hair and swore under her breath. "I swear to Christ, if Shiloh or Vanessa ever stop being workaholics long enough to notice guys, I'll have to bring in another manager just to keep everyone out of trouble with their damned bed partners." She threw up her hands. "Do you have any idea what a blessing it is that Richie's asexual? He's the *one* person in this entire fucking band who I *never* have to worry about causing some kind of penis-related disaster!"

"I get it, all right? What exactly do you want me to say?"

"There's nothing you can say, Jude." She looked him in the eye. "That's the part you don't seem to get. This shit keeps happening, and I find myself having this same conversation with you or with Connor, and all either of you can do is say you're sorry and that it won't happen again when I know damn well that you're only sorry you got caught, and yes it will happen again. How many times does this band have to play second fiddle to stupid personal shit before you all either grow up or break up? Did you think about any—"

"What do you think I did? Sat down with a list of pros and cons?" He shook his head. "You know how this shit goes, Kris."

"No. No, I do not. I know what it's like to be attracted to someone I can't have or shouldn't have, but I also know how to be a fucking adult and show some goddamned restraint." She threw up her hands. "Somehow that concept seems to be lost on every male in this band aside from Richie."

"Yes, I know. I get it." He glared at her. "Look, I get it. I fucked up. If you want to kick me out, just kick me out."

"Kick you out?" She snorted. "Oh. Honey. I'm not letting you off that easy. Not this time."

He widened his eyes. "What?"

Kristy stepped closer, folding her arms and glaring at him. "Here's the thing, Jude. If Running with Scissors can't function as a band because of you and A.J., you're not going anywhere." She shrugged tightly. "You'll just have to be quick about learning the drum parts."

"The—" His stomach dropped. "A.J.'s the drummer."

"For now, yes." She lifted her chin and tightened her jaw. "But if I have to get rid of one of you, I'm keeping the superior musician. Which, unfortunately for all of us, happens to be you."

Jude's stomach dropped into his feet. "You'll kick *him* out and keep me?"

"What else can I do, Jude?"

"But *I'm* the one who—"

"You're the one who fucks up without thinking about how it will affect those around you. I'm doing something you can't seem to grasp, which is putting the needs of the band ahead of everything else. If you can't fix this shit, and this group can't function as a team, then I'll rearrange the band."

He cleared his throat. "Don't kick him out. He doesn't . . . he doesn't deserve that."

"But the rest of us deserve your bullshit?" She shook her head. "I don't think so. Those are your choices, Jude.

You know as well as I do that this band can't deal with another relationship between bandmates. It's too much of a sore spot. So, you can put yourself first and leave me no choice but to kick A.J. out, or you can get your shit together and demonstrate for once that you care about the band. The *whole* band."

"I get it. I do. But aside from leaving, what exactly do you want me to do?"

"Don't you *dare* leave." She stabbed her finger at him again. "I brought you back because we needed you. And you know what? I probably could have found another bassist, but I had a feeling that a year and a half was enough time for you to grow up and get your head out of your ass. I know you, Jude, and I didn't doubt for a second that wherever you went after you left, you were fucking miserable. And I was right, wasn't I?"

He nodded sheepishly.

"You're damn right I was." She narrowed her eyes. "So now I would suggest you fix this shit. You guys are performing tomorrow night, and so help me, if *anyone* isn't there, or if I see *any* of this on that stage, even during sound check, there will be a revised roster before any of you get back to that bus. Got it?"

Jude cringed, not just at the thought of Kristy's wrath, but of how hellish that show was going to be. And how much A.J.'s career was now in his hands, hanging by a thread while Kristy asked the impossible of him. "I can't—"

"Whatever you have to do, do it," she said. "I mean it, though—don't you dare walk away this time, Jude. That's how you handle everything, and if you do it this time, I guarantee you there are no second chances left. You made this bed, so fucking lie in it. Fix the shit with your band. But if you walk out that door, and you leave Running with Scissors in the shambles you left it in before, there will be hell to pay like you wouldn't believe. Am I clear?"

"You are, but I . . ." He swallowed.

She folded her arms tighter. "But you, what?"

He exhaled. "Kristy, I know I screwed up, but I don't know how to fix this one."

"You don't?"

"No. I don't."

She lifted her chin and looked him right in the eye. "Then I would suggest you figure it out. But I don't want to hear anything else about it tonight, or I'm going to be in jail for strangling a fucking bassist."

His throat tightened as if her hands were already around it.

"We'll deal with this tomorrow. For now, I would suggest you and A.J. stay the fuck away from each other." She stabbed a finger at him. "And so help me, if I hear so much as a mattress squeak, I promise the two of you will be playing in shithole no-name bars for the rest of your fucking lives. Am I clear?"

He nodded.

"Go get a motel room. I'll tell A.J. to do the same. Tomorrow . . ." She cursed and waved a hand. "We'll deal with it."

"Okay. Will do."

"Damn right you will. Now get the fuck out of here."

CHAPTER 22

Obeying a text from Kristy, A.J. stayed in a motel a few blocks from the venue. She'd said there'd be a meeting on the bus the next day, so with his stomach in knots, he returned in the morning around the time everyone was usually waking up.

But there was no one around. The tour bus that was always full of people and activity was empty and silent. He took a seat. He texted Kristy but didn't get a response. While he waited—for a text, for someone to show up, for anything—he didn't even let himself tap his fingers or his foot because the echo threatened to drive him crazy.

The door opened. He braced himself, not sure who it was and definitely not sure who he hoped it would be.

He turned his head just as Jude came up the stairwell. Too many feelings twisted in his stomach. *God, I'm glad to see you. No, you're the last person I want to see. Why are you all the way over there? Please, Jude . . . go.*

229

Jude looked around. "Where is everyone?"

"I don't know. I just got here." A.J. pressed back against his seat, stretching his stiff muscles. "Kristy said we're all going to hash it out today, but she didn't say where or when."

"Well, maybe while we have the chance, we should get ourselves on the same page."

A.J. swallowed. "Okay. Yeah. We can, uh, we can do that."

Jude gazed down at him. "How are you holding up?"

He shrugged, his shoulders tighter than they usually were even after a long, grueling show. Beyond that, he was just tired. Numb, in a weird way. "I don't know. You?"

"About the same." Jude gnawed his lip. "Listen, um . . . we shouldn't keep doing this."

Somewhere beneath that layer of numb exhaustion, Jude's admission probably hit him someplace painful. Or brought some panic almost close enough to the surface for him to feel it. But the only thing A.J. really felt was more weight on his shoulders. He sighed. "We probably shouldn't have started doing it in the first place."

"Yeah, I know."

"Maybe . . ." A.J. chewed his lip. "Maybe there's some way we can reason with the group."

"No. Not a chance." Jude shook his head. "Not after Connor and me, and not after Connor and Wyatt."

That bit in beneath A.J.'s skin. He arched an eyebrow. "Seems like the common denominator there is Connor, not us." *Not* me.

"True. But he's still part of the band. And so are we." Jude shifted uncomfortably. "I'd . . . kind of like to keep it that way."

A.J. didn't know what to say to that. His heart sped up.

No. There has to be another option. We can . . . I mean, the band has to understand that . . . Jude . . .

Exhaling, Jude folded and unfolded and refolded his arms. "Look, we agreed in the beginning not to let this interfere with the band."

A.J. nodded. "I guess I didn't think it would be this hard to let it go if it came to this."

Nothing registered on Jude's face. Nothing at all. After a moment, he broke eye contact. "This is probably the only thing we can do. I mean, the sex is great, but it is it really worth losing all of this?" He gestured at their surroundings. The luxury tour bus. The instruments. The empty seats around them as they hashed this out alone.

You really want me to answer that, Jude?

He swallowed. "You tell me."

Jude met his gaze but only for a second.

A.J. gritted his teeth. "You had no problem with me risking my place in the band by getting in Connor's face."

"I don't think this really compares. Do you?"

"Kind of seems like the only difference is whether it's *my* career or *our* careers on the line."

This time, Jude held his gaze. "That's not what's going on here."

A.J. lifted his chin and narrowed his eyes. "Well, since you seem to know what this is versus what that was, what do you want to do?"

"It's not about what either of us wants." Jude looked at him again. "It's about whether I can afford to take *any* risks right now. This band is all I have, A.J. Up until recently, I didn't even have that much. If I piss away this opportunity, the only thing waiting for me is the guest room in my parents' house and a whole lot of job applications for places that probably won't give me the time of day." He swallowed. "If I fuck up with the band, I'm done. I have *nothing*."

A.J. gritted his teeth. "Nothing?"

"Nothing."

"Well, if you don't piss it away, they'll probably kick me out so you can play the drums again anyway, so basically, I'm just sitting here waiting for you to make up your goddamn mind about the band and about me, assuming you can spare a thought for me since I think your priorities are pretty fucking clear right now."

Jude put up his hands. "You know what? I think we're done. And I need a fucking smoke."

"Need some air?" A.J. ground out.

Jude glared at him. "So I'm like Connor now?"

"I don't know." A.J. folded his arms. "In this case, I think I have more in common with Connor, since I'm the one getting dumped by you."

Jude winced, and A.J.'s gut tightened. That was too far. Way too far.

"Jude, I'm—"

"Forget it." Jude took a step toward the stairwell. "I'll . . . I'll see you at sound check."

A.J. stood, ready to beg him to stay and finish talking this thing over, but before he could get the words out, the door slammed behind Jude, leaving A.J. alone on the otherwise empty bus.

He dropped back into his chair.

Well, the last twelve hours or so had been some of the fucking best of his career. A pissing match with Connor. A reassuring but ill-timed kiss. A sleepless night alone. A look at Jude's real priorities.

That last one shouldn't have been a surprise. He supposed it wasn't. After all, he'd known from the start that he and Jude were just fuck buddies. No matter how much time they'd spent together in between recording sessions, no matter how many times they'd just lain there beneath the covers and talked in between making out, they were fuck buddies and nothing more.

Hearing Jude confirm it, though . . . that hurt more than he'd expected. Maybe because it had seemed to come so close on the heels of that tender moment just before Connor had caught them last night. And then A.J. had hit

Jude below the belt, and . . . Fuck. This really was a goddamned disaster.

More and more, he was beginning to understand what had driven Wyatt from the group. His volatile on-again-off-again boyfriend had only been the tip of the iceberg. Working and traveling in close confines with a bunch of artistic types, there was bound to be some friction, and he didn't want to be one of those divas who stormed out when things got heated.

And he understood why this band meant so much to Jude. Why it meant so much to the whole group. No one made it in this business without putting their career ahead of everyone and everything else.

But there was something to be said for not being in the same room, the same bus, and on the same stage, day in and day out, with the person who'd put their career ahead of you—even if you'd known all along that was how things would play out.

What did you expect, A.J.?

He sighed, rubbing both hands over his face.

Ideally, they'd put this behind them and keep working together as professionals. If Connor and Jude were any indication, though, it wasn't that easy. Granted, those two had a much longer and more painful history. Still, the glares and teeth-gnashing between them didn't instill much confidence in A.J. about his future as a bandmate with Jude. Or with Connor, for that matter.

He exhaled. No band had perfect harmony, but this was all rapidly getting out of control. He couldn't cope with the tension, or the guilt for how much of that tension he'd caused.

This wasn't even his band. He was the new guy. The outsider. Hell, the name of the band had been their inside joke since grade school. Whether he liked it or not, he would always play proverbial second fiddle to a prodigal founding member.

Though it was usually Jude who ran for the hills when things got sketchy, that approach was sounding pretty tempting at the moment. Maybe it was time to pack it up. To get away from all this drama, and from the man who'd gotten way too far under his skin.

He closed his eyes. He'd walked on eggshells for so fucking long to make sure he didn't give the band a reason to show him the door, and then he'd gone and handed them one.

Maybe it would be best if he saved them the trouble.

As expected, Kristy had gathered the entire band, ordered them to keep all this shit off the stage and out of the public eye. She'd made it clear in no uncertain terms that they *would* work together and the show *would* go on, or they'd see a side of her only her ex-husband had ever seen. Then she'd dismissed everyone except for Jude with one last warning to make sure tonight's show was on point *or else*.

A.J. was happy that she hadn't held him back to chew him out along with Jude—judging by her expression, that was what she intended to do. He'd gotten the hell out of there. In the back of his mind, he was still considering just packing up and saving everyone the trouble, but he wasn't going to be impulsive about it. He'd see how things went. For now, he did the only thing he could think of—he focused on getting ready for that night's show. They had their early sound check coming up, so he busied himself backstage. God forbid he fucked up that song again. He'd had enough of Connor's wrath for one week.

People moved in and out of the ready room. His drum tech had left a few minutes earlier to take some stands to the stage, and the guitar techs had been wandering back and forth while they all waited for the opening act's sound check to wrap up.

So as he pulled a snare drum case down from the stack, he only vaguely registered footsteps coming in behind him. And stopping.

The silence, though—no movement, no rustling, no speaking—raised the hair on his neck.

He turned around.

If looks could kill, he'd have been a dead man.

A.J. exhaled. "Connor, we have to get set up."

"Yeah, and—"

"Shouldn't you be on vocal rest?"

"Shouldn't you be sucking our bassist's dick?"

A.J. clenched his jaw. Whether Connor was keeping his voice down to protect it before the show, or if he'd reached that level of anger where a person couldn't even shout anymore, he couldn't tell.

Connor folded his arms tightly across his chest. "You want to tell me what the fuck you and—"

"I'm not discussing this again." A.J. turned back to the case and popped the snaps on it. "What's done is done."

"Uh-huh. And what's done is threatening to fuck up my band."

"Your band?" A.J. faced him, gritting his teeth. "Yours? Well, that's impressive. You're finally admitting you think this is your fucking band." His own words startled him—shit, maybe standing up to Connor once had broken the dam completely. Or he was just too damn raw to take any more people coming down on him today.

"Mine. Ours. Whatever." Connor shrugged. "I've spent my entire life working to get this band off the ground. I'm not about to let you fuck it up."

"Yeah?" A.J. stepped toward him, heart pounding and stomach ready to lurch into his throat. "Has it ever occurred to you that you do a fine job of fucking it up yourself?"

Connor blinked, drawing back. "Excuse me?"

"You heard me." *Oh God. He did. He heard me.* A.J. forced his nerves out of his voice. "You ever thought about changing the name of the band to Walking on Eggshells? Keep Connor Happy? Don't Cross Connor? Because that's how it fucking feels around here."

Connor's eyes widened.

A.J. swallowed. Well, he'd already started. No point in stopping now. "You really want to know why I got involved with Jude?"

"I . . ." Connor pushed his shoulders back. "Okay. Why?"

"Because we're two single guys working closely together, and we have a shitload in common." A.J. gestured at Connor. "Just like you and Wyatt."

"Don't you fucking dare—"

"Dare what? Point out the obvious?" A.J. rolled his eyes. "Come on, Connor. We're all each other's social circle now. Not that any of you seem to give two shits what I have to say about anything, but we're traveling together, we're working together, and yes, sometimes we—"

"Wyatt and I knew each other forever," Connor snapped. "You and Jude didn't exactly wait long to start fucking around."

"What we did and when is none of your fucking business. And neither is how we felt about each other."

"Oh yeah? Are you saying— Wait, did you say 'felt'? Like, past?"

A.J. winced, shifting his gaze away. His surge of confidence vanished, and reality slapped him across the face. Yeah. Past tense. One minute it was there, and the next it wasn't. He coughed into his fist. "We, um—"

"Oh really?" Connor folded his arms across his chest. "So tell me again about what you felt for each other?"

A lump tried to rise in A.J.'s throat, and he forced it back. "What do you want me to say? You all obviously don't want us together. There. You got your wish. Happy now?"

Connor blinked. "Oh." Recovering quickly, he glared at A.J. again. "Good. Because the last thing this band needs is—"

"Bandmates doing the same fucking thing you've done *twice* now?" As soon as he said it, A.J. regretted it. He raked a hand through his hair. "I'm sorry. That was uncalled for."

Connor snorted. "And fucking Jude wasn't?"

A.J.'s shoulders sagged. "What do you want, Connor? It's over. It's done. I . . ." He tried to throw up his hands, but that took more work than it should have. "It's done."

"Good. Keep fucking up, and you'll be done too."

Connor didn't wait for a response before he stormed out, leaving A.J. alone with the stacks of instrument cases.

A.J. pinched the bridge of his nose. This day just kept getting better and better.

CHAPTER 23

Jude knew damn well that breaking up with A.J. wouldn't fix everything immediately. That things would get worse before they got better.

And oh, he was right. No one could even look at each other when they arrived for their early sound check. That gathering didn't last long—Connor was too spun up to provide any constructive criticism, and A.J.'s focus didn't seem to extend beyond the songs he already had down. Finally they all agreed to just cut the troublesome song and deal with it—and everything else—later.

The show, however, had to go on.

Running with Scissors had performed while they were at each other's throats before, and their experience served them well that night. From a purely technical standpoint, the show was fine. Instruments were in tune. Vocals were on point. While Connor and Shiloh worked the crowd they were their usual charismatic selves, and every band member played their heart out just like they always did.

Jude just hoped that the fans hadn't caught on to the frosty looks or the very deliberate distance between bandmates. Thank God it was a big stage so they'd all been able to stay away from each other. Tonight, anyway. Some of their upcoming venues were substantially smaller, which meant they needed to get their shit together *stat*.

Practice and professionalism had carried them through, fortunately, but the whole time Jude dreaded what would happen once they were out of sight of their fans.

As soon as the show ended and they were backstage, A.J. disappeared, Connor stormed off, and Vanessa shoved her guitar into a tech's hands before she left too.

Richie and Shiloh stayed, though. And Shiloh's voice was trashed from the show, but that didn't stop her from letting him have it backstage. "Do you get it now? Do you fucking get why none of us wanted anyone—"

"Yes. I do." He raked his hand through his sweaty hair. "Believe me, I get it."

"I mean, even you and A.J. were shooting daggers at each other. What the hell, Jude?" She stepped closer, lips pulling tight across her teeth, and her voice grew louder and more strained as she spoke: "Let me guess—you guys broke up, so now we get the aftermath that we all knew would happen *if anyone started screwing around?*"

"Isn't that what you wanted?" he asked through his teeth. "For us to—"

"No! I mean . . . I mean, yes, but . . ." She groaned. "Goddamn it, Jude! We've worked our asses off. *For years.* Then we almost lost our shot because of you and Connor. And then Connor and Wyatt. And now this? Do you guys just, I mean, not give a shit about anything except yourselves? You *knew* something like this would cause a problem because it's happened time and time *and time* again!"

"Yeah, I did."

"So, why did—"

"Do I really have to spell it out?" Though it hurt like hell to look anyone in the eye, Jude lifted his gaze and met hers. "We were attracted to each other. We got carried away. And . . ." He waved his hand, which shouldn't have taken that much effort. "Look, I'm sorry. It was—"

"You're always sorry for something," Richie snapped. "How about, I don't know, not fucking up once in a while?"

Jude exhaled.

"He's got a point," Shiloh said coldly. "Didn't Kristy tell you and Connor *specifically* to keep your dicks out of—?"

"This was not just sex," Jude growled.

Richie and Shiloh glanced at each other. Then at him.

Shiloh tilted her head. "What the fuck was it, then?"

Jude's heart fell into his stomach. *Yeah, Jude. What was it?*

Well?

Fuck . . .

He leaned forward, covering his face with his hands. "Oh God."

The feeling twisting in his chest right then was one he'd felt exactly one other time in his life. Guilt, regret, and the certainty that there was no going back—that he'd fucked up hard enough he couldn't fix it. This was how he'd felt when he'd woken up next to that bartender and realized he'd just hammered the last nail into the coffin of his and Connor's relationship. And only then, once it had fully slipped through his fingers, had he understood just how much he hadn't wanted to let go after all.

But A.J. . . . this didn't make sense. They were . . . It *was* just sex. Right? Just some chemistry and some sex to keep each other sane. There wasn't . . . They weren't supposed to be . . . They hadn't . . .

Oh God.

They had.

He had.

And now A.J. was gone. Still here, still part of the band, but a few knife-edged words and a slamming door had put miles between them.

"Jude?" Shiloh asked, calmer now.

He exhaled and met her gaze. "Look, we called it off. We're not . . ." *Oh fuck. A.J., I am so sorry.* "We're not sleeping together anymore."

"Mm-hmm. And it's going to be completely back to normal, with no awkwardness and no weirdness?" Her eyebrow rose.

"I . . ." Jude swallowed. "I don't know."

"Jesus," Richie muttered. "Is it really that hard for you idiots to keep your hands off each other? Seriously? And not make it all weird and awkward?"

"For some of us, no," Shiloh said. "Most of us are capable of not letting our hormones control us."

Jude winced. Oh, he'd done okay when it was just hormones drawing him to A.J. Something else was involved now, though, and ignoring that wasn't so easy.

Shiloh exhaled sharply. "How long has this been going on? Before you called it quits, I guess I should say."

"Not as long as you might think." Jude's shoulders sagged, and he gazed up at the ceiling. "It didn't start until after the last tour, if that's what you're wondering."

"Uh-huh. So you guys made it that long without touching each other, and now—"

"Yes. Exactly."

"And you—" She paused. "Look, here's the deal. You guys broke up. Good. You've finally put the band first for once."

Beside her, Richie nodded in agreement.

Shiloh folded her arms. "Speaking for the entire band, I want to make one thing abundantly clear."

Jude gritted his teeth. He wondered if this was another instance of the band coming to a consensus without including A.J. It made sense this time, since A.J. was part of the problem, but the irony wasn't lost on him.

"Okay," he said. "Go ahead."

"If you two lay a hand on each other again," she said coolly, "you're done. You're out of here."

Great. So if they touched, Jude was out. If the band couldn't function as a unit, A.J. was out.

But he just nodded. "Understood."

"Good. Now I need a fucking beer." With that, Shiloh turned on her heel and left.

Richie hovered there for a moment, alternately watching Jude and Shiloh. Then, without a word, he followed her.

Jude pressed his elbows into his thighs and rubbed his face. He wished his bandmates had stayed. At least then he could listen to them berating him instead of being alone with his own thoughts. He'd let them eviscerate him, too. He didn't have it in him to get defensive, and besides, every last member of Running with Scissors could come in here and verbally rip him to pieces, and it still wouldn't come close to hurting as much as realizing he was in love with A.J. That he'd managed to not only fuck things up with A.J., but had put A.J.'s career on the line.

There wasn't much he could do to smooth this whole thing over, but one thing was for damn sure—he was not getting A.J. thrown out of this band. Whatever happened, if anyone left Running with Scissors, it would be him.

But that was a last resort. He wanted to be a part of this band as much as A.J. did, and that meant this tense, awkward air between them had to go so they could work together. Like it or not, they needed to sit down and have a serious talk.

He got his chance a couple of hours later. He'd showered and changed clothes and was outside smoking his umpteenth cigarette when A.J. came back to the bus.

Their eyes met.

A.J.'s jaw tightened, and he lowered his gaze, shoving his hands into his coat pockets as he continued toward the bus.

"Wait," Jude said.

A.J. stopped, but his expression didn't change.

"Can we, um . . . can we talk?"

"I guess."

Jude hesitated. Then he pulled another cigarette out, but didn't light it yet. "I wanted to apologize." As if he hadn't been doing that left, right, and center lately. Did anyone even believe him anymore?

A.J. kept his gaze down and didn't say anything.

Jude lit his cigarette, took a drag, and carefully turned his head so he wouldn't blow smoke in A.J.'s face. "We need to settle things somehow. At least enough that we can get along."

"Okay. Yeah, you're probably right." A.J. exhaled, avoiding Jude's gaze. "Question is, how do we get there from here?"

"I wish I knew. But, for the record, I *am* sorry. About the whole thing. I knew damn well from the beginning that if we started fucking around, there was—"

"Don't." A.J.'s tone had a hard edge. "Just . . . can we let that part go?"

Jude put his cigarette between his lips. "Yeah. I just wanted to be clear that—"

"Fine. Whatever." A.J. rocked from his heels to the balls of his feet. "It's done."

"It is." Jude tapped the ashes onto the pavement just for something to do with his hand. "Look, we both owe it to the band. They need us." *I need you. But I can't have you. God this hurts . . .*

As he sucked in some more smoke, he shoved his feelings for A.J. as far beneath the surface as he could—there was no point in letting them show now. "They need us, and I think we both need them."

A.J. winced but nodded. "Yeah. I know. After what happened, I've been worried like hell they're going to boot us both."

"No, they won't." *Over my dead body are you getting thrown out.* "I think they're waiting to see if we're going to fuck up further, or if we can still be professionals."

A.J. swallowed. "Can we?"

"I think so. I think we can be bandmates at the very least." He brought his cigarette up to his mouth. "Maybe we can figure out friends as we go."

A.J. scratched the back of his neck and then met Jude's eyes. "It's hard to pretend we're not attracted to each other, but I do want to be adults about this. We still have to work together as musicians if nothing else. And yes, I'd like to be friends." The unspoken "eventually" was there, but Jude could accept that. Maybe it still hurt too much for A.J. to throw his arms around him and pretend they'd never had it out like that. At this point, Jude would take what he could get.

"Okay." He forced a smile. "We'll take it a little at a time. But . . . bandmates. Friends at some point. I'm good with that."

A.J. hesitated and then managed a small smile as well. "Okay. I can live with that too."

They held each other's gazes for a moment, and it occurred to Jude that he had no idea what the protocol was for ending a conversation like this. It felt weird not to have his arms around A.J. in the first place. A handshake would be way too detached and formal. So what the fuck were they supposed to do?

Finally, A.J. gestured at the bus. "I'm going to turn in. It's been a long day."

"It has." Jude held up his cigarette. "I'm just going to finish this and then do the same."

Another awkward pause. Eye contact. Silence. Distance. So fucking much distance.

Then without another word, A.J. continued past Jude and boarded the bus. The door shut, and Jude closed his eyes and exhaled.

Well, that was what he'd set out to do. They'd put aside the bullshit, and now they could be friends—sort of—and bandmates again. It was the best possible outcome for everyone involved.

So why did he feel worse?

It was almost like back in the old days, when he and Connor would be at each other's throats. They hadn't even been able to be in the same room, and it would have taken an act of Congress to make them hash it out before they were damn good and ready, but he'd known all along that eventually, they'd calm the fuck down, look each other in the eye, have some violent makeup sex, and *then* talk it through. Maybe when he and A.J. had separated, he'd held out that same hope that this was temporary. That they were cooling down, collecting their thoughts, and would work it out beneath the sheets once they'd fucked it out of their systems.

But, no. They were friends. Bandmates. There was no choosing between A.J. and the music, only between the music and going back to LA with his tail between his legs. A.J. wasn't an option. Jude couldn't be the reason A.J. lost his place in this band.

This was how it had to be. This was the right thing.

So when the hell would it stop hurting?

Not surprisingly, Jude couldn't sleep that night. His conscience alone had him wide awake. Then there was his knotted stomach, the band's ultimatum, the echoes of everything that had been spoken since he and A.J. were discovered—it all conspired to keep him staring at the rack above him while the rest of the band slept.

From where he lay, he could hear two soft, familiar breathing patterns.

Connor. A.J.

They were both asleep right now, but it hadn't been like that all night. Both had tossed and turned. Occasionally, someone had sighed with what sounded like frustration. Connor had gotten up and disappeared for a while earlier. Needed some air, Jude guessed.

For now, though, they were asleep, at least for the moment. Unlike Jude.

Lying there in the stillness, he thought he was going to go insane. In the past, he'd loved listening to Connor breathing next to him. Especially in their latter days, when those peaceful postcoital nights had been getting fewer and further between. He should've known it was time to call it quits when even that gentle rhythm wasn't enough to relax him. Maybe if he'd taken that hint and broken up with Connor then, a lot of heartache could've been avoided. But it had taken him months, until things had deteriorated beyond repair and he'd bedded that bartender like an idiot.

Now he was a few feet away from Connor, listening to that same sound as it almost synced with A.J.'s breathing.

A.J.

Fuck.

He rubbed his hand over his face. He'd made damn sure to savor every second he and A.J. had been able to spend together before the tour because they'd known there wouldn't be much time on the road. Now that was biting him in the ass. He'd memorized everything about

A.J. The way he buried his face in the pillow when he was asleep. The steady rise and fall of his chest, and the whisper of his breath across the pillowcase.

Finally, he swung his legs over the side of his rack, grabbed his cigarettes, and hurried off the bus. He didn't even bother putting shoes on. Though the night was chilly, especially since he was only wearing a pair of sweatpants, it was more comfortable than the warm, peaceful bus.

He smoked the first cigarette too quickly. As he lit the second while the first still smoldered on the ground, he was surprised his hands weren't shaking more. Between the cold, the rush of nicotine, and his mind being all over the place, it was a miracle he could work his lighter.

As he took a drag—slower this time—his thoughts drifted back to his bandmates.

Kristy's threat wasn't an idle one. Either he put this band back on the rails, or shit was going to get real. And even without her threat, he needed to find some way to right everything. He owed it to his bandmates. No matter how hard it was to face them, there was no way in hell he was walking away and leaving them in the lurch again.

True, they could replace him easily enough. They might be screwed for a few shows, but a bassist could be found. And if he walked, then A.J.'s position would be secure. Of course everyone would assume he was just being Jude and running when shit hit the fan, but he could handle that as long as it meant A.J. was still part of the band. It was simply out of the question to let A.J. take the fall. He didn't deserve to lose his job because everyone was tired of a pattern that Jude and Connor had set long before his arrival.

And more than anything, he couldn't do that to A.J. Even if this had been entirely A.J.'s fault, Jude wouldn't have been able to.

"You had no problem with me risking my place in the band by getting in Connor's face."

"I don't think this really compares. Do you?"

"Kind of seems like the only difference is whether it's my *career or* our *careers on the line."*

Jude winced. He swore into the cool air, blowing out a cloud of smoke at the same time. A.J. was right, wasn't he? Sure, A.J. had needed to stand up for himself the other night, but Jude had promised to have his back. And he had. Right up until . . .

He closed his eyes and took another drag. Things should have been better now, though. After all, they'd agreed to be friends. That should've been enough. But he couldn't convince himself that it was. It had only been a few hours since they'd talked, but during those few hours, they'd barely looked at each other. A.J. actively avoided him, and if Jude was honest with himself, he did the same. Not because he wanted to be away from A.J., but because it hurt too much to be around him.

The longer he stood out here alone, the lower his heart sank. Back when he'd first rejoined the band, A.J. had seemed to find any excuse imaginable to just happen by while Jude was having a smoke. He'd even come out in the middle of the night. They'd shoot the shit and enjoy some time to themselves, and he'd stupidly believed they were just being friendly.

No. They'd been circling closer to each other. Finding excuses to be in the same space.

A.J. wasn't coming out tonight. On the bus tomorrow, he wouldn't join in if Jude started tapping his fingers. Maybe, with time, they'd be friends, but standing out here alone, Jude couldn't make himself believe that he could be "just friends" with A.J. any more than their relationship had been "just sex."

I fucked up worse than I thought, didn't I?

He'd been kidding himself if he'd ever believed things between him and A.J. were strictly physical. The attraction had been there from the start, and the sex had been unreal, but everything between them had been different from anything he'd had with a casual fuck buddy in the past. In fact, it only compared to one person he'd ever slept with—Connor.

He dropped his cigarette on the ground. He was barefoot, so he didn't stomp it out, but right then he doubted he'd have felt the burn anyway. He was too caught up in this growing ache in his chest.

What the hell did I do? And how the hell did I do it twice?

He could move on from what he'd had with ex-lovers and ex-boyfriends. What he'd pissed away in both Connor and A.J., though? That was something much deeper. They'd been friends. There'd been intimacy there that didn't only show up when the clothes came off. Now Connor hated him and A.J. couldn't stand the sight of him.

The more he realized how similar those two relationships were, the deeper the truth cut. Not only how much he'd hurt Connor, but how much he really felt for A.J. They weren't just fuck buddies. Hadn't been from the start.

"What is it going to take for you to stop getting a good thing and fucking it up?"

He sniffed sharply. *Yeah, Jude. What* is *it going to take?*

Something. He had to do something. What, he didn't know, but maybe once he'd slept on it, he'd figure it out. Standing here all night wasn't going to fix anything.

He quietly boarded the bus again and crept back to the sleeping area. He settled into his bunk, but unsurprisingly, sleep didn't come.

A.J. breathed. Connor breathed.

And Jude prayed like hell for a way to fix everything he'd fucked up.

CHAPTER 24

Jude looked like shit the next day.

A.J. wasn't surprised. He'd heard him get up and leave during the night, and whenever he was in his bunk, he'd been tossing and turning. More than once, A.J. had considered going out and checking on him, making sure he wasn't completely falling apart, but . . . no. That would have only made things weird. Weird*er*.

So he'd stayed in his bunk and listened as Jude returned, pretending to be asleep. After a while, he really had fallen asleep. This morning, judging by the circles under Jude's eyes and the way he was dragging ass and sucking down coffee, A.J. had been the lucky one.

This is what he wanted. He'll be fine and so will I.

Eventually.

Throughout the day, as the band got ready for that night's show, A.J. avoided Jude as much as he could. If

251

they had to be in the same room, they were never alone. Twice, Jude tried to pull him aside and talk to him, but A.J. . . . he just couldn't. Every time they'd talked so far, A.J. had felt worse afterward, so he wasn't in a hurry to do it again.

"Can we talk?" Jude asked an hour or so before they were to leave the bus for sound check.

A.J. debated it but then shook his head. "I'd really rather not."

Jude watched him. A.J. cringed inwardly, certain Jude was about to push it.

Please. Not tonight. Just . . . not now.

After a moment, though, Jude nodded. "Okay," he said simply, and just like that, he was gone. Off the bus, out of sight.

A.J. exhaled, leaning against the table. Maybe he should hear him out. Was he being a dick by refusing to even listen to whatever Jude had to say? Maybe. Maybe not. He had no idea. They *had* agreed to be friends, after all.

But for tonight, at least, he couldn't cope with it. Letting go of Jude shouldn't have been this hard—they'd been fuck buddies, for God's sake—and he didn't want Jude to see that it was.

The door opened again, and his heart skipped. Fuck. So much for backing off.

But it wasn't Jude.

Shiloh came up the steps and when she saw him, cocked her head. "Hey. Are you, um, doing okay? I just saw Jude leave."

"You should be on vocal rest."

"I can handle a conversation if I'm concerned about a bandmate." Her eyebrows pinched together. "*Are* you doing okay?"

He shrugged as he shifted his gaze away. "If I'm not, it's my own damn fault."

"A.J." When he turned, she sighed. "Look, I can be angry about what happened and still care about how you're doing."

"Yeah, you can. Do you?"

"Yes." She gestured over her shoulder. "Did something happen? With Jude?"

"No." He rubbed his neck. God, he was stiff today. "He was just getting something, and I'm about to go find food." Good enough excuses, he decided.

She watched him quietly. "You guys seem to be doing okay with each other. No screaming matches, anyway."

Maybe we're better actors than musicians.

"What else can we do?" he asked. "We were together. Now we're not. But we still have to work together." He shrugged. "So we are."

And it's going to drive me insane.

"I know, but . . ." She took a breath. "To be honest, I'm surprised you're both handling it as well as you are."

"It's only been two days. Give us time."

"I'm serious. I mean, the tension is . . . well, it is what it is. But you and I have both been through Wyatt and Connor fighting on the bus, and I watched Connor and Jude screaming at each other every chance they had." She lifted a shoulder in a tight half-shrug. "Considering you guys aren't even together anymore, you're just staying out of each other's way. Not dragging the rest of the band into it." She smiled a little. "I appreciate that."

"Don't mention it," he muttered.

She touched his arm. "I know you guys didn't do this to be malicious. And I know what you're doing now is hard."

He swallowed and met her gaze. "We owe it to you guys. The band is important to both of us. We can learn to live with this part."

"Thank you." She squeezed his arm and then withdrew her hand. "We all have to be there for each other out here on the road. So if you need anything, even if you just want to talk, I'm here. Okay?"

A.J. nodded. It was weird, getting sympathy and support from one of the people who'd felt most betrayed by him getting involved with Jude. And it made him feel worse for not resisting the temptation. His bandmates were good people. They worked hard. They deserved better.

"Thanks," he murmured. "I'm, uh, okay for now, though."

"The offer's there if you need it."

He nodded. "You should . . . your voice. You—"

"I know. But it was worth it to make sure you're all right."

Well, now he felt like a complete jackass. Shiloh actually cared about him. Or maybe she was just feeling him out to make sure he and Jude didn't kill each other onstage that night.

While Shiloh made herself some tea and rested her voice, A.J. left the bus, ostensibly to find his drum tech and start setting up his rig. Really, he just wanted to get outside and be alone for a few minutes. To get some air, as Connor always did.

And of course, the minute he stepped off the bus, there was Jude.

Bleary-eyed. Quiet. Smoking against the venue wall.

Their eyes met. The question was still there in Jude's expression.

Can we talk?

A.J. looked away and kept walking. Maybe they'd talk eventually. Maybe he'd be okay eventually.

But not tonight.

CHAPTER 25

Three or four days later—being on the road did weird things to Jude's perception of time—the band was on some straight, flat stretch of interstate again. He couldn't quite remember where the next show was. Somewhere in Michigan or something? Wherever.

They'd pulled into a truck stop in the middle of nowhere, and everyone was slowly trickling back to the bus. He was outside smoking, of course. Connor and Kristy were still out, but no one was in a huge hurry, and Jude admittedly didn't mind a break from Connor's presence.

Especially since he couldn't get a break from A.J.'s. As he'd expected, touring and performing with his now-ex was tough, but they were getting through it. One show at a time. One mile at a time. One quiet but civil moment of eye contact at a time.

Today, though, he was restless. He needed to talk to A.J., and whether they liked it or not, it couldn't wait. After all, they'd promised the band and each other that they'd be professional. Even if starting the conversation wasn't the most comfortable prospect in the world, it was necessary.

Suck it up. The band comes first.

He put out his cigarette, took a deep breath, and boarded the bus.

A.J. hadn't yet settled in. He was rummaging around in a duffel bag, his Kindle and MP3 player on a cushion as if to let the others know he planned to sit there.

"Hey." Jude muffled a cough. "Do you have a few minutes?"

A.J. lifted his gaze.

Behind him, Shiloh lowered her book. Vanessa pulled out one of her earbuds. Jude was pretty sure he sensed Richie's gaze on his back.

A.J. glanced around as if searching for an escape.

"About the music," Jude added quietly.

A.J. met his gaze again. "Um. Okay?"

Jude resisted the urge to find something for his fingers to tap. "There's a . . . a section of 'Eagle Eyes' that I think, um, needs some work."

Standing straighter, A.J. narrowed his eyes. "Problem with the percussion?"

"Well, the rhythm section. Both of us."

"What do you mean?"

"I think we're drowning each other out. I'm wondering if we should move a couple of parts around."

A.J. shifted a little, some of the tension leaving his posture as he slid his hands into his pockets. "You mean during the chorus, right?"

"Yeah. The thing is, it works in the recording, but live . . ." Jude shook his head. "Is it just me?"

A.J. gnawed his lip. His eyes lost focus, and he bobbed his head subtly, as if nodding to the unheard beat.

After moment, he met Jude's gaze. "No, it's not just you. What do you suggest?"

Behind him, Vanessa and Shiloh exchanged wide-eyed glances.

"I'm not sure," Jude said. "I mean, it's a solid drum part. I don't think we should kill it."

"But the bass line is good too."

"I know. I'm . . . I mean, maybe we should try a few things during sound check tomorrow night."

A.J. nodded. "Yeah. Okay. I can have my tech set me up early, and we can give it a try."

"Sure. Good. I can be there. Maybe half hour before sound check?"

"Okay."

Jude smiled. "All right."

They held each other's gazes, and some of that awkwardness tried to creep in, but then they broke eye contact and went their separate ways. A.J. settled into his seat with his book and music. Jude went into the back to dig out his phone charger.

As soon as he was away from everyone else, behind the curtain dividing the sleeping area from the rest of the bus, he closed his eyes and released a breath. So that hadn't been as painful as he'd expected. Difficult, yes, but they'd gotten through it. Tomorrow night, they'd rehearse together, figure out why the song wasn't working, and have it sorted out before the show.

We've got this. We can do this.

The curtain squeaked across its tracks. He turned around as Shiloh stepped in.

She closed the curtain behind her. "Hey."

He swallowed. "Hey."

"So, um . . ." She folded her arms loosely. "Do you, uh, want any of the rest of us to be there early tomorrow night?"

"No, I think we can sort it out. It's mostly a bass and percussion issue, so—"

"That's not what I meant." She tilted her head. "Are you two . . ."

"Oh." Jude waved his hand. "No, no. We'll be fine. You saw us out there." He gestured past her. "We're good."

She held his gaze, and after a moment, she nodded. "Yeah. You seem to be."

"So, why are we having this conversation?"

"Well, I . . ." Shiloh shifted her weight. "I don't know. Maybe you guys have this under control more than I thought you did."

"Thanks?"

She laughed softly. "You know what I mean. We're all kind of on edge."

"Yeah." He sighed, resting his forearm along the upper rack—A.J.'s, he realized a second too late—and pressing his forehead against it. "I know you are. And I'm sorry."

Shiloh was quiet for a few seconds. Then she stepped a little closer. "I know this is hard for you guys, but . . . thank you. For being civil."

"We said we would be." He closed his eyes. "And yeah, it's hard."

So much harder than it should be.

She touched his arm. "I believe it. But after you and Connor, and after Wyatt and Connor, I have to admit, I expected—"

"You do realize Connor is the common denominator there, right?" He'd known it was true when A.J. said it, but it really clicked now that he'd repeated it to Shiloh.

"Yeah." She withdrew her hand. "Trust me, I'm well aware of that."

He raised his head. "But?"

Shiloh swallowed. "But I also know that anyone is going to struggle when they're in close confines with someone they'd just as soon be away from."

I don't want to be away from him.

Who am I kidding? I want to be on the other side of the world from him.

Bullshit. I want—

He shook himself and raked a hand through his hair. "We promised you guys we'd make this work. If it's tough, it's our problem."

"And there was a time when you would've made it *our* problem."

He glared at her, but before he could speak, she put up her hand.

"Jude, you know what I mean. You've changed. You've grown up a lot." She smiled. "I just wanted you to know I appreciate that."

He exhaled, relaxing a bit. "Thanks for not kicking us out. Giving us a chance to get our shit together."

"Isn't like we had much choice. We need you. Both of you."

"It's mutual, believe me."

"I know." She stepped closer and hugged him gently. "I know this is hard. But . . . I think you guys will be okay."

A lump of unwelcome emotion rose in Jude's throat, but he tamped it down. "I guess we'll see, won't we?"

She let him go. "You'll be fine. Just let me know if you guys need anyone there tomorrow night."

He smirked. "You think we need adult supervision?"

"Oh. Sweetie." She laughed and rolled her eyes. "I *know* you need adult supervision."

Jude chuckled. "Shut up."

She winked and then returned to the main part of the bus, shutting the curtain behind her.

He kneaded some tension out of his neck and shoulders. Another smoke would probably do him some good, but . . . no. He was already on the verge of chain-smoking. They all had to be on the bus for long hours at a stretch, and he needed to be able to cope with that, so he resisted the temptation.

And speaking of temptation . . .

He tried to push thoughts of A.J. out of his mind. It was even harder now, though. They had gotten along, hadn't they? It was still awkward, but the aftermath of their breakup wasn't the nuclear fallout of his and Connor's. And their relationship hadn't been as volatile, either.

He gazed at the divider, as if he could somehow see A.J. through it. What if they could make it work? What if they could put the band first and still be together?

It wouldn't be worth the risk. There was too much on the line.

Wasn't there?

He shook himself. *You're being an idiot. It's over. Let it go.*

But what if we didn't have to—

Let it. Go.

He tamped down on those thoughts. It was over. It was done. The band needed him more than A.J. did, and A.J. needed the band too much for Jude to be this selfish. It didn't matter how much he wanted A.J.—it was *done*.

So he found the phone charger he'd been looking for, joined the rest of the group in the living area, and settled in for the next few hours on the road.

And tried like hell not to sweat over tomorrow night's sound check.

CHAPTER 26

Forty-five minutes before sound check, A.J. was ready.

He sat at his drum set, warming up his hands and arms with a few easy cadences. Or at least that's what he told himself. He didn't need to warm up until closer to the beginning of the show, but he did need to do something with all this nervous energy before Jude joined him.

Ever since their brief discussion yesterday, he'd questioned Jude's motives. Was this just a ploy to get him alone? An attempt to show the band that they could work together?

But then he'd listened to 'Eagle Eyes,' and replayed the live version in his mind, and he'd had to admit—Jude was right. Something was off. No matter how much he tried to tell himself otherwise, there was no pretending they didn't have a legitimate reason for some one-on-one stage time.

We're bandmates. We can work together. Why am I being such an idiot about this?

Naturally, Jude picked that exact moment to step out from backstage.

A.J. gulped. Right. *That* was why he was being such an idiot—because Jude was still smoking hot, and A.J. was still way more attracted to him than he needed to be.

Jude stopped in front of the drums, which were on a slightly raised platform, and set his water bottle down. "You ready?"

Not really.

"Yeah. I'm ready." A.J. idly clicked his drumsticks on the edge of the snare. "So, should we go through it once and see if we can hear the problem?"

"Sounds like a good idea." Jude adjusted the bass's strap, pulled a guitar pick from his pocket, and looked up at him. "Count us in?"

A.J. hit the sticks together to set the tempo and then called out, "Two, three, four!"

And they were off. Eyes locked, nodding in time with the beat, they played through the first and second verse of the troublesome song. Thank God for muscle memory. With no flashing strobes or swirling spotlights to pull his focus away from Jude, he was lucky he knew when and where to hit the drumheads.

Fortunately, though, even without the rest of the band—no guitars, no vocals—the song came together well enough.

And then . . . it didn't. Two beats into the chorus, and it was just noise. The drums overpowered the bass, and the bass seemed to numb the whole percussion line, smoothing the minute gaps between beats that were supposed to be sharp and distinct.

They both stopped.

"You're right." He scowled. "There's definitely a problem there."

"Yeah, and I don't get it—it sounds fine on the album."

A.J. tapped his heel on the foot of the stool. "Let me hear it again. Start three bars before the chorus."

"Can do."

A.J. counted them off, and they played the transition again. Not halfway through, Jude put up a hand, and they stopped.

"I think I figured it out."

A.J. raised his eyebrows.

"Right before the chorus starts, back off for a bar and a half. Let me play you in, and then I'll back off until the end of the chorus. When you come in, blast the intro *hard*."

Well, that was a possible solution. A.J. wasn't sure how effective it would be, but it was certainly worth a shot. So, when they played it again, A.J. backed off per Jude's suggestion, letting the bass take over. Jude crescendoed more dramatically than he had previously, and when A.J. came in, he played loud and hard. The drums still drowned out the bass, but now it sounded like a deliberate effect—as if Jude's part was an intro to A.J.'s drum solo. An overture of sorts.

They both stopped, and A.J. reached for his water bottle. "I think this works."

"Yeah. Me too. Go through it a few more times just to make sure?"

A.J. took a swig of water. Then he picked up his sticks again, and they rehearsed the modified transition until it was concert-ready.

By the time they'd been through the song several times, he was definitely confident they'd fixed the problem. He stood, dropping his drumsticks in the can beside his seat. "We'll run through it with the rest of the band during sound check, but I think we're good now."

Jude nodded. "Yeah, it sounds great." He smiled, though it seemed a little forced. "Thanks for . . . you know . . ."

A.J.'s smile probably wasn't much more convincing. "Don't mention it. We're in this together."

Jude took a breath like he was about to speak, but paused. And the pause went on. And on. And he was looking at A.J., a weird expression that seemed like a mix of hurt and . . . something. A.J. couldn't quite put his finger on it, especially as the awkwardness between them swelled to the point of unbearable.

Then Jude rolled his shoulders and cleared his throat. "Yeah. We are. In this together, I mean." He leaned down to get his own water. "I'm going to go grab a smoke before everyone else gets here."

"Okay. Yeah." *That was weird.* "See you at sound check."

"Yeah. See you then."

With that, Jude left, and as he walked offstage, he walked right past Vanessa and Richie, who were on their way in with their guitar techs. The techs kept walking, guitars and coiled cords in hand, but Vanessa and Richie halted. They glanced at Jude, then each other, then A.J.

"So, uh . . ." Richie raised his eyebrows as A.J. stepped down off his platform. "You guys cool?"

"Yeah." A.J. waved a hand. "Just had to work out some issues with 'Eagle Eyes.'"

Vanessa studied him. "So it's not . . ."

"No. We're fine." He forced a smile. "Don't worry about it."

Richie furrowed his brow, lips tightening, but didn't say anything.

Vanessa glanced in the direction Jude had gone. "He's coming back for sound check, though, right?"

"Yeah, yeah. He just went out for a smoke."

"Oh." She looked at Richie. They both shrugged. "Well, Connor and Shiloh are on their way in. Guess we'd better get set up."

They continued past him.

He rubbed his eyes with his thumb and forefinger.

The whole thing *had* gone smoothly. It wasn't easy, being onstage alone with Jude, but he'd done it. They'd done it. And he was okay.

Maybe they really could do this after all.

As the tour went on, A.J. kept to himself more and more. He was professional onstage, during interviews, and any other time he was expected to interact with Jude. They'd proven they could be cordial to each other, and maybe they'd work on this whole "being friends" thing later. For now, he needed a little time to regroup. "Friends" would have to wait until he could look at Jude without feeling that ache in his chest.

God. He was going insane. What the hell was the matter with him? This wasn't how a person got over a fuck buddy.

Whatever. Whatever Jude had been, it was time for A.J. to get over him.

The buses continued weaving their way across the country, and the band continued performing, leaving 'Unseen' off the set list and all their bullshit off the stage.

In Chicago, apparently Richie had caught wind of a club that everyone was suddenly dying to check out. As everyone got ready to leave, Shiloh stopped beside the table where A.J. had been reading.

She adjusted her purse on her bare shoulder. "Are you sure you don't want to come? An evening away from the bus would probably do you some good." Her forehead creased slightly; though she hadn't come out and said it, she'd been more sympathetic toward him than he'd probably had any right to expect. She was still pissed at Jude and let him know every chance she had, but she'd practically handled A.J. with kid gloves. Or maybe that had to do with him blowing up at Connor, considering that had happened the same night she'd found out about him and Jude.

He shook his head. "I think I'm going to stay here."

"Okay." She offered him a card. "This is where we're going. If you change your mind, you're always welcome to join us."

He took the card and smiled up at her. "Thanks."

His bandmates left, and he was grateful for the solitude. He was exhausted, he was done with people, and he hoped like hell they stayed at the club till last call. Maybe he could even get some sleep—he'd been sucking down coffee all day, and it hadn't helped. He'd given up expecting anything short of cocaine-laced Red Bull to wake him up after a few nights in a row of shitty sleep.

Whether or not he slept tonight, at least now he had some time alone with his thoughts. Not nearly enough, but an evening would help. What he really wanted, though, was to get a ticket home. Get the hell out of here. Go somewhere he could decompress without the added pressures of traveling and performing.

But of course, the apartment he had back in Los Angeles wouldn't work. He and Jude had spent so much time there, and they'd had so much sex in his bed, that the place was probably haunted by the ghost of their relationship.

Relationship? Yeah, that was giving it a bit too much credit. His dick had had a relationship with Jude's ass, and that was about as far as it went.

The band hadn't been gone fifteen minutes before the bus door opened. He swallowed a curse—so much for being alone. Hopefully somebody had just forgotten something and would leave again in a few—

Oh goddamn it.

He locked eyes with Jude. Muffling a cough, he sat up. "Everyone else went to a club." Shoving the card across the table, he added, "Address is there if you want to join them."

"I didn't come here to find them. I came to find you."

A.J.'s gut knotted. *I was afraid of that.* He rose. "Well. You found me."

"Yeah." Jude swallowed. "Can we talk?"

"We probably shouldn't."

Jude flinched.

A.J. leaned against the counter. "What good will it do?"

"Only one way to find out."

He sighed. All the pent-up fury—at Jude, at the band, at himself, at their frustrating circumstances—had worn him down. God, he was just done. With all of this. "Fine. Talk."

Jude cleared his throat. "Look, I've been thinking and I . . ." He rubbed a hand over his face. "I think I made a mistake. When I told you we couldn't do this."

A.J. studied him, and the hair prickled on the back of his neck. "We can't get back together. That—what we were doing—it's over. It—"

"It doesn't have to be."

"Yes, it does. I can't . . ." He released his breath. Just the thought of putting this all into words made him want to collapse. "The secrecy, and the conflict, and all the tension—I can't do it. In fact, I can't deal with any of it. Not with you, and not with everyone else. I haven't said anything yet, but I'm here until the end of the tour or until they can find someone to replace me." He laughed bitterly. "Well, you'll replace me, I'm sure, so I guess it's until they replace you on bass. And then . . . then I'm out."

"A.J., you . . . Don't. Don't do this."

"Why the fuck not?"

"Don't be stupid like I was and throw this band away."

"Isn't that exactly what I'd be doing if I stayed with you?"

Jude winced.

"What do I do?" A.J. swallowed. "If I stay in the band, I'm face-to-face with you all the time. There's no going back and pretending we didn't—"

"No, there isn't. But maybe we can move forward." Jude straightened, pushing his shoulders back. "You're a permanent member of this band. They just brought me back to fill in for Wyatt. If . . . if anyone's getting kicked out, it should be me."

"But this is—"

"I don't want you to leave the band, and not just because you're an amazing, hard-working, talented musician. I don't . . . I don't want you to leave, because—"

"Jude, you founded this band. They don't have to like you to know that you're a better musician than any of us." A.J. shook his head. "And I know how much Running with Scissors means to you. If *you* leave, or they kick you out, you're going to regret it and so will they. *And* you're going to resent *me*."

"And if I stay—"

"Then we'll deal with it," A.J. snapped. "There aren't any other options. You can't just walk away like you always do."

"But you can?"

They held each other's gazes for a long, silent moment.

"Look," Jude said finally, "the thing is, it isn't just a matter of walking away from the band or not. One way or the other, I have to give up something, and given the choice, I'd rather have you."

A.J. straightened. "Do you *hear* yourself?"

"Yes, I do." Jude took a breath. "And yes, this band means the world to me. But what it is now? Everything it's become in the last two years?" He shook his head. "That's been with you, not me. If they can't cope with us being together and being in the band, then I'm out. Not you."

A.J. stared at him. "Jude, this is *your* band."

"Not anymore." Jude met his gaze. "Not unless they'll let me stay even though I'm in love with you."

A.J.'s heart stopped. "You . . . what?"

Jude swallowed. "I love you, A.J."

His shoulders drooped. "Jude, we can't . . ."

"We can." Jude stepped closer. "We shouldn't. I know we shouldn't. But yes, we *can*."

Sighing, A.J. raked a hand through his hair, and didn't even care that he'd probably fucked it all up. "We both need this band. And the band needs us. *Both* of us." He lowered his hand and met Jude's gaze. "We can't."

Jude took a deep breath. "You're right that the band needs us, and that we need the band, but I'm starting to think that what I needed all along was someone like you."

A.J. tightened his jaw. "Someone to talk you down when—"

"No, no. Not that. I mean . . . someone who's . . ." He paused, eyes unfocused as he seemed to be searching for the words. "I just . . . I like being around you. I guess it sounds kind of stupid, but I've never had that with someone I've dated. With Connor, it was always volatile, even when things were good, and even when we were just friends. It was always hot or cold—never in between. Other guys, it's . . . There's never really been anything there, you know? Maybe the sex was good, or maybe we liked the same bands. But with you . . . With you, it's like I just want to be with you. Even if we can't do anything because the band is around, and we have to act like we're barely even friends, I'm cool with that because I'm with you." He swallowed hard and met A.J.'s eyes. "I've never had that before."

A.J.'s chest ached, and he struggled to hold Jude's gaze. "I've never had that before either." He kneaded his stiff neck. "I don't know what to do, though."

"Well . . ." Jude cleared his throat. "If there's ever been something I should be running away from, it's you, but I can't. I don't want to. I just . . . everything keeps coming back to you."

A.J. sighed. He stepped closer, but couldn't make himself reach for Jude. "How do we deal with the band, though?"

"They'll decide if I stay or go." Jude reached across the void and touched A.J.'s cheek. "This part is up to you."

A.J. closed his eyes and pressed against Jude's hand. After a moment, he whispered, "And if you stay in the band, then you're on bass."

"Yeah. I am."

"But . . . you're a drummer, and—"

"A.J." When A.J. opened his eyes, Jude smiled. "I'm a musician. Plain and simple. As long as I can get up onstage and play, I'm happy. The only thing I can't get around or compromise on is you."

"I can't . . ." Exhaling, A.J. finally closed the rest of the distance and wrapped his arms around him. "This has been killing me. You've been right here, and I couldn't touch you."

"I know the feeling." Jude kissed A.J.'s forehead. "Staying away from you just . . ." He shuddered and held A.J. tighter. "I can't do it."

"Neither can I. And I don't want to compromise on you either." A.J. lifted his chin. He gazed in Jude's eyes for a moment, wondering if he dared, and then to hell with it—he drew Jude in and kissed him.

Jesus. There was no question that they'd been stupid to get involved with each other, but there was also no question that they were in too deep to just pretend it didn't mean anything. Or that this wasn't going to end with one of them getting deep in the other.

He had never been reckless with his career, but right then, standing there in Jude's arms and losing himself in Jude's kiss, he couldn't talk himself into being rational and reasonable.

Jude's lips left his just enough to murmur, "I want you so bad right now."

"Me too." A.J. shivered, digging his nails into Jude's back. "Don't . . . don't have any condoms, though."

"I do."

A.J. lifted his head and met Jude's gaze. "You do?"

Jude nodded.

A.J. glanced past him. "How much time do you think we have?"

"How much do you think we need?"

A.J. grinned. Then he grabbed Jude's shirt, pulled him closer, and just before their lips met, he said, "As much as we can fucking get."

L.A. WITT

CHAPTER 27

That kiss took Jude right back to the very first time, when they'd frantically made out for a few fleeting seconds after a show.

Especially when A.J. pushed him back a little and panted, "What if . . . we get caught?" Despite the worry in his tone, he didn't let go, and in fact tilted his head to bare more flesh to Jude.

"We already got caught." Jude pulled him back in and let his teeth graze the side of A.J.'s neck. "Won't—" He hissed as A.J.'s fingers slid beneath his shirt. "Won't make much difference if we get caught again."

That was bullshit, and he knew it—getting caught again would be a goddamned disaster—but it must've convinced A.J. because he dragged Jude's shirt up over his head. Or like Jude, A.J. was just too turned on to care about the consequences right then. The only consequences that mattered at that moment were the ones that would come if Jude got up and walked away like he was supposed to, and that wasn't happening. Not this time.

"Wait." A.J. met his gaze. "Wait. We should—" He gulped.

Jude's heart sank. He wanted A.J. so bad. So, so damn bad.

But . . .

"We shouldn't . . . not here." A.J. licked his lips. "Everyone else could come back early. They . . . they don't need to catch us like this. We've put them through enough." He grabbed his wallet off the table and handed Jude's shirt back. "Let's go somewhere else."

Jude glanced at his shirt, then at A.J. "Like where?"

"There's got to be a hotel around here somewhere."

Jude's hard-on—not to mention his bank account—wanted to protest, but the longer they argued about this, the longer he'd have to wait before he could have A.J. And the more likely someone was to come in and bust them, so it was now or never. "Let's go." He put his shirt back on, and they hurried out of the bus.

A cab took them to a hotel in one of the slightly shadier parts of Chicago, but he didn't care if they were in the heart of Compton at that point. They had condoms and lube, and they had time, and they were about to have privacy. Nothing else mattered.

A.J. paid the cab while Jude went in to secure a room, and finally—*fucking finally*—they had a place to themselves off a noisy street with no one around to bust them.

Clear of the door, Jude kicked it shut, and it hadn't even clicked before A.J. came at him. He grabbed Jude's belt, dragged him closer, and kissed him. Christ, he was aggressive. They kissed and stumbled, tugging at each other's clothes and feeling around for skin and for hard cocks under far too many layers of fabric.

"Get . . . get out of these clothes." A.J. stepped back and took off his own shirt. "I can't fuck you when you're dressed."

Holy shit. Jude couldn't get undressed fast enough. He didn't care where anything landed—as far as he was concerned, once a piece of clothing was off his body, it ceased to exist. All that mattered was getting naked and getting into bed with A.J.

Once they'd stripped, they didn't even bother turning down the bed, and tumbled onto the covers together— kissing, groping, clawing at each other.

A.J. pushed him onto his back and climbed on top, and Jude pulled him down into another long, breathless kiss. The thrill of doing something dangerous and reckless was gone. This wasn't a stolen kiss. They hadn't set out for a stealthy fuck, hoping like hell they didn't get caught, but nevertheless they were almost completely silent, just like the very first time. Breathing, moving, touching, but not saying a word. Not even moaning. Nothing he could say right then would've done the moment justice anyway—he was too overwhelmed to form a coherent thought, never mind speak it.

A.J. broke the kiss, and then he moved, and suddenly Jude was sure he was dreaming because A.J. had his lips around Jude's dick. His hands too. And God in heaven, the man knew what he was doing.

He didn't try to take Jude's whole cock, just focused his lips and tongue on the head while his hands stroked the rest. Featherlight fingertips teased Jude's balls, A.J.'s tongue swirled around the head of his dick, every motion as soft as it was deliberate—he had to grip the headboard to anchor himself in the present. Jesus. A.J. didn't do *anything* halfway.

"Shit, you're gonna . . ." Jude groaned, trying to blink his eyes into focus so he could watch him. Because, hell, was there anything hotter in this entire world than A.J. enthusiastically and expertly working this kind of magic?

Creases formed between his eyebrows, and his little moans vibrated against sensitive skin, driving Jude insane just like the hot huffs of breath A.J. released now and then.

"Still can't believe how . . ." Jude swept his tongue across his lips. "How good you are at—"

Right then, A.J.'s eyes flicked up. Those blue eyes that had been the subject of more fantasies than he could count lately, the most heart-stopping, defining feature of the man he'd almost let go, and now they were fixed on him, pupils blown and eyelashes wet, and . . .

And Jude fell apart.

A.J. stroked and sucked and teased him all the way through one hell of an orgasm. Spine arching off the mattress, toes curling, eyes rolling back—he hadn't come like that in a long, *long* time, and A.J. didn't let off until Jude nudged his forehead.

"Holy . . . shit." Jude stared up at the water-stained ceiling, his eyes still tearing up even as his vision cleared.

"I've missed doing that," A.J. said as he settled beside him. "You sound fucking hot when you come, you know—" Jude cut him off with a kiss, and A.J. didn't protest at all. They pulled each other close again, making out just like before except Jude's head spun faster this time and there was a hint of salt in A.J.'s mouth. Though Jude had already come, and wasn't hard anymore, he was still turned on as all hell.

"Fuck me right now," he panted. "Right . . . now."

"But you just came. You'll be sore. I—"

"Don't care. Now."

A.J. kissed him again, harder this time. "Condoms?"

"In my pocket. Gimme a sec."

"I'll get them."

Jude released him. A.J. moved away, and Jude just breathed for a moment, still coming down from his orgasm and completely coming unglued at the thought of A.J. fucking him. He hadn't even realized how much he'd been craving A.J.'s touch until tonight, and with as long as it had been since they'd had sex, and considering he had no idea when they'd have this opportunity again, he wanted it all *now*.

A.J. knelt on the bed beside him and rolled on the condom. "I want you on your stomach again." He flashed a wicked grin as he reached for the lube. "You're tight as hell like that."

Jude's skin broke out in goose bumps. Without a word, he shifted onto his stomach, and his heart started going crazy as A.J. got on top of him once more.

A.J. pressed his cock against Jude's ass. "You're lucky I didn't wind up fucking you in the back of the cab." He kissed his neck. "I've been so turned on since we left."

"Wouldn't have . . . wouldn't have stopped you."

A.J. laughed quietly, and he pressed a little harder. He breached him and in the same moment released a breath across Jude's neck, and Jude couldn't decide which was hotter. Hell, it didn't matter. A.J. was inside him, against him, and *God, don't stop*.

A.J.'s knee pushed Jude's leg forward. Now Jude could barely move, but A.J. could. Jude held on to the pillow, eyes squeezed shut as A.J. started thrusting. He found the most delicious rhythm, and all Jude could do was lie there and take it.

"God, I could do this all night," A.J. groaned.

"Please do."

A.J. dug his fingers into Jude's hip and held him in place while he fucked him harder.

Jude kneaded the pillow, wishing he could move, wishing he could touch A.J., but damn, this felt good—and from the sharp, hot breaths and the soft, profane whimpers, A.J. was enjoying the hell out of it too.

"Oh shit . . ." A.J. buried his face against Jude's neck. "Fuck, I'm gonna . . ."

Jude rolled his hips as much as his position allowed, which wasn't much, but it must have been enough—A.J. swore again, and then exhaled hard beneath Jude's ear, and shuddered. His hips jerked a few times as his cock pulsed inside Jude, and then he collapsed over him.

"Fuck, I needed that," A.J. slurred.

"Me too."

A.J. kissed the side of his neck. Then he withdrew, and Jude rolled onto his back on the mattress while A.J. stepped away with the condom. When he returned, they pulled each other close on top of the covers and kissed lazily as they caught their breath.

The dust slowly settled, and though they drew apart enough to look at each other, they didn't let go.

"I love you," A.J. whispered.

"I love you too." Jude ran trembling fingers through A.J.'s hair.

A.J. smiled and then brushed his lips across Jude's. "So what do we do now?"

"Well." Jude pushed himself up on his elbow and met A.J.'s gaze. "We sit down with the band and, if you'll pardon the pun, face the music."

"How do you think they'll take it?"

Jude swallowed. "I can guarantee Connor isn't going to be happy."

"Yeah, I know."

"Whatever happens is up to the band. But as far as you and me . . ." Jude caressed A.J.'s face. "I want to make this work."

"Me too." A.J. kissed him lightly. "We should clean ourselves up and head back to the bus." He stretched his arms and twisted his back until it cracked. "If we're going to talk to the band, we should get it over with."

"Good point." Jude didn't want to let him go, but he didn't stop him from getting up. "But maybe we should give them tonight. I mean, they're out partying and having a good time. Let's let them have that, and we can talk about this tomorrow."

"Fair enough. Especially if it means *we* have tonight."

Jude smiled. "Excellent point."

And he pulled A.J. into another kiss.

Jude was wide awake, but A.J. slept soundly beside him. The faint light coming in from outside illuminated the very edges of him, picking out his profile as he snored softly with his back to Jude.

Jude envied his ability to sleep tonight. Then again, after the way they'd fucked, and how exhausted and shaky A.J.'d been after the second time, it was a miracle he'd been able to stay awake long enough to share a shower before he'd collapsed in a heap. If he was going to lose any sleep over this, it would apparently have to wait until *after* his body had recovered.

Jude was exhausted too, but not enough to pass out like A.J. had. And he didn't really mind—he just enjoyed being beside A.J., skin to skin while his body still ached from some long-overdue sex.

Everything in their world was far from settled. Though for once in his life he hadn't run away from something, he was probably about to get his walking papers from Running with Scissors.

But *this* part was settled. It was all out in the open, and despite the potential consequences that would come when they told everyone else, A.J. was lying beside him.

Whatever happened once they sat down with the band, at least he had tonight. He had this. Even if it was just a few more hours before A.J. woke up and they slipped back onto the bus, they had tonight.

And tomorrow, it really was time to man up and face the music.

CHAPTER 28

After the show the next night, the band scattered in search of food. A.J. and Jude returned to the buses, though, and quickly showered and decompressed so they'd be ready when the others came back.

When the band arrived, A.J. and Jude were outside, and Jude was halfway through his second cigarette.

A.J. took a deep breath, and they exchanged glances.

Well. Here goes nothing.

Jude cleared his throat and turned to the others. "You guys have a minute?"

Their bandmates halted, and they all eyed A.J. and Jude.

"For what?" Vanessa asked.

"We need to talk." Jude glanced at A.J. "As a band."

Shiloh's eyes darted back and forth between them, and as her shoulders sank, she rolled her eyes and mouthed, *Oh fuck* . . .

Vanessa's expression hardened. "Is this about you two?"

"Yes," A.J. said quietly.

"I thought this thing was all over and settled," Richie said. "Why do we have to bring it up now?"

"You guys are fucking again, aren't you?" Vanessa folded her arms and glared at Jude. "Is this talk going to be the 'We're in love and you can't stop us' bullshit? Because you can shove that up your ass along with him." She nodded toward A.J. and then stalked past them and stomped onto the bus.

One by one, everyone boarded and took their places—Vanessa and Richie on the couch, Shiloh at the table. Connor stood beside the table, and A.J. and Jude both stood beside the kitchenette, staying an arm's-length or so apart.

Every band member fidgeted under the weight of the heavy silence.

"All right, look." Jude exhaled. "This is what it is. A.J. and I didn't set out to get involved in the first place, but we . . . we did. And—"

"Yeah, we know," Shiloh said through her teeth. "And it was over. So what the hell happened?"

A.J. and Jude glanced at each other.

"Oh for fuck's sake," Vanessa muttered.

Connor winced, clenching his jaw and looking away.

"I mean . . ." Vanessa threw up her hands. "I just have to ask—how did it even get to that point? You two fucking in the first place? You knew what this band has been through, and you—"

"How does anything ever get to that point?" Jude asked calmly. "It happened. I'm not sure what else you want me to say."

"Bullshit," she threw back. "You're both grown men. You had to know at some point before this thing got out of control. You couldn't back off and put the fucking band first? Especially after the way things have blown up in the past? And then you *still* don't see why it's a problem to start fucking each other *again*?"

Connor bristled, but said nothing.

"What did you expect me to do?" Jude snapped, suddenly angry. "You all kept me at arm's length—and that's being pretty fucking generous to you—from the time I came back into the band, and yet now you're telling me that getting involved with A.J. is what's causing all the tension. Is the tension only acceptable if it's me who feels like a fucking outcast? Jesus, you guys. Yeah, I fucked up. I know I did, and I spent a year and a goddamned half kicking myself for it. But doesn't it tell you something that I quit my job on a whim and came back when you needed me? That I was as desperate to be a part of this as you were desperate for someone to fill in for Wyatt? A.J. was the only one who didn't treat me like a fucking pariah when I came back."

"So?" Vanessa growled. "We're all on guard because of your bullshit, so you fucked him just to get back at—"

"No. No." Jude exhaled. "I'm sorry, that's . . . that's not what I meant. The thing is, I was alone. He was alone. And we—"

"You know what?" A.J. broke in, and every head turned toward him. "Enough. There's no point arguing about why it happened, or who felt what. Can we just skip to the part where we talk about where we go from here?" His stomach twisted—confrontation still made him queasy, but so did the direction the conversation had been taking. "Because beating dead horses is only going to make things worse."

"He's right." Shiloh glanced at A.J. and nodded. "We might as well be civil about this."

"Civil?" Connor rolled his eyes. "Seriously? Didn't you make it clear that if they touched each other again, Jude was gone?"

"Yes, I did," she snapped. "Because the last *two* times a couple of bandmates broke up, it's turned into a screaming match that almost split up the band. Whatever happens tonight, I'm not going to let that part happen again. What's done is done. Now we get to sort this shit out, and yes, even if this does end with somebody getting the boot, we're going to be civil about it. *All* of us."

Connor glared at her for a moment, but wisely backed down.

Jude cleared his throat. "Look, we want this to be civil too. And yes, it was a mistake to fuck around with someone in the band." He swallowed, pushing his shoulders back. "But I'm not going to pretend it was a mistake to get involved with A.J."

"That's very sweet," Vanessa spat. "But what the hell happens if the two of you break up?"

"We already did," A.J. said. "Yeah, it hurt to be around each other, but we managed. And so did all of you."

She rubbed the bridge of her nose. "Except now you're back together."

"Yeah," A.J. said.

"He does have a point," Richie said. "Even after they broke up, they still worked together. It wasn't comfortable, but . . ." He shrugged tightly.

Shiloh groaned, squeezing her eyes shut and balling her fists.

Jude took a breath. "Listen, I've put the band through hell because of my personal life before, and I'm not out to do that again. I didn't set out . . ." He shifted his gaze to A.J., and swallowed hard as he took A.J.'s hand. Facing the other members, he said, "I didn't set out to feel this way about him. And I'm sorry to put you all in this position again. There's no way I can promise how this will turn out one way or another, but . . . you have my word that the needs of the band are going to be my priority."

A.J. nodded. "Same here. Neither of us wants to fuck up the band."

"So we're leaving the next step up to all of you," Jude said. "If you want me out, then I'm out."

"Oh, great. Thanks." Shiloh scowled. "I don't know what we can say, you know? It's done. You're both in the band. You're seeing each other. So . . . what *can* we do? You've got us all backed into a corner here."

"She's right," Vanessa said. "You're not giving us much of a choice here. We need you both. And . . ." She glanced back and forth between them. "You both obviously need each other too."

Jude swallowed. "If . . . if we can't make this work as a band, you don't have to fire me. If you want me to, I'll stay on until you find a bassist, and I'll walk."

"So, that's it?" Shiloh gave a sharp half shrug. "You're choosing him over the band?"

"I want both. And if I can't have both, then I won't leave you guys in the lurch this time. I promise. I'm here until someone can take my place. And I'll understand if that's what has to happen."

"We're still cornered," Vanessa said through her teeth.

Jude moistened his lips, glancing at A.J. "Then tell me what you want me to do."

Everyone exchanged uncertain looks. For a long moment, no one spoke.

"What do we want you to do?" Shiloh said. "Well, I . . . I'd like . . ." Then she pushed out a ragged breath. "You know what? I'm fucking tired of this band hitting a wall every time one of you gets into a relationship. I haven't been on a date in three fucking years. I couldn't call my mom on her birthday because I was on vocal rest. I bust my ass, just like Vanessa and Richie and—" Shiloh's voice cracked. She sniffed sharply and set her jaw as she composed herself. "Just . . . after all the work it's taken to get to this point, and all the shit we've all given up to get this far, could one of you act for five goddamn seconds like any of that *means* something?"

"It does mean something, Shiloh," Jude said quietly. "This band means everything to me, and it killed me to be away from it for that long."

She swallowed. "Then why . . .?"

"I couldn't explain why if I tried." He took a deep breath. "It happened, and I can't change it. And I can't change what I feel for A.J."

Beside them, Connor cursed under his breath.

Jude went on, "I want to make this work. We're both committed to the band, and to handling our own relationship separately."

Shiloh held his gaze for a long moment. A.J.'s heart lodged itself in his throat, and everyone seemed to be waiting for her to speak, as if they all intended to go along with her verdict.

Finally, her shoulders dropped. "I'm not going to tell you how to run your relationships. And I don't want either of you out of the band. But if this continues, you have got to understand how much trust we're all putting on you to not screw us over again."

"Totally understood," A.J. said.

Jude nodded. "Absolutely."

Vanessa chewed her lip. "Well, you guys have been okay. And you've proven you can work together even after you've split." After a moment, she sighed. "I still don't think we have much choice, but I . . . I guess I can live with it. The first sign of drama, though . . ." She shot them both a pointed look.

Richie shrugged. "I don't really give a fuck what you guys do on your own, as long as you can play onstage and nobody's fighting on the bus."

"I'm completely okay with that," A.J. said. "Jude's important to me, but so's the band. I don't want to fuck it up or fuck up my place in it."

One by one, every head turned. Every pair of eyes flicked in the same direction. And finally, Jude joined them, looking right at Connor.

A million different emotions seemed to be trying to play out on Connor's face. His lips tightened. His Adam's apple jumped.

Then, abruptly, he turned on his heel and walked out, throwing over his shoulder, "Fuck this, I'm done."

The door slammed. Shiloh glared at Jude. "I don't care what you have to say to him, you had *better* fucking fix this."

"I know." Jude glanced at A.J. "I'm on it."

And with that, he was gone.

CHAPTER 29

Jude had long ago learned that there was no reasoning with Connor when he reached this point, but damn it, this had all gone on long enough. The door banged shut behind him, and he jogged after Connor, who was on his way into the venue's mostly deserted staging area. The other door was about to slam, but Jude caught it and strode after him. "Connor, wait." He gritted his teeth. "Just fucking *stop* already."

Connor spun around. "Why?"

"Because we need to talk."

"Yeah? About what?" Connor stepped closer, eyes narrow. "I think it's pretty clear that your priorities are where you put your dick first, *then* the band you claim to care so much about."

"You know that isn't true."

"Oh really? Because I seem to recall you fucking around with someone else, and then ditching the band because you couldn't stand the sight of me anymore." His voice vibrated with anger, but the faintest wobble betrayed the other emotions underneath. And there were few things Jude had ever seen that cut deeper than the faint shine of tears in Connor's eyes. It had hurt back then, back when his anger hadn't been able to hide the look of betrayal, and it hurt like hell now.

Jude pulled in a breath. "Connor, I'm sorry."

Connor folded his arms. "For which part?"

"All of it. Just . . ." Jude struggled to look his ex in the eye. "*All* of it."

"That covers a lot of ground," Connor growled.

Jude exhaled slowly, struggling to stay calm. "I'm not the only one whose relationships have fucked up the band."

"Don't even go there, Jude." Connor's tone was flat but taut. "Do not go there."

"Actually, I think we both need to go there. You and me, you and Wyatt, me and A.J.—we all fucked up, and—"

"Then fucking leave again," Connor snapped. "Let's keep the trend going. Leave like you did the first time, and like Wyatt did, and don't let the goddamned door hit you on the—"

"Connor." Jude patted the air with both hands. "I didn't come out here to fight with you. I'm saying we've both fucked up, and neither of us can change any of that. And yes, if I could change any of that, I would, but I can't. The only thing I can do now is try to make things right *now*."

"You're on a roll, then. Didn't Kristy specifically tell us all to keep our dicks out of the other band members? You know, so we wouldn't—"

"I get it. I swear to God, I do."

"Do you?" Connor waved his arm in the direction they'd both come from. "Then why the hell did I walk in on you sucking face with A.J.? And why did the whole band just have to listen to you assholes tell us you're going to keep fucking anyway? Or did you just have this little epiphany in the last ten fucking seconds?"

Anger surged in Jude's chest, but he took a breath. Getting into a screaming match with Connor would get them nowhere. Injecting as much calm as he could into his voice, he said, "Look, I came back to the band because you guys needed me, and I needed you guys."

"Yeah? Why's that?" Connor's eyes narrowed, masking the shine and making him look equal parts annoyed and bored. "Ran out of dicks to suck in Los Angeles?"

"No," Jude said through his teeth. "I've been flailing ever since I left. It was . . . Fuck, it was the biggest mistake I ever made besides cheating on you."

Connor flinched. His features hardened, and that undercurrent of hurt dissipated as he glared down his nose at Jude. "You keep saying that shit was a mistake, and that you're sorry. But you obviously weren't sorry enough to keep your hands off another band member."

"I . . . That wasn't what I set out to—"

"Yeah, yeah. Whatever you say, you self-righteous son of a bitch. What was it you said when you came back? That you're going to put the needs of the band first this time? Really?" He rolled his eyes. "Spare me, asshole. Where was all that shit two years ago? You didn't give a fuck about the band when you fucked that bartender behind my back, but suddenly—"

"Don't even go there," Jude snarled. "You can say what you want about me, but don't you dare imply that I didn't care about the band."

"Well, did you? Because last time I saw you, you were walking the fuck away—"

"Because I couldn't cope with being around you, all right? I didn't want to leave. I . . . Fuck, Connor. I was giving up the band. I was giving up my best friend. I was giving up someone I'd fallen pretty fucking hard for." Jude forced back the lump rising in his throat. "You'd better believe it wasn't an easy decision, and it hurt. It's hurt ever since."

"Obviously not enough to keep your dick out of A.J., but then . . ." He laughed bitterly. "We all know what happens when your dick is in control."

Jude flinched. "That isn't what happened back then, and you know it."

"Isn't it?" Connor folded his arms. "Then what *did* happen?"

"What happened was . . ." Jude hesitated. Then he dropped his gaze. "What happened was I fucked up, all right? I was pissed off, and instead of coming to you and talking about it like I should have, I—"

"You fucked a bartender. In the same bed where you'd been fucking me."

"Yeah. That." He pushed his shoulders back and met Connor's eyes. "It was a mistake. I knew what I was doing, and I did it anyway, and I've hated myself for it ever since." He released a breath. "I'm sorry. Okay? I know it doesn't change a damn thing, and I could say it a million times and it wouldn't change a thing, but there hasn't been a day that's gone by that I haven't regretted cheating on you or leaving the band right when we all needed each other."

Connor tensed. Then he exhaled sharply. "Fuck it. I'm going to get some—"

"You don't need some air this time," Jude snapped. "And if you do, I'm coming with you, because I could use a goddamned smoke. But wherever you go, we're going together, because we're fucking settling this. *Now.*"

"Whatever, man." Connor turned to go. "I'm done."

"Would you quit walking away every time something—"

"Oh, fuck you." Connor spun around and got in Jude's face, stabbing a finger at his chest and almost hitting him. "Fuck you, Jude. I might walk away and cool down, but at least I come the fuck back. You walk away and disappear, and leave people behind who you claim to care about, and people who you've even managed to convince you love, and you never come back until someone fucking begs you to." He stabbed his finger again, and this time thumped the middle of Jude's chest. "You want to tell someone not to walk away? Start with yourself, asshole."

Jude was ready to throw Wyatt in Connor's face again, but held back. He wanted to settle this, not throw gas on the inferno.

And Wyatt would be gas on the inferno, wouldn't he? Just like Jude's presence was salt in the open wound.

Jesus. No wonder Connor was so pissed about him being involved with A.J. The wound Jude had left was apparently still fresh, and Wyatt hadn't left all that long ago, so that was likely a raw nerve too. And now Jude was sleeping with another band member right under his nose. Practically in his face. God, as good as Connor was at hiding things, he must've been a wreck right now. Just having Jude back in the band must've been painful as hell, and to add this . . .

Jude swallowed. "Looks, whatever happened with Wyatt, it obviously still hurts."

Connor winced, turning away and tightening his arms across his chest.

Speaking as gently as he could, Jude said, "But there had to be a reason you two hooked up even though you knew what could happen. The road's lonely. We all have to lean on each other. And . . . things happen. They happened between us, they happened between you and Wyatt, and—"

"And they happened between you and A.J.," Connor growled.

"Yeah. They did. And—"

"Don't you dare compare those to each other. They're not the same at all."

"Why not?"

"Because Wyatt was the one who helped me pick up the pieces after the love of my life—" His teeth snapped together.

Jude's heart skipped. "Connor . . ."

Connor rubbed an unsteady hand over his face. "You weren't there. He was."

"I also wasn't the love of your life."

Connor dropped his hand, and when he met Jude's gaze, his wasn't just full of hurt, it was full of tears. He started to speak, but then cursed and swiped at his eyes.

"Look at us," Jude whispered. "Look at where we were before we split up. Don't you think we both deserve better than that?"

Connor leaned against the wall, and when he wiped his eyes this time, it didn't do any good.

With his heart in his throat, Jude stepped closer. He expected Connor to recoil, but he didn't, so Jude wrapped his arms around him.

And Connor broke down.

Jude struggled to hold on to Connor as well as keep his own composure together. They'd known each other since they were kids, and he'd never seen Connor cry. Not when his first girlfriend dumped him their freshman year, not when he ran with Mrs. Newman's scissors and gave himself that scar—he was always stoic to the point of callous.

But not tonight.

Eyes closed, Jude stroked Connor's hair. "I'm so sorry I hurt you."

"I loved you, Jude," Connor whispered. "More than anything."

Jude choked back his own tears. "I loved you too." He held Connor tighter. "I did something stupid out of anger, and there hasn't been a day that I haven't wished I could undo all of that shit."

"But why?" Connor drew back and looked up at him, eyes red and wet. "I know we were in a bad spot, but . . ."

Jude shook his head. "I've been asking myself the same thing ever since. We weren't going to make it, but it shouldn't have ended like that."

Connor flinched. "We could have . . ."

"No. If we'd been more mature, we could've put it to bed and stayed friends, but we wouldn't have pulled off more than that."

Connor sniffed sharply and wiped his eyes again. The tension was returning to his posture, but he didn't speak.

"Let me throw you a hypothetical," Jude said. "What if I *hadn't* cheated on you? And I hadn't left the band when I did? Where do you think we'd be now?"

Connor's brow furrowed. "What do you mean?"

"I mean, do you think we *ever* would have gotten our shit together?"

Connor quirked his lips, and his eyes lost focus for a moment. Then he shrugged. "I don't know what could've happened. Just that one day you were there, and I thought we could fix things, and then you were gone."

"Think about it." Jude sighed. "Look at us, Connor. The only difference between what we're doing right now and what we did back then is that we're not going to have makeup sex afterward."

Connor dropped his gaze.

"It's true. You know—"

"So, what if it is?" Connor waved his hand. "Since we were doomed to fail, that justifies what—"

"No, I'm not justifying anything. I'm just saying that maybe we need to let it go and put it behind us. It's over. It's done. And . . ." Jude paused. "And to be honest, I miss my friend."

Connor blinked.

Jude took a breath. "Every time we're in the same room, we dig this thing a little deeper, but . . . what if we stopped? What happened, happened. But what if we just accepted that our relationship was never going to work, and tried to pick up the pieces we have left?"

Connor's expression softened slightly. "I don't think we even have those pieces left."

"I think we do. It'll never be what it was before, but we were friends for a lot longer than we dated. And yeah, we had a good thing for a while, but there's no going back. You weren't happy. I wasn't happy. The band was miserable." Jude swallowed. "And if I could go back and change it, I would."

"No, you wouldn't." Connor sighed and slowly lifted his gaze. "Because if all of that hadn't happened, you never would've met A.J."

Jude couldn't find a single trace of anger in Connor's tone. Just the unmistakable timbre of bone-deep resignation.

"I get it." Connor slumped against the wall and rubbed his temples. "The thing is, I lost you. I lost Wyatt. The band has almost fallen apart, and we've somehow kept it together, but it's . . ." He released a long breath and lifted his gaze. "This is all I've got, man. The band. This is it."

"You think I don't know that? I just spent a year and a half figuring out exactly what happens when something like this goes away. I get it. And I don't want to go through it again. I also don't want to put you through it again. Any of it."

"So we're just supposed to forget everything?"

"Not forget it. Maybe, I don't know, try to start over. To tell you the truth, I regretted losing you as a friend a lot more than losing you as a boyfriend."

Connor winced. "Jude, I loved you."

"I know. And I loved you too." Jude swallowed. "I don't . . . I don't think that's something that'll ever change."

Connor met his eyes.

Jude took his hand. "I can apologize a million different ways, but it's never going to change what I did. And what I did is never going to change the fact that I loved you then and I love you now. Maybe if I'd been more mature when we dated, I'd have found a different way to let you know I was unhappy. We could have put things down gently instead of crashing and burning. But we can't go back in time. And we can't just let this thing keep eating us both alive." He squeezed Connor's hand. "I'm not asking you to pretend I didn't do what I did. I'm just asking you to believe that the person I am now is not one who's going to hurt you again."

Connor didn't speak. Jude wasn't sure what else to add, so he let the silence linger, waiting for Connor to say something. Anything.

Finally, Connor whispered, "How long would you guys have gone before you told us?"

"I don't know. I don't think we'd gotten that far yet."

Connor laughed, quietly, but genuinely. "I'm kind of amazed you managed to keep it on the down-low for as long as you did."

Jude cocked his head. "How long do you think we were keeping it quiet?"

"I knew something was going on before I saw you together. I've . . . known for a while."

Jude blinked. "But, I mean, when you caught us, you—"

"I know." Connor ran a hand through his hair, slowly, as if the gesture required energy he didn't have. "I think seeing you together just pissed me off because it confirmed what I already knew."

"But . . . *how?*"

Connor sighed heavily. "Jude, I know you. I know when you're hiding something. And I know—" He hesitated. "I know what it means when you look at someone the way I kept seeing you look at A.J."

Jude's throat tightened. "I'm sorry you had to see that. I . . . We should've told you."

"I don't know. I guess I didn't give you much choice there." He wiped his eyes again with the back of his hand and stood a little straighter. "I guess it was bound to blow up either way."

"Yeah. And for what it's worth, we didn't just jump into this thing. We both tried not to, actually. But . . ."

"I guess I can understand that. A.J.'s hot, and you're . . ." He met Jude's gaze and managed a slight smile. "He's got good taste in men."

Jude laughed, heat rushing into his cheeks.

Connor rubbed the back of his neck. "I'm sorry. And maybe you're right. That we're better off being friends and bandmates."

"I think that would beat the hell out of what we've been since I came back."

"Yeah. Me too. It'd be a lot better."

Their eyes met, and they both smiled. Then, for the second time that night, Jude hugged Connor, and for the longest time neither let go.

"I know I'm not an easy person to work with or live with," Connor whispered. "But God, I missed you."

"I missed you too. And I can't say enough that I am so sorry. I fucked things up with you and the band, and I'm—"

"I know." Connor hugged him tighter. "Just don't leave this time."

"Wild horses couldn't drag me away from this band." Jude released him and met his gaze. "If you and the band want me to stay, I'll—"

"We'd be stupid to let you go again."

They exchanged one last glance and slight smiles, and then started back toward the bus. There was no telling how things would go now, but if nothing else, the two of them had finally buried the hatchet. This was how it should've ended back then. If they'd both been a little more mature, if Jude had been a hell of a lot less impulsive, maybe they could've put their relationship to rest peacefully like this.

However the rest of this evening went, he was thankful for a second chance with his best friend, and for a second chance to let go of his first love.

CHAPTER 30

Jude and Connor had been gone for ages, and no one had said a word. The band sat in silence, exchanging uncomfortable looks and fidgeting.

A.J. kept tapping his foot and drumming his fingers. Richie alternated between squirming in a chair and wandering to the kitchenette as if something appetizing might have materialized since the previous seven or eight trips. Shiloh played on her phone, but nothing seemed to hold her interest for very long, and each time she put it aside, she tossed it onto the table harder than the time before. As twitchy as Vanessa was, A.J. wouldn't have been surprised if she was seriously considering hunting down a pot dealer in town. At this rate, he was ready to ask her to pick something up for him.

Not that he expected any requests to be met with responses besides *Go fuck yourself.*

His face burned. His insides threatened to fold in on themselves. He tried not to tap or drum or fucking breathe, because he didn't want to attract any attention to himself. If he could've vanished into the woodwork, he would have. Whatever was happening between Connor and Jude right then might be worse than this, but probably not by much.

Shiloh cleared her throat, the subtle sound making everyone on the bus jump. When A.J. turned to her, his chest tightened—she was looking right back at him.

After a few long, uncomfortable seconds, she said, "While we're digging things up, I'm curious about what you said that night we all found out about you and Jude. That you didn't like being treated like a stand-in." She lifted her eyebrows. "Is that really how you've felt?"

A.J. dropped his gaze. "I . . . Yeah. It is."

"But . . ." She shook her head. "Why?"

He exhaled. "I guess I've just always felt like an outsider. Kind of . . . like all it would take was one fuckup, and I'd be gone."

"What? No!" She pursed her lips. "I mean, you auditioned against shitloads of drummers. We didn't pick you because you were 'okay' until something else came along."

"She's right," Richie said quietly. "We didn't hire you on because you were a placeholder until we found someone more permanent. I don't think any of us thought you were temporary."

A.J. leaned forward, resting his elbows on his knees. "Except you guys have been together since you were in school. I'm the new kid. I'll—"

"You were the new kid two albums ago, hon." Shiloh got up and moved to the chair closest to A.J.'s. She took a seat and reached for his arm. "You've really felt that way this whole time?"

He hesitated, suddenly feeling less like the new kid and more like a colossal idiot. Then he sighed and nodded.

"Yeah. I mean, I guess sometimes I think I'm along for the ride, but don't have much of a voice."

She cocked her head. "You don't think you can speak up?"

"I've tried." He swallowed, then sighed, shaking his head. "It's stupid. But I guess it's kind of like being the new kid in school, you know? Trying to be part of the group and all." He paused. "I mean, I know I'm a damn good drummer. But . . ."

"I get it," Shiloh said. "I'm just sorry we didn't catch on sooner that you felt like that. Or that you thought we didn't want your input on things. I had no idea."

"Same here," Vanessa said.

Richie nodded. "Yeah. I thought we were cool, man."

"We are. We . . ." A.J. took a breath. "You guys have been great. Honestly. But you're a tight group."

"Yeah, we are." Shiloh glanced at the others, and faced him. "But we want you to be part of it. Not just onstage."

He swallowed against the ache in his throat. Hearing them say it was a relief, but it didn't do much for his conscience. He and Jude had jeopardized everything this group had worked for, so he couldn't help feeling like he didn't deserve the place they'd given him. "I'm sorry, guys. For all this with Jude. It—"

"We'll deal with that." Shiloh's tone was terse, but gentle at the same time. "We've bounced back from worse. As long as he and Connor don't kill each other." She took his hand and squeezed it. "But we're not throwing you out. Okay?"

He nodded. "What about Jude?"

She and Vanessa exchanged glances. "I don't know. A lot of that depends on what happens out there." She gestured at the door.

"It also depends on if Kristy doesn't kill him." Richie held up the phone he'd been playing on. "She's on her way, and she's pissed."

"As well she should be." Vanessa looked at A.J. "Sorry, man."

"It's okay. I get why she's pissed. And I mean it—I'm really sorry for what happened. And we tried to keep it quiet because we didn't want to rock the boat or fuck up the band." He paused, and more to himself, added, "I just couldn't help feeling this way about him."

Shiloh peered at him. "You guys aren't just screwing around, are you?"

"No." A.J. held her gaze, though it was a challenge. "Maybe in the beginning, but now—"

The door opened, and they all froze.

Connor came in first. Then Jude.

Everyone tensed. Both guys were quiet, expressions betraying nothing.

Then they glanced at each other, and Connor took a deep breath. Facing the band, he said, "So, Jude and I . . . It's settled."

"Define 'settled,'" Shiloh said.

"He means we're good," Jude said. "About everything."

The whole band stared at them.

Vanessa blinked. "Like . . . you guys really . . ." Her eyes darted back and forth between them. "Like, buried the hatchet? For real?"

Both guys nodded.

"And you're . . ." Shiloh raised her eyebrows. "Connor, you're okay with them . . ."

"Yeah," Connor said, his voice soft and completely devoid of hostility. "As long as it doesn't mess with the band, it's their business."

"But . . ." Vanessa glanced at Connor, and then turned to A.J. and Jude. "But there's still no guarantee that things won't go to shit if you two go to shit. If you guys keep doing what you're doing, how do we know the band won't fall apart?"

"What she said." Shiloh shot Jude a pointed look. "Because I am not joking—this thing fucks with the band, there's going to be hell to pay."

Connor cleared his throat. "I . . . don't think it's going to be a problem."

Every head snapped toward him.

He shifted a little, cheeks coloring. "Look, let's face it—most of the drama in this band has been because of Jude and me. Or, well, because of me. Feelings happen, and people hook up even when it's not a good idea, but . . ." He swallowed. "We're all adults here."

He turned to A.J. and Jude. A.J.'s heart clenched. He'd never seen this side of Connor—a little contrite, a little sad, and—considering the discussion was about Jude's love life—civil. Connor held Jude's gaze for a second before lowering his. "I don't see why we can't all make this work."

"You're sure about this?" Shiloh asked gently. "I mean, you're really okay with it?"

"Yeah." Connor pushed his shoulders back. "Look, Jude and I had a lot of shit we needed to sort out. And I think . . . I think I let a lot of that come into play with me and Wyatt." Some more color bloomed in his cheeks. "I should probably call him too."

A.J. tensed.

"He's not coming back," Shiloh said firmly. "You two can sort your shit out all you want, but we've got a bassist and a drummer."

Connor glanced at A.J., and for a split second, A.J. was sure the lead singer was about to stomp all over everything he'd just settled with their bandmates. Instead, Connor nodded. "I know. Wyatt deserves closure, though. God knows I needed it." He gestured at Jude. "Things would've been a lot better for all of us if Jude and I had figured that out a long time ago."

"Live and learn," Jude said quietly. "We're good now. I'm sure you and Wyatt can sort it out too."

"I hope so." Connor leaned against the table. "But I'll deal with that. As far as the band, I agree with Shiloh. We've got a bassist and a drummer."

Jude took a breath like he was about to say something, but right then, the bus door opened again, and as Kristy stepped aboard, everyone straightened like soldiers snapping to attention.

Their manager scanned the group, pausing on each band member in turn. "So, what's the verdict?"

"The verdict is that the band comes first." Jude took A.J.'s hand, and though Connor was looking right at them, he didn't flinch. "Whatever happens between us stays between us."

"Mm-hmm." She eyed them both dubiously. "And you all know things like that are easier said than done, right?"

"We know," Connor said. "But high school's over. We should, you know, probably act like it."

"I've been telling you that for a long time."

"I know. And . . ." Connor paused, and then looked A.J. in the eye. "You've got a really good guy. Just . . . you know . . ." He grinned. "Keep the son of a bitch in line, will you?"

"Yeah, yeah." Jude rolled his eyes and laughed quietly.

Every jaw in the room fell open, including A.J.'s.

Kristy blinked. "Okay, that?" She gestured at Connor and then Jude. "That's not what I expected to see tonight."

"I'll take it," Shiloh said. "If it means Connor's easier to live with and you two aren't plotting to kill each other."

Connor and Jude exchanged glances and laughed. Connor clapped Jude's shoulder. "I think we'll be okay."

"For both of your sake," Kristy said, "I would hope so." She paused. "So, we're all in agreement, then? Everyone can live with this, and Jude and A.J. are going to be adults if things don't work out between them?"

Murmured affirmatives rippled through the group.

She exhaled. "All right. Well, we'll see how this plays out, but I'm holding every last one of you to this." She turned to A.J. and Jude. "Especially you two."

"Understood," they both said.

"Good. Now, everyone get some sleep. We're back on the road at first light."

"Yes, ma'am," Connor said, saluting playfully.

She rolled her eyes, but laughed. As everyone dispersed, A.J. released his breath.

Jude put a hand on his back. "You okay?"

"Yeah." A.J. eyed him. "You look like you could use a smoke."

"Like you wouldn't believe."

L.A. WITT

CHAPTER 31

Outside the bus, Jude and A.J. stood in silence for the longest time. Neither of them spoke until after he'd crushed the cigarette under his foot.

"You okay?" A.J. asked finally.

Jude chewed on the question for a while. "I think so, yeah. I . . ." He met A.J.'s gaze. "I mean, this is settled, right? Everything's good with the band. It's just been so up in the air and crazy, it feels kind of weird now."

A.J. laughed quietly. "Yeah, when things have been tense for a long time, peace doesn't feel normal anymore." He rolled his eyes. "Ask me how I know."

Jude blew out a breath. "I'm glad it's over, though."

A.J. slid his hands into his pockets. "Do you think it *is* over?"

"What do you mean?"

"I mean, everyone says they're okay with us now, but . . ." He studied Jude. "How long before someone sets someone else off?"

Jude shook his head. "I think we'll be fine this time. Especially since Connor and I hashed things out. We were all pretty sane and functional as a group before he and I started butting heads."

"It's hard to imagine this being a sane and functional group."

Jude laughed. "I promise. We can be." He wrapped his arms around A.J. and kissed his cheek. "It'll be okay. I'm sure we'll all butt heads, but I think . . . I think the worst is over."

"God, I hope so." A.J. lifted his gaze. "Did you really mean what you said? About letting the band boot you out, but staying with me?"

Jude nodded. "Yeah, I did."

"What if they'd kicked you out? What would you have done?"

Jude ran his fingers through A.J.'s hair. "Only thing I could do—man up and face the music. Bow out gracefully. See if I could find another band. Do the long-distance thing with you if I had to while you're touring."

A.J. swallowed. "But you'd give up . . . I mean, this is your band."

"Yeah, it is. And it's the band I want to be a part of, but if push came to shove, there are others. I can still be a musician regardless of whether Running with Scissors lets me stay, just like I can handle being a bassist if I can't be a drummer." He caressed A.J.'s cheek. "But there's only one you. I've already used up a second chance with you, and I'm not about to find out if there's a third one."

"Well, that part's over. You're back with me, we're both still in the band—can't really ask for much more than that, aside from the ability to erase the past."

"I'm not even sure I'd want that."

"You wouldn't?"

Jude thought for a moment and then shook his head. "No. I mean, I regret a lot of things I've done. And I seriously regret what I did to Connor and the band." He ran the pad of his thumb along A.J.'s jaw. "But as Connor of all people pointed out to me, it's hard to come out and say I'd go back and change it, because then I never would've met you."

A.J. swallowed. "In that case, is it wrong for me to be glad things worked out the way they did?"

Jude smiled. "If that's wrong, I don't want to be right. I mean, maybe we'd have found each other some other way. Who knows." He pressed a gentle kiss to A.J.'s forehead. "But we did find each other this way. The end doesn't necessarily justify the means, but . . ."

A.J. nodded. "Yeah, I understand. Maybe we all had to fuck up a few times in order to get it right."

"Maybe. And, I mean, there's no way we can guarantee what will or won't happen in the future. Maybe this will work out. Maybe it won't." Jude slipped his hand into A.J.'s. "We'll just have to take it one day at a time, and whatever happens, keep it between us."

A.J. looked down at their hands. After a moment, he asked, "You really think Connor's okay with this?"

"I think he's more okay with it than he was earlier. We . . . probably should've cleared the air a long, long time ago. About everything." Jude exhaled. "I mean, we should've gotten our shit together before I quit the band, but definitely when I came back. Before . . ." He glanced at A.J. "Before we hooked up."

"Except we didn't know we were going to."

"No, but I did know things were going to go to shit with Connor eventually." He stared out into the night. "And one of these days I will learn that ignoring something with him won't make it go away." He paused and then laughed softly. "Funny thing is, he said he's actually known about us for a while."

A.J.'s eyes widened. "He did? How?"

"I guess I gave it away." Jude cradled both sides of A.J.'s neck and leaned in, pausing just long enough to whisper, "He saw the way I look at you."

A.J.'s lips parted, but before he could speak, Jude kissed him.

"Guess I wasn't as subtle as I thought I was," Jude said after he pulled away. "But it's kind of hard not to look at you like this."

A.J. smiled, sending a shiver through Jude, but the smile didn't last. "If he's known all along, why didn't he say anything?"

"The same reason he and I never settled our bullshit two years ago—Connor's as good as I am at avoiding uncomfortable subjects." Jude brushed away a few spiky strands that had fallen onto A.J.'s forehead. "Maybe he thought it would go away if he ignored it long enough."

"Yeah." A.J. laughed. "Just like if I ignored how much I wanted you, it would go away, right?"

"Glad I'm not the only one who had that problem."

A.J. smiled again, and it stayed this time, especially as he wrapped his arms around Jude. "I'm glad this worked out."

"Me too. I love you, A.J."

"I love you too." A.J. pulled him closer. "And here I was worried that you'd elbow me out of the band."

Jude laughed and kissed him softly. "Not a chance. Even if we hadn't hooked up, you're the drummer of Running with Scissors now. That was never going to change."

A.J. studied him for a moment, and as he exhaled, he shook some tension out of his shoulders. "It's funny. After everything tonight, I'm starting to actually believe that."

"You'd better believe it. You're a damn good drummer." Jude kissed him again, and this time neither pulled away. A.J.'s fingers drifted up into Jude's hair, and Jude slid his hands into A.J.'s back pockets. When he broke the kiss, it was just enough to murmur, "Think anyone will notice if we sneak off for a little while?"

A.J. grinned. "I think they'd all be surprised if we didn't."

"Good point." Jude kissed him once more.

"Maybe we should go find a horizontal surface somewhere."

"Maybe we should. And we will." Their lips brushed. "In a minute." And Jude claimed a deep kiss. A.J. didn't protest—he tightened his fingers in Jude's hair, gripped it *hard*, just right to let him know exactly what kind of night awaited him when they finally did hunt down a horizontal surface, but even that wasn't enough for Jude to let him go yet. Kissing A.J. like this—out in the open, no longer afraid of getting caught or shy about admitting he was in love—gave him more of a rush than the music or the nicotine. He could quit anytime he wanted, but he didn't want to, so he held A.J. tight and let the kiss go on and on.

Even as he lost himself in making out with A.J. and turning him on, Jude couldn't believe they were here. That this was real, and that everything had worked out like this. If he could've gone back and unhurt Connor and their bandmates, if he could've erased the night with the bartender and skipped over that miserable year and a half in a cubicle, he would've in a heartbeat. And yet, maybe it was best that all those things had happened. He'd regret the damage he'd done until the day he died, but he couldn't ignore that those events had brought him to this moment, standing here outside the Running with Scissors tour bus with A.J. in his arms. It had been a long and fucked-up road paved with his stupid mistakes, but somehow they'd wound up here. All those missteps and wrong turns had inexplicably been leading them to this.

In a weird way, it was all the mistakes—the face-plants, the dick moves, idiot decisions—that made him believe he and Connor and A.J. and the band were on the right track now. No one wanted to go back to that bullshit.

As he held A.J. beneath the streetlights, feeling calmer and more at peace than he had in ages, he knew there was no going back. There was only going forward.

And as long as he was going forward with A.J. and Running with Scissors, Jude had no doubt he was finally on the right road.

The End

about the

AUTHOR

L.A. Witt and her husband have been exiled from Spain and sent to live in Maine because rhymes are fun. She now divides her time between writing, assuring people she is aware that Maine is cold, wondering where to put her next tattoo, and trying to reason with a surly Maine coon. Rumor has it her arch nemesis, Lauren Gallagher, is also somewhere in the wilds of New England, which is why L.A. is also spending a portion of her time training a team of spec ops lobsters. Authors Ann Gallagher and Lori A. Witt have been asked to assist in lobster training, but they "have books to write" and "need to focus on our careers" and "don't you think this rivalry has gotten a little out of hand?" They're probably just helping Lauren raise her army of squirrels trained to ride moose into battle.

Website: www.gallagherwitt.com
Email: gallagherwitt@gmail.com
Twitter: @GallagherWitt

31827119R00182